WEAVER

Ingrid Seymour

PenDreams • BIRMINGHAM

Published by PenDreams

Cover design by Andreea Vraciu

Manufactured in the United States of America
Copyright © 2018 by Ingrid Seymour

ISBN: 9780991093441

℘ *Chapter 1* ℘
Sam

Manacles bound Sam's wrists.

There was a stiff metal bar between them that kept her hands apart. They were special handcuffs meant to prevent her from reaching for her broken vinculums. They fulfilled their purpose. The only problem: they were on the wrong Morphid.

They should have been on Danata. *That witch!* And Sam would have paid prime dollar to be the one to shackle the evil Regent.

The contraption had been on Sam for about a week, an eternity since she'd been torn away from Greg, her Keeper, her love. Pain gripped her heart at the memories of their violent separation. She shook herself and pressed her forehead to bent knees, trying to hide from her own grief, but it was useless.

Her sorrow turned to anger, and she refocused her attention on the metal bar. Not for the first time, she pressed her hands to the floor, placed a foot to the bar and pulled. She clenched her teeth, using all her strength in an attempt to bend the metal. If she could just curve it enough so the tips of her fingers could touch, she would weave her broken link back to Greg's.

Nothing.

The bar remained as straight as it always did, no matter how many times she wrestled with it.

Winded, she reclined, resting her back to the side of a narrow bed. She was in one of Rothblade Castle's windowless cells, where Danata kept her least-welcomed guests. There was but a bed and a small washroom attached to the room. Everything else was rock and coldness.

Sam wanted to cross her arms and rest them on top of her knees. She was tired of only being able to keep them straight or folded at the elbows. Every position was awkward.

Feeling defeated, she settled for placing her forearms on the top of her kneecaps and staring at the stupid metal bar. The palms of her hands faced each other. She extended her fingers, reaching, imagining them becoming elastic, able to bridge the gap that separated them.

Her back itched. She moved from side to side to scratch it against the bed. A curse escaped her lips. Being bound like this was maddening. Doing just about anything was awkward or flat-out impossible. Meal times challenged her dexterity as she struggled to take the utensils to her mouth. It would have been more practical to eat with her hands, but she refused to be humiliated to that level. When she'd believed herself human, she'd dreamed of being a five-star chef. That dream was gone now, but at least she could keep her dignity.

She hadn't changed clothes in a week, not to mention showered. She didn't even want to think how dire things would be if the washroom didn't have a stupid bidet. *Gross!*

Sam sniffed her t-shirt, wondering how badly she stank. Not too bad, it seemed, though she was probably the worst judge in the matter. If Greg was here, he would set her straight. "You smell like a wet dog," he would say.

His sparkling blue gaze and easy smile flashed before her. Sam swallowed thickly and did her best to ignore the pain that filled her chest. If she allowed her feelings to take over, the tears would begin again and then there would be no stopping them. Thinking of Greg was torture, and sadness would kill her if she allowed herself to dwell. And since she had no intention of dying, she refrained. No way would she let Danata get away with the horrors she'd perpetrated on her and so many others. The Regent would pay for her viciousness.

In an effort to keep her circular thoughts at bay, Sam stood up and started pacing, awkwardly holding her hands in front of her. She walked from one corner of the room to the next, and the next, and the next. She had pushed the bed to the middle of the room just for the purpose of walking in circles. A caged tiger had nothing on her.

God, how much longer would she have to endure this solitude? Sam's best guess was that she's been locked up for a week, a rough estimate since she had no way to tell time—not even a hint of sunlight.

And what if this was it? What if her fate was far worse than death and she was meant to become an old woman between these bare walls? So far no one had come to see her. Unless those who delivered her meals counted. They brought water and bread and a plastic fork to pick at the small rations of bland meat and vegetables—barely enough to stay alive. It was ridiculous, but it probably amused Danata to treat her as if it were the Middle Ages.

Sam passed by the small washroom for the tenth time. Her pace had gotten faster and faster as she went. Her heart raced and a hammer pounded inside her head, keeping time with her steps. Panic. She knew it, but didn't seem able to do anything to stop it.

Her breathing quickly grew ragged. Her chest felt strange, as if a hand were squeezing the air from her lungs, the life from her heart.

She bent over panting, hands on her knees. Her honey-colored hair fell in front of her. It was matted and oily.

Greg Greg Greg.

His name flashed like a neon sign that could not be turned off or ignored.

There was a hole in her soul, an empty space voided of life. Worst of all, the hole was growing, and it would keep growing until it gave an unobstructed view through her ribs. Because Greg had been an integral part of her, and his love and connection had filled her to the brim. Now, she was empty.

Exhausted from her grief, Sam collapsed on the bed. She buried her face in the rough blanket and put the pillow over her head. A muffled scream rang in her ears and left her throat feeling raw. Her hands squeezed handfuls of blanket, but the pain remained. Nothing made it go away, not even sleep. Dreams haunted her, and every night she relived the moment of her separation from Greg.

The agony was such that, often, Sam wished she hadn't intervened in that desperate instant when Danata ripped them apart. She had sensed the impending tragedy and had allowed her Weaver instincts to take over. If she'd done nothing, she would have ended up like Jacob's dad—absent, almost catatonic. Instead, here she was: totally aware of how much she'd lost.

Somehow, she'd saved her consciousness, but oblivion might have been better. At least, she would have spared herself the pain, the anguish, the enormous loneliness that weighed on her heart like a ton of bricks.

The certainty that Greg shared her "wakeful" fate made it all worse because it meant he was suffering just as much.

Sam rolled over onto her back. She stared at the stone ceiling. There were no light bulbs, candelabra or anything remotely modern. The room was as it must have been hundreds of years ago. Her only source of light was an old lamp that seemed to run on a battery, and she kept expecting to go out.

"Stupid Fate!" she muttered.

Stupid caste. Stupid Morphids.

She was in a constant battle with herself, hopelessly wishing she were human, free from the whims of these invisible powers that now ruled her life.

Sam didn't want to be a Regent. She didn't want to be a Weaver. She would have rather remain the adoptive daughter of two callous parents, a plain human girl.

Instead, she was a creature born to suffer.

A sound by the heavy wooden door pulled Sam away from her pity party. Even though she didn't have a watch, she knew it wasn't meal time. They'd delivered a tray about an hour ago. Breakfast, judging by the dry oatmeal and cold tea she'd barely managed to stomach. No one ever came between meals.

She sat up, and stared at the door as it creaked opened, her chest filling with apprehension. She should have felt relief that someone was here. At times the loneliness, the lack of human contact, was nearly maddening—but being alone was better than any visitors Rothblade Castle had to offer.

The door swung open slowly. Sam's throat went dry at the sight of the person at the threshold.

Yes, utter solitude would have been preferable.

Danata strolled into the room, the tails of a lavender dress flowing behind her. Her black hair was arranged on top of her head like a beehive. Her skin was pale and smooth, and her lips painted in the color of blood. Her overdone gown touched the floor, *whooshing* gently with her every step. Her sleeves were long and tight, all the way to her wrists.

"Hello, dear," she said. "I trust you have been enjoying our hospitality." She pointed toward the food tray on the floor.

Sam's mouth opened and closed. She wanted to tell Danata where she could stick her hospitality, but the words stuck in her throat. She couldn't speak. All she could do was stare into the Regent's violet eyes and remember the satisfaction that had flashed there when Danata had reached for Sam's vinculum and ripped it in two.

"I see your week of seclusion has worked wonders on your manners," Danata said. "You were always too vociferous for my taste. You've been useless long enough, however. I have a task for you, one I think you'll enjoy greatly. Follow me."

Danata turned on her heel and walked out of the room, making Sam wish she'd been condemned to die a lonely old woman.

ℰℴ *Chapter 2* ℭℛ
Greg

Greg stood in front of the old English house, his back to the front door. He was glancing toward the forest across the way, inhaling the fresh air, trying to clear his mind. The trees in the distance were dark green, the grass beneath them yellowish, dying in the cold weather.

He zipped up his jacket and cracked his neck. The house with all its inhabitants was stifling, so he spent a lot of time out here, calmer in the solitude.

It had been a week since he'd woken up screaming Sam's name over and over, reliving the moment he'd been ripped from her, and to his endless frustration, nothing had been done to rescue her. All her parents, Roanna and Bernard, had done so far was talk, and analyze, then analyze some more.

To be fair, they weren't entirely to blame for the infuriating lack of action. MORF, Morphid Order for Regency Fealty, and its commander, Luana Mirante, were just as guilty.

Greg was at his last straw. Just a moment ago, as they'd been discussing their options for the *nth* time, he'd completely lost it and had threatened to leave to find Sam on his own.

How many times could they ponder the possible places where they might be keeping her prisoner? Rothblade Castle was the logical answer, and if that was wrong, didn't they have to start somewhere? But they were scared. The place was "too protected", "impenetrable," they said.

At this point, Greg didn't care how many of Veridan's wards, hexes and curses surrounded the castle. Living like this was not living. He had to find Sam. She was still out there. He knew it deep in his bone marrow. Even if his Keeper skills were gone, he was sure of it—no matter what Mirante or anyone else asked him to consider.

And when he found her, she would weave their vinculums back together, and they would be restored. Greg didn't care that Portos believed Danata had figured out a way to stifle Sam's powers. He didn't care that they insisted he should be patient. If they didn't decide what to do soon, he would take matters into his own hands. He'd told them that much before he stormed out of the house.

Not that they took him seriously. They thought him useless without his link to Sam, without his Keeper senses, because he couldn't locate her and wasn't immune to magic anymore.

Useless as a human, Mirante had said under her breath when she thought he wasn't listening.

And maybe she was right. He felt the lack of power within him almost as much as he felt Sam's absence. Still, doing something was preferable to sitting here, staring at the dusty antiques that cluttered the old house.

The front door opened behind him. Greg's shoulders stiffened. He didn't look back to see who was coming out, but he didn't need to. The fast, short steps hurrying in his direction said it all. He relaxed and was about to turn when a small body crashed against his back and thin arms wrapped around his waist.

"I thought you left me," Jacob said. "I thought you went to find Sam without me."

Greg put a hand on one of the boy's arms and gave it a reassuring squeeze. "I didn't leave you," he said. "I'm right here."

Since Veridan had murdered Jacob's father, the boy had clung to Greg as if he were a big brother. He slept curled up next to him, sat by him at every meal, followed him everywhere. To others, the clingy behavior might have become annoying, but not to Greg. The kid was impossible not to love. And even if that weren't the case, Greg would have loved him for the simple fact that Sam did.

Peeling Jacob's arms off his waist, Greg turned, but as soon as they were facing each other the boy hugged him again, pressing his little face to Greg's stomach.

Damn.

His chest tightened with a tangle of emotions.

"Promise me you won't leave me," Jacob begged.

Greg ruffled his dirty blond hair, removed his arms from his waist again, and leaned down to look him in the eye. He hated himself for what he was going to say, but he couldn't lie to the boy. Jacob trusted him, and he wouldn't break that trust, even if lying would have been easier.

"I can't promise you that, buddy. I don't want to leave you, but I may have no choice."

"I can help," Jacob sobbed. "I miss Sam, too."

Greg smiled. "I know you do, but—"

Before he could say anything else, the front door opened again, saving him from the difficult task. He looked over Jacob's shoulder, then straightened.

Ashby, Perry, and Brooke strode out of the house and crossed the short gravel walkway to meet them.

Greg looked down at Jacob. "We'll talk later, okay?"

He patted the boy's shoulder and walked away from the approaching trio.

"Greg, wait up!" Brooke said.

Against his better judgment, he stopped mid-stride. He wasn't in the mood to talk to them, but how many conversations could he postpone?

"Hey, sweetie," Brooke told Jacob. "Why don't you go inside and get you some hot chocolate? Calisto and Joao are making some. They have marshmallows."

Jacob's eyes went from Brooke to Greg and back again, a silent question in his eyes.

"It's okay, Jake. Go get some hot chocolate," Greg said.

"I don't want hot chocolate. You're just trying to get rid of me."

Greg raised his eyebrows, giving him a "please just go" look.

Jacob sighed and, after an unhappy huff ran back into the house. Greg waited until the door closed, then glanced back at his friends.

"You're freaking the boy out, mate," Perry said. "He thought you'd left him."

"If for no other reason than the boy," Ashby added, "you should stop talking about leaving."

"He's the only reason I'm still here," Greg said.

"Make sure not to tell him that," Perry said, shaking his head.

"How much longer do they expect me to sit here staring at the walls? Aren't you sick of waiting?"

"As long as it takes to figure out a plan that works," Ashby said. "We shouldn't do anything rash."

Brooke scoffed. "Rash is his middle name." She scratched her arm, then snickered. "Rash, get it?"

Perry snickered too, but Greg and Ashby ignored her.

"Stop being a blockhead, Greg." Ashby shook his head. "Rothblade Castle is a physical and magical fortress. You can't just waltz in to rescue Sam."

"Now you're just spewing Mirante's same crap."

"I want Sam back, too," Brooke said. "But getting captured or killed isn't going to help anybody. You always act now and ask questions later, but maybe this isn't the time for that."

"They don't even trust us with all they know," Greg said.

"Now, he's right about that," Perry said. Walking to the low stone wall that surrounded the house, he hopped on it like a skillful crow and stretched to his full height, scanning the forest. "But they're not going to tell us their plans—not after we led Veridan to Sam."

"They've assured us otherwise," Ashby said.

Perry scoffed. "And you believe them?"

Ashby opened his mouth to answer, but closed it without saying anything.

Brooke lowered her gaze to the ground. "We did screw up, guys." More than any of them, she was stuck on the fact that Veridan had used her to track Sam down to the homeless shelter.

So in Greg's book, that made her the wrong person to take advice from. Guilt wasn't a good counselor.

"I think we should wait and let them do their job," she said, though without confidence. "It's only been a week, and it has to take more than that to hatch a plan against Danata, right? Plus, they're grown-ups, they know what they're doing."

"Yeah, grown-ups like Veridan and Danata," Greg sneered.

"That's different. Those two are evil. We're talking about Sam's mom and dad. Of course, they care. They have to do everything in their power to get her back safely. Right?" Brooke asked.

Greg shook his head. "Maybe, but Mirante is the one running the show, and she cares more about dethroning Danata than anything else."

He paused, quarreling with his emotions. He hadn't said his next words out loud to anyone, but he needed the pain of embarrassment, the pain of failure, to jolt him.

"I was supposed to protect her." He choked out the words. "I was supposed to keep her safe, and I failed her. I have to do something. She would come to me, if our situations were reversed. Can you imagine how she's feeling? She must be wondering where we are, why we haven't come for her. If I find her, if I get close enough, she can weave us back together, and then I would be able to defend her again."

Greg's eyes flashed to Ashby. Sam hadn't weaved their broken link. Was Greg a jackass for mentioning this? It was true that Fate had given her Ashby for a Companion, but Fate had also taken him away, hadn't it? Still, Greg couldn't help the guilt that rose in him, especially now that he knew exactly what Ashby had gone through.

"I'm sorry," he murmured. "I didn't mean to say—"

Ashby put a hand up. "No need. I've come to terms with it. You know that."

Was that true? Was it possible to ever come to terms with such a loss?

No. It couldn't be, and Greg didn't intent to go on living like this. He was going to find Sam. He was going to put an end to the pain.

He peered at Perry. In Greg's mind, he was the only one talking sense. Maybe, just maybe, the sorcerer would lend a hand. Greg had a feeling he would.

❧ Chapter 3 ☙
Sam

Sam stepped outside of the chamber that had served as her prison cell for the last week, and took a deep breath. In the hall, the two guards flanked her and forced her to follow the Regent's brisk steps. The men seemed familiar. Sam recalled their hard faces from the last time she'd been held prisoner, the day Danata had ripped her from Ashby. What were their names? Simeon and Omar, she thought.

Apprehension twisted in her gut. This couldn't be good.

Sam looked sideways at the guards. They kept their eyes straight ahead as if she weren't there. The urge to run possessed Sam, but it was a stupid flight instinct as useless as fake butter on toast.

Her nervous hands pulled on her dirty t-shirt as she forced one foot in front of the other. Their steps echoed in the barren stone hall. Sam tried to memorize the labyrinthine corridors but quickly got disoriented. There were no windows. Everything was made of gray rock, and the hangings on the walls were ancient, just like the spare pieces of furniture strewn about. It all depressed her even more.

The first time she'd been here—when Ashby brought her with him right after her metamorphosis—the place had seemed magnificent. They'd waited for Portos in a large entrance hall that hung with beautiful tapestries and gleamed with marble floors. The place had been open—nothing like these claustrophobic halls Danata had relegated her to.

But now, as she followed, Sam realized she'd been spared from an even grimmer area of the castle. Gradually, the halls grew narrower and darker, making her feel as if she was headed straight for the bowels of hell. When they passed a heavy wooden door and began to descend down a dimly-lit, closed-in staircase, she became certain of it.

Her heart hammered, knocking against her ribcage as if it would break out. She wrung her t-shirt more fiercely, wishing instead to place her hands on her chest, but the manacles made it impossible. Swallowing thickly, she wondered where Danata was taking her.

Images of medieval torturing devices popped into Sam's mind. She looked over her shoulder at the guards who now were forced to walk in single file. They still avoided her gaze, but even in the gloom, she detected shame in the eyes of the guard directly behind her, Omar, if she recalled correctly. He knew what awaited her, and he didn't like to be part of it.

Sam froze mid step. "Please don't take me down there," she begged in a barely audible whisper.

Foolishly, she hoped the man would take pity on her, but all she got was a rough "Come on, move!" and a shove that send her to her knees.

A hand slipped around Sam's arm.

"Just do as you're told," Omar mumbled, pulling Sam to her feet.

She trembled, staring down at the bottom of the steps where Danata waited.

"What is the matter? Hurry up and get that girl down here. I don't have all day," she snapped.

Gathering her courage, Sam jerked her arm out of Omar's grip and decided she wouldn't be a coward like these men. Whatever Danata had in store for her, it couldn't last forever or be worse than the empty feeling that slowly gnawed away at her bones. And if death awaited, at least it meant her desolation would also come to an end.

Sam walked down the rest of the steps until she reached Danata. The Regent appraised her, stopping at her manacled hands as she twirled a small key in a leather strap. She smiled.

"Follow me." Danata turned and led the way into a brightly illuminated hall that was nothing like the dark, dingy staircase they'd just left.

Sam blinked as the narrow hall opened into a wide area with several metal doors, kept secure by electronic keypads. Proper lighting spilled from modern sconces attached to white walls. Clearly, the area had gone through some upgrades recently.

The strong smell of bleach and anti-septic stung Sam's throat. She sniffled and pressed her nose to the sleeve of her t-shirt. This was nothing like the dank dungeon Sam had imagined, but that didn't mean the creepy feeling clogging her chest was going anywhere, on the contrary.

For some reason she couldn't put her finger on, this felt much worse.

***

"There's something I'd like to see," Danata said, the delightful timbre in her voice redoubling Sam's dread.

Vivid images popped into Sam's head: manacles much worse than the ones she already wore, wooden contraptions that would stretch her limbs to a painful snapping point, electrical cords, drills. A knot clogged her throat. She swallowed and forced it to pass. There was no way out of this place, and no one to help her. She had to face this with courage.

Clearly enjoying Sam's state of dread, Danata walked to the end of the hall, faced the last door on the left, and slowly entered a code in its security keypad. A beep sounded with every touch.

"Come closer," the Regent said, swinging the door open.

Sam hesitated.

Danata tapped her foot impatiently.

Thinking of Greg who never shied away from a challenged no matter how dangerous, she began to walk.

I'll get through this, she told herself. No way she'd give this woman the satisfaction of seeing her broken. One step after the other, Sam kept her breaths even and reached Danata. Once there, she took a moment, prepared herself for the worst, then turned toward the cell.

At the sight of what waited beyond the door, Sam's heart caught in her throat. The fibers that made up her body seemed to tremble, unbalancing her to the point of vertigo. She put a hand out, looking for a handhold, but all she found was Danata's arm. She immediately recoiled.

"Enter." Danata put out a hand in invitation.

Sam shook her head, not at the torture devices she'd imagined, but at the decrepit woman who sat curled up atop a dirty cot. Her back was against the wall, and her knees pulled up to her chest. She wore a long, dirty dress, her toes peeking out from under its ragged seams. Cracked, yellowing toenails betrayed her age and perhaps some debilitating disease. Her hair also looked unhealthy, matted and dry, with wiry strands shooting in every direction. She stared at Sam and Danata with huge, brown eyes that seemed lost in the folds of her brown skin.

Compelled by some invisible force, Sam stepped into the room, a hand stretched toward the woman.

Danata followed, her steps finicky as if she was entering a pigsty and didn't want to get her dress dirty. She wrinkled her nose at the pungent body odor emanating from the woman.

Sam's chest boiled with anger, and more than ever, she became aware of the depths of her hatred toward the Regent. Sam didn't need to use her skill to know that this poor woman was one of Danata's unfortunate victims. And yet, the Regent was acting as if the poor wretch was to blame for her own deplorable state.

"I want you to meet Anima," Danata said, as if she were introducing a longtime friend and not one the casualties of her cruelty. "She used to be part of my sister's council, but had a . . . change of heart when I became Regent."

Anima hugged herself tighter, staring at Danata like a scared child who's expecting a second beating. There seemed to be no recognition in her eyes, though, just the type of primal fear a warm-blooded animal exhibits in front of a predator.

Danata faced Sam, wearing an expression that seemed foreign on her cold features. Sam tried to decipher what the look in her eyes meant, but came up empty.

After a moment, Danata said, "I have, in my life, made many mistakes . . ."

Sam frowned at the foreign sounds escaping through the Regent's lips. Was this contrition? An apology? No, that was impossible. Anger, sarcasm, and ill-intention were Danata's native language, not this. Sam's distrust hardened further.

"Anima is one of those mistakes," Danata said. "She made me very angry once, even though she should have known better. Everyone is aware that my temper is . . . my biggest flaw." She averted her gaze as if embarrassed.

Sam didn't buy her act. Not for a second.

"No one is perfect, my dear Samantha," Danata continued. "But many aren't aware of their shortcomings. I am, and I'm paying for them. I lost my son." Her eyes wavered.

It's all an act, Sam assured herself. There was no way a monster like Danata could feel regret. If she grieved for her son, it was for selfish reasons—nothing else.

Suddenly, as if catching herself, Danata's face hardened into a more familiar expression of indifference. Was the woman's cold heart actually capable of true motherly emotions that she must fight to keep hidden?

"When I ripped Anima from her husband," Danata said, "I was young and inexperienced. I regretted it immediately and countless times since. She was a remarkable individual, but there was no way back. Not until now." She turned her violet gaze to Sam.

So here it was: the reason Danata was bothering to keep Sam alive.

The woman smiled. "I never expected to be able to correct my mistake, but then you came along. My anti-thesis. Everything I am not."

The last words were full of venom and caused the world to right itself. This was the woman Sam knew, through and through.

Danata took two steps toward Anima. "When I learned of what you are capable of, I immediately thought of Anima. She has never left my thoughts."

"Really?" Sam asked, displaying the full extent of her skepticism. "Is that why you keep her in a cell? Why she's in such poor condition?"

"Poor condition?" Danata looked around, feigning surprise. "She's kept in a clean area. The staff provides her with food and clothing. She has medical care, if needed. Keep in mind that these people show no interest in caring for themselves, and my staff isn't quite adept to the task. All things considered, I think this is quite charitable."

Sam scoffed in disgust. There was no point in arguing. Danata knew about charity as much as a lion knew about hollandaise sauce.

"But that's not why we're here, is it? We're here to help her." Danata said in a sensible tone.

"Oh, please! Drop the act," Sam snapped, tired of the Regent's antics.

Danata straightened, arching an eyebrow. "I don't expect you to understand or sympathize with me. That's not why I brought you here." She turned, gestured to one of the guards and said, "Go get him."

Get who? Who was she talking about? Greg? Ashby? Had she captured them too? Sam's heart smashed against her ribs like a caged animal.

Danata continued, "I brought you here to amend a mistake, to help Anima and her husband."

Relief washed over Sam, along with a healthy dose of guilt. Danata hadn't captured Greg or Ashby. She was talking about the second victim or her so-called mistake: Anima's Companion.

"If you want to help them, you are welcome to. They deserve better, even if they betrayed me. Their punishment has certainly exceeded their crime."

Then Danata stepped aside and let Anima's husband through.

℘ Chapter 4 ⌘
Perry

Perry sat by himself in the kitchen of Mirante's old house, eating a bowl of cereal. He missed Brooke by his side already. Her curvy shape, her teasing hands. He smiled to himself.

"There you are." Greg walked in, brightening when he noticed Perry. "I've been looking for you."

Perry set his spoon down. "I'm here, mate."

Greg pulled out a chair and sat across from Perry, an intense look in his eyes that didn't bode well. Perry picked his spoon back up and took a bite of his Honey Monster Puffs, pretending not to notice Greg's anxiousness.

"You hungry?" he asked, pushing the cereal box in Greg's direction.

"No, I . . ." Greg paused for a moment, then just came out with it. "Take me to Rothblade Castle."

Perry blinked. "Excuse me?"

"Use your magic to transfer me to Rothblade Castle," Greg elaborated. "Do this one thing for me."

"Bog off, mate. You know I can't do that," he said. "I'm not allowed to go there. Portos would have my head. Just leave me alone. I'm not in the mood for this. I just had to take Brooke back to her house, and it wasn't fun saying goodbye."

Mirante had ordered him to "get rid" of the human and erase her memories. Worst yet, Ashby hadn't backed him up, saying Perry would thank him later since Brooke would be safer until it was all over. The bastard.

Greg kept going as if he hadn't heard a word Perry said. "You could take me somewhere nearby, then tell me how to get there."

The desperation in Greg's eyes made the cereal taste sour in Perry's mouth. He shook his head. "What for? You wouldn't be able to get in. If it was that easy, we'd have already gone and attacked."

"I thought you understood." Greg ground his teeth.

Perry frowned at him, but said nothing. One had to be cautious with Greg and his volatile temper.

"I thought you saw through their bullshit," Greg said. "Thought you would help me."

He heaved a heavy sigh. "Maybe, but . . . I still can't take you there."

"I'm going either way," Greg said, as if the threat would make a difference. It didn't.

"That's your decision, but I won't be bloody responsible for it." Perry's chair scraped the floor as he stood.

Greg jumped to his feet, fists clenched. He looked mad, ready to force him to listen. A week ago, Perry would have been worried, but now he couldn't help but feel sorry for the bloke. Greg was no match for Perry—not without his Keeper immunity to magic.

"I don't need your help," Greg said after a tense moment. "I don't need anyone's help. I'll find her and bring her back."

Greg turned to leave. Perry put a hand on his arm.

"You'll be no help to her if you're dead."

"No one understands," Greg said. "Not even Ashby. I *have* to help her." Greg shook with anger.

Perry took a step back and held both hands up as Greg's knuckles turned white.

"Believe it or not, we're all trying to help her," Perry said.

Greg took a step closer. Unable to help himself, Perry placed a hand to the amulet on his chest, his conduit for magic.

"Really?" Greg asked, his eyes falling to the pendant. "Well, don't all trip on each other trying to do it."

To Perry's relief, Greg shook himself and stomped out of the kitchen without letting his anger get the best of him.

Perry rolled his shoulders back and cracked his neck. The bloke was intense, and if Portos' plan to keep him in check didn't start to work soon, they would lose him.

❧ *Chapter 5* ☙
Sam

Shuffling steps followed the clank of a metal door. Sam waited, resisting the urge to use her skill to confirm her suspicions. She held her breath as the guard pushed Anima's husband into the room and forced him to sit next to his wife.

The old man was as disheveled as his Companion. Sam was disturbed to see that his watery eyes showed no recognition of his wife. Instead, they held only terror and focused entirely on Danata and the guard.

After weaving her father, Bernard, Sam had used her powers only twice and in completely different ways. Jacob's father and the homeless woman at the New York shelter hadn't had a Companion to weave them back to. Their Integrals had died. So Sam's task had been to repair what was left of their vinculums to allow the two poor souls a reprieve from the intense grief caused by the severing.

This, however, was different. She was faced with two severed Companions, two Morphids who could still be made whole, two souls who could have peace again. How could she deny them that?

"Well, girl," Danata said. "You're here for a reason. Make yourself useful."

Sam clenched her teeth. The urge to help the couple was overwhelming. Her instincts felt afire with purpose and determination to set things right. Yet, a part of her told her not to listen to her instincts. This was Danata asking her to fix what she'd purposely broken. The woman could not be trusted.

"That urge you feel to reach for their vinculums," Danata whispered, "I feel it, too. And when the deed is done, I also feel satisfaction as I'm sure you do. Is it wrong to obey one's nature? In this instance," she pointed at Anima, "I think it was."

Did the Regent really regret what she'd done to these people? Maybe after what she'd done to Ashby, she'd had time to think and feel remorse. Did she truly want to make amends?

No. Sam shook her head. *She has no heart. I can't trust her.* Sam fought her instincts. The need to reach and weave the broken links made her tremble. She went down on her knees, curling herself and her need into a ball. Vomit rose to her throat, burning her vocal cords. She swallowed hard, fists clenched as she fought to control the maddening urge to make the frail ribbons of light whole.

"Help her to her feet," Danata ordered.

Non-too-gently, Simeon gripped Sam's arm and forced her up. Shivers rippled down her body, raising the small hairs on the back of her arms. Legs trembling, she focused on a spot on the floor, still fighting.

"What's the matter?" Danata asked in a sweet tone.

Sam couldn't have answered even if she'd wanted to. Her throat was full of bile, and her tongue was trapped between her teeth. Instead, she shook her head and steeled her will against her instincts—even if the task made her feel evil. These people *needed* her help, yet Sam couldn't give them the respite they deserved. Danata's ulterior plans might be worse than the cure.

"Unbind her hands," Danata said, handing Simeon the small key she'd been twirling.

He took it, stuck it in one of Sam's manacles, and released her hands. Involuntarily, her fingers fluttered upward, reaching for the broken links. With a grunt of realization and effort, she pulled her hands back and pressed them against her stomach.

"I don't understand. I thought you'd want to help them," Danata said. "You're the only one who can undo what I did."

"What do you want from them? You must be after something," Sam said, her voice breaking.

"What do I want from them?" Danata repeated, frowning. "I just . . ." She paused, her eyes shifting from side to side. After a moment, she seemed to reconsider what she was going to say and waved a dismissive hand in the air. "All right, I admit there's something Anima can do for me, but that doesn't mean you should pass the opportunity to improve her situation. Don't do it for me. Do it for them."

"You tore me from Greg, tore me from Ashby," Sam said. "Why should I do anything that benefits you in any way?"

"You sought to destroy me, child."

"You're crazy. I never set out to destroy you. I never asked for any of this."

"You brought my sister back. Getting rid of her was not easy, and now . . ."

"What you do is evil."

"I can't help it any more than you can," Danata said, then abruptly walked out of the cell, ordering the guard to follow.

For a moment, Sam thought Danata would have her locked in the cell, but the Regent simply stood outside the door, quiet and expectant. Apparently, she had nothing else to say, and she meant to wait until Sam succumbed to her instincts.

Almost mechanically, Sam turned to face the couple. They sat next to each other, yet miles apart. It was as if they were strangers and not Companions fated to love each other unconditionally.

Tears prickled in the back of her eyes. She thought of her own torn links, faded and frayed, floating above her. She dare not look up. If she did, she would be tempted to repair one of the vinculums, and what would be the use of that with Danata standing right outside the door?

Sam recoiled within herself, fighting her nature. After a moment, an incessant sound began in the back of her head, relentless and increasing in pitch by the instant. She covered her ears, the struggle more than she could bear.

Had Danata told the truth? Was she like Sam? Unable to control her instincts? Forced to *rip* all of those who came in contact with her? No. Sam refused to believe it. Danata had had time to understand her skill and learn to control it. Morphids could make their own decisions rather than be blindly controlled by Fate.

The pain inside Sam reached a breaking point.

Of their own accord, her hands shot upward, beckoning for the two halves of the broken vinculum. As soon as they touched her trembling fingers, the bonds turned electric and reached out for each other. She felt the yearning, the weight of the years spent in isolation. And she knew, then, that she had no other choice but to rebuild the broken minds and souls of these two people.

She began to weave.

Blinding light sifted through her fingers. She squinted until she could see the broken strands as they twined together, meeting and embracing with tangible relief. Faster than the first time she'd done it, the links weaved themselves into *one* flawless ribbon of light. When the job was done, the entire room seemed to exhale with relief. Energy flowed into Sam, immensely satisfying and almost enough to make her feel whole again.

She blinked and looked at the couple. For a moment, they sat immobile, numb as before, but then their eyelids fluttered. They wet their lips and swallowed as if parched. Anima inhaled deeply and planted a hand on her chest. Reginald held his head and shook it between knobby fingers, a deep moan sounding in the back of his throat.

Anima said something, a mumbled word Sam couldn't understand. At the sound of her voice, Reginald released his head and glanced up. His deep dark eyes filled with wonder, surprise, and something like regret.

"Ani-ma?" he said.

Slowly, his wife's eyes swiveled in his direction. The same wonder and surprise pooled inside her equally dark eyes. With trembling fingers, she reached for his face.

She frowned at his beard as she caressed it. "So much gray," she said.

"Anima," Reginald repeated, his voice clearer and tinted with a plea.

"Where have you been?" Anima asked.

"I—I . . ." He seemed to search his mind, then looked around the room.

When he noticed Sam, he frowned. Anima followed his gaze. A thrill of recognition went down the woman's face.

"You," she said in shock. "Oh, no!" She looked like she'd seen a ghost.

***

Anima's eyes widened and filled with something like terror. Sam's insides froze. Why was she looking at Sam as if she were a nightmare come to life?

The woman opened her mouth to say something—to scream, perhaps—but as her gaze drifted above Sam's shoulder, she stopped.

Danata stepped back into the room, making the atmosphere feel icier than it already did. Anima's terrified expression redoubled and was joined by her husband's. Visibly shaking, they pulled close together and embraced.

"You," Reginald said in a broken voice. "What have you done to us?"

"Take him away," Danata ordered the guards.

The two men walked into the cell and tried to take Reginald away, but Anima clung to him, crying out in heartbreaking fear.

Danata rolled her eyes and watched with disdain as Simeon's beefy hands took hold of Anima's arms, while Omar forced Reginald to his feet and shoved him out of the cell with such force that the old man crashed to the floor in a heap of bones.

He pushed up. "Anima," he rasped, his watery, fear-filled eyes searching for his wife as Omar dragged him out of sight back to where he'd come from.

"Stop!" Sam screamed. "What are you doing?"

"You stay out of this," Danata ordered.

"You evil monster," Sam cried out, launching toward Danata.

"Oy!" Simeon let go of Anima to try to help the Regent.

Danata needed no help, however. She was fierce and violent all on her own and, with a twinkle in her eyes, grabbed a handful of Sam's hair, slapped her across the face, and threw her to the floor. She loomed over Sam, lips pulled back in a savage grimace.

Sam crashed against her side, jamming her elbow. Pain shot up to her shoulder, but it was her face that hurt the most. Wincing, she rubbed her cheek.

"I told you to stay out of it," Danata snarled, then walked toward Anima with evil intent. "Hold the girl back," she ordered.

Simeon's tall, black boots appeared in front of Sam. She recoiled, tears stinging the back of her eyes.

"Hello, Anima," Danata purred behind the guard.

Through Simeon's thick legs, Sam watched Anima shrink away on her cot, pressing her back against a corner of the cell.

"Stay away from me, monster," she said.

"Is it possible you never foresaw this?" Danata asked, sweeping a hand in a circle to demonstrate the cell. "Isn't that ironic?

"How long? How long since you—"

"Does it really matter? You're here, *have been* here half your life."

"And yet it's not enough. What do you want now?" Anima asked in a weak, scratchy voice, then in a strange gesture, stuffed her hands under her armpits and tensed all over.

"I want you to show me more. *Everything*," Danata said.

Anima's eyes danced around the room. She looked like someone trying to grasp the full extent of her situation.

"Leave us alone," the old woman pleaded.

"*Us*? You mean that useless man?" Danata pointed in the general direction of the door. "He's fine, don't worry about him."

"He's my husband."

"A burden I would say, but I didn't bring you back to discuss *him*. Although you should be happy you are *rejoined*."

Anima's eyes wandered to Sam. Danata turned sideways in order to look at both of them.

"It seems you've seen the girl in your visions," Danata said. "She scares you. Why?"

Anima shook her head, but said nothing.

"She's your savior," Danata said, her tone heavy with sarcasm. "You shouldn't be scared of her."

Tears overflowed Sam's eyes as helplessness filled her. Why hadn't she fought harder to resist her instincts?

Anima's gaze remained on Sam. The woman's chin quivered, but there was no terror in her eyes anymore, only sadness.

"She's just a girl. Freshly morphed," Anima said to herself more than anyone else.

"A girl who can undo what I do."

"Yes," Anima said, sinking lower into her cot. Her eyes closed and opened again, fluttering. She seemed ready to pass out, and Sam thought that would be a blessing.

"I think I remember you," Anima said after a moment.

A strange feeling washed over Sam. She rubbed her arms to dispel a shiver. Danata stood straighter, honing her attention on Anima.

"I've seen you," the woman said. "It's been a long time, but I would never forget your face. It's . . . Samantha, right?"

Goosebumps rippled in Sam's arms. "Yes, ma'am."

Anima nodded very slowly. "I'm glad you're here. It means . . ." Anima stopped, her eyes shifting toward Danata. As if catching herself, she pressed her lips together, leaned her head back and closed her eyes.

Sam glanced sideways at Danata, expecting her to explode in demands to know *everything*—whatever that meant. But to Sam's surprise the Regent stood calmly, scrutinizing Anima with care.

Simeon frowned at Sam, looking as confused as she was. She glowered back, refusing to share in their mutual puzzlement. He returned the glare and scratched his head, a clueless expression on his idiot face.

"You'll pay for this," Sam whispered so only he could hear her. The man clenched a fist and raised it a bit, but after a quick flick of his eyes in Danata's direction, he let out a breath and brought it down.

After a long moment, Anima took a shuddering breath. She flexed her neck from side to side, and finally opened her eyes. Unlike before, something gleamed in the depths of her dark gaze, now.

"I see even your son has abandoned you," the old woman said with a chuckle.

"Where is he? Tell me!" Danata demanded.

Anima ignored the question. "Ashby is a man now, and he's chosen to place his loyalty elsewhere. In case you're wondering, he *doesn't* love you anymore."

At the words, Danata's face disfigured into a mask of pain. She quickly disguised her feelings, but not before they revealed how devastating this piece of information was.

"He grew up smart . . . like his father." Anima shook her head. "You're not better off than me. You've lost everything."

Danata spoke through thin lips. "I have lost nothing. What matters to me is still safely in my grip."

"You've always lied to yourself, Danata," Anima said with a pity so profound and sincere that it made Sam wonder if the woman was a saint.

"My course is altered," Danata said. "It's been altered a hundred times over."

Anima nodded. "Yes, it certainly has been, though not for the better."

Danata took a step forward, stamping her foot on the floor. Anima flinched and pushed back, looking as if she wished to melt into the wall.

"Now, you *will* show me what I need to know," Danata said through clenched teeth.

Anima barked out a weak laugh. "Why would I do such a thing now? After you've stolen my life, my youth, my Companion?"

"I would think carefully, if I were you." Danata cut a sharp glance in Sam's direction.

"I don't need to," Anima said in a quiet tone that was more commanding than Danata's near growl.

"If you don't, you'll suffer a hundred times what you've suffered so far." The Regent leaned forward, bringing her face close to Anima's. "You'll give me what I want because I have her," she pointed a finger at Sam without even looking back, "I can tear you apart from your beloved Reginald a thousand times in a day, if I want to."

Sam gasped and pressed a hand to her mouth. Horror washed over her, but as it passed, her chest slowly filled with fury. The witch was crazy if she thought Sam would play along.

"No, you won't," she said in an even, sure tone. She would prevail over her instincts if it killed her.

Allowing Anima and Reginald to live separated from each other would be a cruel injustice, but Sam knew the pain and anguish that ripping caused. It had to be far worse than the numbness that followed. She would not let them go through that.

Danata regarded Sam for a moment, then laughed. "What makes you think you'll have a choice?"

"I don't care what you do to me," Sam said, even as her stomach clenched.

"We'll see about that. Take her back to her cell," Danata ordered. "And summon the High Sorcerer to my office."

Simeon grabbed Sam's arm and pulled her toward the door. Her gaze lingered on Anima, silently trying to tell her it would be all right. Anima smiled sadly, her dark eyes full of something that looked and felt like forgiveness.

Sam's heart broke as the guard dragged her out. Glancing one last time over her shoulder, Sam caught a glimpse of Danata's hands gripping the newly remade vinculum.

Unable to watch, Sam closed her eyes.

The couple's cries of pain and desolation filled Sam's ears as they echoed through the cavernous hall like the laments of two condemned ghosts.

She staggered onward, ahead of the guard, her already-broken heart splitting into a million more pieces.

ℰ Chapter 6 ℭ
Veridan

A mixture of fear and excitement ran through Veridan's veins. The sight of his nebula was glorious. When he began this task several years ago, he never dreamed it would grow to this size and amass this level of energy.

He was so close. So close.

He could almost feel it, taste it, and it had a delightful flavor, better than anything he'd ever sampled.

More delightful still was the fact that the nebula seemed to be growing exponentially now.

Oh, if only it'd been this way since the beginning, but his progress had been excruciatingly slow. How many times had he found himself at the brink of giving up? How often had he reigned in his hatred toward Danata, the inconvenient conduit to all this power?

He fidgeted, feeling oddly restless. For a long time, the idea of reaching his goal had consumed him day and night, but now, his obsession had reached a fiery pitch. He had to find more victims for Danata, more lambs to guide to the slaughter, so her *ripping* hands could unleash the last bursts of power that would complete his nebula.

But these last few weeks had been frustrating. Danata was distracted, focused on those infernal kids that demanded more attention than any snotty brat had a right to.

Sure, the ripping of Samantha and her Keeper had been a great addition to his stock of power—something that had pleased him to no end, especially considering how the energy from their vinculum had visibly enlarged the nebula. But enough was enough. Danata's obsession with MORF and Ashby had to end. It would lead Veridan nowhere, unless she agreed to his most recent proposal, one that would help her find the insolent boy. Of course, she would never consent, not considering what she'd have to give up.

In the past, Danata's fixation would have suited Veridan. Heads tended to roll when she was upset, but now that he was so close, it was an inconvenient waste of time. Why, oh why did the heartless woman have to possess motherly instincts? Of all things!

Veridan cursed under his breath. Depending on Danata was a damnable thing. He wished he could leave, go elsewhere to find what he needed, but there was nowhere else to go, no other individual that could do what she could. He knew the nebula would have never gotten this far without her—other means of acquiring energy weren't as effective and high-yielding as ripping—but the embers of his patience were nearly extinguished.

Maybe he should talk to her again, convince her that Ashby was a lost cause, tempt her with promises of Roanna's capture. But he was afraid to push too hard, afraid to raise suspicion.

Patience, Veridan. Patience. Her blindfold could fall at any minute.

One never knew with Danata and her unpredictable temper. Chances were she would soon get tired of pining over Ashby. Stranger things had happened.

At least the infernal girl couldn't weave anyone together anymore—not locked up as she was. That was a relief. She'd caused enough damage during her stint in New York City, repairing broken links and stealing energy from his nebula in the process. But he'd taken care of her, made her pay, too. He'd worked too hard to let her spoil things.

With a sigh, Veridan reached out a hand to the nebula as if to pet it. The lost souls and essences trapped inside writhed in its center. The surface gleamed, reflecting the light of the surrounding candles Veridan had lit with the flick of his wrist.

"We're almost there," he addressed the souls trapped within, the way he would a group of children. "Just a little longer, and you'll see. Morphids will finally be what we're meant to be—not these sniveling creatures who hide and pretend not to exist. This world has taken much from us. But no more. Your sacrifice won't be in vain, and Morphidkind will thank you one day. Your suffering will be remembered. I'll make sure of it. Humans will learn who we are. We won't be a race of dwindling numbers, always struggling to survive. We will show them our greatness, and the pride our ancestors wore like a badge of honor will be pinned to our chests as we walk the earth with our heads held high."

Veridan smiled, the corners of his mouth stretching away from each other. The gesture felt strange but, nonetheless, genuine.

These thoughts filled him with pleasure, an emotion he'd nearly forgotten.

Morphids had come from a different realm a long time ago. The exact reason that drove them to abandon their land was unknown, as well as the history of most of the individuals who had arrived. Moreover, most of the knowledge that referred to the original settlers had been lost through the centuries, perhaps even on purpose.

There were many theories that attempted to explain why Morphids had come to this sad human realm. Most blamed the event on things like famine, disease, or war.

Whatever the reason, Veridan's passion for knowledge about his kind had started when he was no more than a child, the day his grandfather died and left him a few ancient texts as inheritance. That was when his quest for Nymphalia had begun.

"We will rise from this obscurity," Veridan said. "We will overpower those who have stifled us and have caused our numbers to dwindle. We will—"

The nebula throbbed.

A shiver traveling down his spine, the Sorcerer took a step back to better judge what he feared most.

Like a huge black heart, his cloud of power had grown bigger for an instant, then had shrunk.

He shook his head. *Why? How?!*

The Weaver girl was locked up, and she was the only one capable of stealing from him. Had she escaped? No, he would have heard a commotion, or received summons from Danata.

Again, his gaze roved around, traveling from one end of the nebula to the other, quickly calculating its size. There was no denying it. It was smaller.

"No no no!"

Seething with anger, Veridan rushed out of the small alcove and stepped into his adjacent chamber. He picked up a fresh shirt from his wardrobe and slipped it on, determined to discover what had caused this.

A few ideas crossed his mind—one including that meddling fool, Portos—but he refused to believe that someone other than the girl was to blame for the change. No one knew of his plans, after all.

Once he was properly attired in a tie, black jacket and trousers, he rushed toward the door, then remembering he hadn't locked the alcove, turned back. Key in hand, he placed a hand on the doorknob and had to do a double take.

The nebula had gone to its original size.

He frowned, confused. Was he seeing things?

No. He wasn't some feeble-minded fool. Something *had* happened. Something Danata was to blame for. He was certain of it. Finally locking the door, Veridan straightened his jacket and cufflinks, his features relaxing as he went through the motions. He had almost reached the required level of coolness, when a firm knock sounded at the door.

"High Sorcerer," a gruff voice said from outside his door.

"What is it?" he demanded.

"The Regent requires your presence in her office."

But of course. "Tell her I'll be right there," he nearly growled.

***

"You summoned me," Veridan said as he entered Danata's office and closed the door behind him.

The floor-to-ceiling windows that made up the front wall were dimmed, impeding the office staff from looking in. The Sorcerer had passed the workers on his way in, while they peered at him sideways with a mixture of curiosity and wicked contentment. That could only mean Danata was in a mood, and they were glad someone else would take the brunt of her rage today.

The Regent stood behind her desk, holding a glass in her hand. She gave Veridan a quick glance, then returned her attention to her drink, a healthy amount of Veridan's spell-made, energizing potion, a brew she could hardly do without these days. Once she'd drunk half of the amber liquid, she set the glass down on a silver tray and finally gave Veridan her full attention.

"I've changed my mind about your proposal," she said, her face twisted in a pain-filled grimace that allowed him to grasp her meaning right away.

With a sideways glance toward her nearly-empty decanter, Danata took a seat at her desk. Veridan sat too, crossing his legs nonchalantly and acting, for all the world, as if her decision meant nothing to him.

Quelling his delight, he conjured a slight grimace. "Are you certain?"

"When have you known me to dither?"

"Never, my Regent," he said, doing his best to suppress a smile.

"I guess I will now learn exactly how my victims feel," she said.

"In a way."

"And are you certain there is no turning back once . . . ?"

"I am."

Danata waved a hand in the air. "It doesn't matter. What Ashby has done to me, to his own mother, is unforgivable. He has disobeyed me, abandoned me, left me no reason to be loyal to him. I tried to make amends. There'll be no reason to harbor regrets."

"I'm sure there won't be."

The boy was the only occupant in Danata's otherwise empty heart, and the void his absence would leave behind might very well become her first true regret. But he wasn't about to tell her that.

Or perhaps not. He, himself, had felt little regret when he'd dissolved his filial bond with his parents—that first bit of pure energy that had served as the seed to his nebula.

"Did you feel your parents' absence after dissolving your bond?" Danata asked, as if reading his mind.

So she wasn't so certain as she made it sound. At least the question related to her well-being and not Ashby's. That was something.

"As a matter of fact, I felt free, liberated." It was true. His parents and their morals had always felt like a load on his back. "But you must remember, my Regent. You saw us interact afterward. Neither I nor them mourned the loss."

She nodded as if recalling.

Not that his own experience offered any sort of guarantee. He'd only performed the spell once. Parents and their offspring didn't go around wishing to dissolve their bond, and if they did, they didn't come to Veridan for help, unfortunately. Shame the spell required one of the parties to be a willing participant. Otherwise, he would be done with his quest.

"And you suffered no ill effects?" she asked.

"None whatsoever."

Danata stood and began pacing behind her desk. "It doesn't matter, I suppose. Our current situation demands risks, and I've never shied away from them. My sister and her MORF rebels are organizing. They've been far too quiet lately, and that's not a good sign. We must find them, sooner rather than later. I will not allow Roanna to take back the Regency. Our kind needs a strong leader, not my simpering sister. Under her rule our numbers will dwindle further. We've only begun to undo the damage she and her predecessors did. We cannot lose ground."

This was true. Roanna was never aggressive enough in trying to solve Morphidkind's dwindling population. She'd governed with a weak hand, trying to get everyone to agree on a course of action rather than dictating one. Not that Danata was a better choice than her sister. True, she had no trouble choosing a path—whether that path was the most reasonable was an entirely different matter.

Regardless, neither Danata nor Roanna would be able to fix this problem. He was the only one equipped to do that.

"I agree," he said. "MORF is dangerous for us all. Action is most certainly required." He wouldn't mind finally getting his revenge on that stupid Keeper, too, and it would involve a fair amount of satisfying torture.

"Are you sure the girl doesn't know where MORF is?" Danata asked yet again.

"Yes, My Regent," he assured for the fourth time. "I searched her mind carefully." Danata didn't seem convinced for some reason. Ashby's betrayal had made her more distrustful than ever.

"If only the Seer had talked," Danata mumbled to herself.

"Seer, my Regent?"

What was she talking about? There were no trustworthy Seers left. Romera Silvercreek was a joke, and Veridan wasn't aware of any newly morphed Seers. The cast was extremely rare. Finders were more common, though not as effective.

After a moment of reflection, one person came to memory. Someone he had nearly forgotten in all these years: Anima Altenbeck.

The woman had been useless since the day Danata ripped her from her husband almost twenty years ago. Except now there was the Weaver.

So this is what had happened to his nebula. The Regent and the girl playing tug of war.

Despite himself, Veridan almost laughed. Oh, this woman was delightful in her evil creativity, enough to make Machiavelli take offense.

"Yes, a Seer," Danata said. "Anima Altenbeck. I'm sure you remember her. In case you're wondering, the woman is as stubborn as ever. She wouldn't tell me where to find MORF."

Slowly, Veridan's amusement died. Why hadn't Danata consulted him before using the girl for this purpose? And what if she tried again and made the effects on his nebula permanent? Even trapped in a cell and in the Regency's hands, the Weaver was a greater liability than he'd anticipated.

It seemed the girl had outlived her usefulness. She'd served her purpose well, her two severed vinculums bringing him ever closer to his goal and keeping Danata distracted. But he would not risk it all for a foolish girl, no matter what *Fate* or anyone thought of her.

Veridan raised his eyebrows to indicate he understood what Danata had been up to. They had communicated this way for many years. Tacitly. They were of the same wicked mind and soul, after all. Same as the girl, he would have to do away with Danata. It would be a shame, considering the benefits the woman provided, but there was no other choice. Sometimes, he liked to imagine that she would delight in his plans. But in truth, she would be angry to realize he'd been using her all along. She wasn't a reliable accomplice, in any case.

He stood, tugging on his cuffs. "I think we'd best find out where MORF is before it's too late. Cutting the filial bond will allow me to trace Ashby's exact location." He extended a hand in invitation.

Allowing him to do the spell would be the last useful thing Danata would do for him.

***

Danata lay on her bed, wearing a light, white nightgown. She stared straight at the canopy of her four-poster bed, her face impassive, though the rapid pulsation at her throat betrayed how she truly felt.

Veridan pulled the curtains shut, inviting shadows into the room. Removing his jacket, he walked to a lamp in the corner and turned it on. After folding his jacket, he draped it over the back of a gilded chair and approached the bed.

The Regent didn't meet his gaze as he unbuttoned his shirt and pulled out his amulet.

From his memory, he brought the words of the spell he'd found in one of his grandfather's ancients texts—those wonderful books that had changed his life so completely.

Enunciating the words, Veridan kept a hand on his amulet as he lowered the other to Danata's stomach and rested it gently over the silky fabric. The Regent closed her eyes and bit her lower lip.

The Sorcerer's words repeated in a loop, slowly sifting through the various energies that surged through the Regent. There was the energy of self that made her who she was, a Ripper, a temperamental creature. There were obscure forces he had no name for, some that perhaps had something to do with Fate, even if Veridan preferred to deny their existence.

Finally, there was a force almost as strong as the force of self. It was embedded deep within her core, intertwined with everything else.

Veridan's voice increased to a feverish crescendo. Danata's body stiffened like a plank, and she began to vibrate. Her eyelashes fluttered. A sheen of sweat peppered her forehead and soaked her nightgown.

In his mind's eye, he could see the strands of the filial bond holding tightly, refusing to let go. They fought him, and to some degree, so did Danata. She was willing, but not as ready as she pretended to be.

One by one, his fingers clenched to make a fist over the Regent's stomach. He imagined that each one caught a strand of the stubborn bond until he had a hold of a small section of the filial connection.

It writhed, trying to get free, but his grip and his spell were sure, relentless. When he was certain of his hold, Veridan turned his fist, leaned backward, and yanked with all his magical and physical strength.

Danata's back arched, her middle coming off the bed as her feet and head dangled, and her clenched fists brought up handfuls of the duvet. A raw cry of pain tore through the arc of her neck. Her dark hair swung from side to side as she fought.

Slowly, the filial bond slithered out of her, like a snake from its lair.

Veridan walked backward, pulling, the spell fast on his lips, while the filial link wriggled out and out and out until, with a snap, it came free of Danata's body.

With a final scream, the Regent collapsed back on the bed, her body limp, her face pale.

The bond turned black in the Sorcerer's hand and, like the ashes of a burnt piece of paper, disintegrated and drifted to the floor.

Veridan let go of his amulet and wobbled on weak legs. He wiped sweaty hands on his pants and, in spite of his desire to collapse on the floor, he tended to the Regent.

She opened her eyes. "Did it work?" she rasped.

Veridan nodded. "I know exactly where Ashby is."

ೞ Chapter 7 ಛ
Ashby

Many miles away, a scream of anguish broke through the lips of a blond boy with onyx-black eyes.

Alone in his room, he fell to his knees screaming and clutching his middle, feeling for all the world as if his very soul was being pulled out through his navel.

After the pain subsided, he pressed his forehead to his knees while a frigid shiver ran up his spine as if someone were watching him.

ℰ᠔ Chapter 8 ℭℛ
Greg

After his futile conversation with Perry, Greg climbed the steps to the small bedroom he'd occupied this past week and slammed the door behind him. His chest pumped up and down. His head pounded with a horrible headache. If he stayed here, he would go crazy. He knew it. He had to leave.

With resolve, he walked to the corner of the room where his old backpack sat, stuffed with what little he owned. Sam's own backpack lay next to it. It gave him a pang just looking at it.

They were the bug-out bags they'd used when they fled and left Indiana behind. Mateo had brought them from New York. He'd come here—transferred by Portos—and had joined the senior Morphids in their interminable planning. That day, Greg saw Mateo and Roanna sharing a heart-warming moment. It turned out they hadn't seen each other since Danata stole the regency seventeen years before. Their hushed conversation had taken place in Ashby's absence. The poor fool was still in the dark about the fact that Mateo was his father. Greg didn't understand the secrecy, but it was none of his business.

He shouldered his backpack. There wasn't much inside, but it was enough. He had money to catch a train and make his way to Sam and that was all that mattered.

Pausing for a moment, he thought of Jacob. Greg didn't want to sneak out like a coward, but remaining calm in the face of the boy's supplications was unlikely to happen.

He guessed that, at this hour, Jacob was playing in the backyard as it had become his habit. Squaring his shoulders, Greg exited the room. As he started to descend the steps, Katsu came out of his own room and joined him.

"Hello," he said with a head bob.

Greg nodded back and hurried his step, the pack bouncing on his back.

The young, Japanese Morphid was a new addition to MORF's ranks. He'd arrived only yesterday, transferred by Portos from Tokyo. The old Sorcerer had dropped Katsu off without much of an explanation and had left on another errand, mission or whatever—Greg wasn't privy to the details, which was part of the problem. Everyone came and went, and no one told him anything worthwhile. All Greg knew was that Katsu belonged to the Warrior caste and, presumably, was here to become a member of the Mirante's army, the one she insisted was needed to defeat Danata.

As they both reached the bottom of the stairs, the Warrior smiled with an enthusiasm that made Greg uncomfortable. He was around Greg's age, but there was something about his happy demeanor that made him seem much younger.

"Where are you going, Greg-san? May I accompany you? I'd like to get to know you," Katsu said.

Since the Warrior had arrived, he'd shown a particular interest in Greg. It was nothing new. Greg had become accustomed to the curiosity of the MORF members who came and went through the old house. It seemed they all wanted a glimpse of the rare, ruined Keeper, and Katsu was no exception. Well, too bad. Greg wasn't in the mood to make friends. There was only one person he cared about, and she wasn't here.

"No, thank you," Greg said rudely and headed for the front door.

Katsu followed, his gaze flicking to Greg's backpack. "You're not coming back, are you?"

Ignoring the intrusive question, Greg pushed out the door, hoping to get rid of this pain-in-the-ass dude, but Katsu seemed undeterred by the rudeness.

Outside, the sky was gray, the sun a faint insinuation behind the heavy clouds. Greg pressed forward, boots crunching gravel underfoot. Katsu followed close behind.

"Look," Greg turned, his anger getting the better of him.

Katsu halted a mere two paces away. He smiled expectantly, waiting for Greg to speak. Something about the Warrior's eager expression gave Greg pause. He cleared his throat and tamed his words as best he could.

"I wish I had time to talk to you, but it's not possible at the moment. Maybe some other time."

Katsu inclined his head respectfully. "My apologies, but we must speak now, before you make a mistake."

Greg frowned, becoming suspicious. "Who put you up to this?"

Katsu's cheeks reddened slightly, giving him away.

"Who?" Greg pressed.

Katsu heaved a sigh and nodded in resignation. "Portos."

"Well, you and Portos can go to—"

"Please don't say anything unpleasant."

"Just leave me alone," Greg faced the road again and started walking.

"You don't have to feel like a weakling, Greg-san. You're big and strong, and I—"

Greg whirled, anger fizzing through him. "I may have lost my powers, but I'm not a weakling or a coward. You all are the ones hiding behind old furniture." He made a dismissive gesture toward the house.

"Good, that's good." Katsu nodded several times. "But you must know . . . it isn't hiding when you are biding your time."

"All that means is that no one here cares about Sam. She has no time. A monster is keeping her prisoner."

"I understand she's strong." Katsu held Greg's gaze. An insinuation twinkled in his eyes.

Chest growing tight with a strange sensation, Greg dropped his backpack and took a step forward. He looked down at Katsu, nostrils flaring.

"You should stay out of things you know nothing about." Greg's voice was barely more than a rumble in the back of his throat.

"From what I've been told about Sam, I think she'll be able to hold her own." Katsu shrugged dismissively.

Angry words buzzed in Greg's head, but they never made it past his lips. Instead, they provided the fuel for an abrupt shove that sent Katsu staggering back a few steps.

The Warrior smiled and rolled his shoulders. "Maybe you just want to ease your own suffering, your *separation anxiety*. Maybe you're using her as an excuse."

It wasn't true, not even remotely, but something snapped inside of Greg, and without thinking, he charged forward, a balled fist preceding him. In his mind, he almost heard Katsu's jaw crack. But, in reality, his fist never connected with its target because, with the speed of lightning, Katsu dodged to one side and easily avoided the blow.

"Umm, not bad," Katsu said, raising an eyebrow and nodding his head.

Greg tried again, moving faster this time. His punch came closer but still missed, whizzing by several inches from the Warrior's ear. Cocky confidence shone in Katsu's eyes. His caste meant he was an expert in hand-to-hand combat, not to mention dexterous with any type of weapon, and Greg was asking for a beating. Except, he couldn't muster enough sense to care. What he did muster was more speed—enough that, this time, his knuckle grazed Katsu's cheek.

The Warrior's eyes went wide with surprise. He hadn't been expecting that.

Confidence growing, Greg went for another punch. It was a mistake. Katsu was done with the game, and in one swift motion, got hold of Greg's arm and flipped him to the ground.

Greg blinked at the gravel, a cloud of dust wafting into his nose. He tried to get up, but the Warrior had his arm in a lock and bent in painful warning.

"Hmm, I guess Portos was right," Katsu said in Greg's ear.

"Right about what?" Greg growled.

"You could still be a valuable asset to MORF."

"I don't care about MORF."

"You should. They want me to train you."

"Train me?" Greg laughed. "What good are fighting skills against magic? It's like taking a knife to a gunfight."

"Think a sword, a special one that would—" Katsu stopped abruptly, his body tensing.

Greg bent his neck to look back over his shoulder, but Katsu's attention wasn't on Greg anymore. Instead, it'd shifted to the field beyond. Greg strained to follow his gaze, stretching to see past the tall grass that lined the adjacent road. He saw nothing.

He was about to ask what was the matter, when the Warrior let Greg go, jumping to his feet.

Greg wasted no time and followed suit. He beat at his dusty pants as he let his gaze rove across the field. He still saw nothing to warrant Katsu's change in attitude. The Warrior stood stiffly, fists clenched at his sides. He said something in Japanese. A curse. Greg was certain.

"What is it?" Greg asked.

Katsu's nose twitched, scenting the air, and his dark eyes shone as if piercing some invisible barrier. "We have to get out of here!"

"What? Why?" Greg asked, but he got no answer because Katsu was already halfway to the front door, running as if savage samurai were chasing him.

Greg watched in confusion, rubbing the back of his neck. He didn't have to wonder long, though, because the instant Katsu entered the house, a strange *twang* reverberated through the air, making everything go wavy around Greg. He stared at the zigzagging house, swaying on his feet.

Disoriented, he turned and faced the field again, ears ringing. The air and the grass seemed to undulate, as if he were looking at them through a heat wave. He shook his head and pressed at his temples, trying to clear his senses. His vision tunneled, and what he saw in the distance froze him to the depths of his very soul.

A large group of people stood shoulder to shoulder in the middle of the field. There were about twenty of them, all dressed in what looked like armor and holding swords, shields, and all manner of medieval-looking weapons that glinted even in the poor light.

With effortless precision, the line of warriors parted, and a familiar figure filled the vacated space. Greg squinted at it, his stomach churning in recognition.

Veridan stood flanked by warriors, his head held high.

Their gazes held, and even from a distance, Greg could feel the Sorcerer's vengeful intensity. A crooked smile tipped Veridan's lips. He acknowledged Greg by inclining his head, then slowly lifted a hand, and with a flourish, pointed toward the house.

Like dogs released from their leashes, the small army began to run at a full pelt. Greg's first instinct was to stand his ground and face Veridan. But the notion disappeared as soon as he remembered how useless he'd become.

"Shit!" he cursed under his breath and ran into the house.

***

"Jacob!" Greg yelled as he slammed the door behind him.

Inside, it was chaos already, people running out of rooms and rushing toward the back of the house.

"In here. Hurry, hurry!" someone directed, jerking an arm toward the kitchen where they'd been instructed to congregate in case of an emergency.

Hoping Jacob was already in there, Greg shoved a console table against the door, sending knickknacks crashing to the floor, then spun on his heel and rushed toward the kitchen. He passed the parlor where Bernard, Mateo, and Ashby were gathering scattered papers and dumping them in a box.

He stopped to help, but Bernard waved him off. "We're done. Go!"

"How in the hell did he find us?" Mateo asked as Greg rushed ahead.

How in the hell, indeed. The house was supposed to be warded by powerful spells.

Skidding into the kitchen, Greg's eyes darted around the room. Empty.

He waited, heart hammering against his chest, the smell of freshly-baked cookies sending his senses for a spin. After two beats that felt like an eternity, Portos and Perry materialized next to the refrigerator. Bernard, Ashby and Mateo, box in tow, rushed past Greg and sidled next to the Sorcerers. Five pairs of eyes swiveled in Greg's direction, expectantly.

"Hurry, boy," Portos urged.

"Where's Jacob? Greg demanded. "Did you already take him?"

Portos and Perry exchange questioning glances.

"Did you . . . ?" Portos asked.

Perry shook his head.

"Dammit!" Greg growled, then turned to leave.

"Get back here," Portos ordered.

But even if Greg were willing to leave Jacob behind, he hadn't been taking the transferring potion they'd all been instructed to drink every day. He hadn't planned on needing it.

"Ashby, not you!" He heard Mateo protest as Greg ran back toward the stairs that lead to the bedrooms. His boots pounded against the hardwood floor. Down the hall, the console table he'd propped against the door seemed to mock him.

"Greg, get back!" Perry and Ashby were in pursuit.

He kept going.

Several MORF members ran past in the opposite direction, glancing at Greg as if he'd lost his mind. At least they served to distract Perry and Ashby who—at Greg's backward glance—seemed torn on who to help.

When he reached the stairs, he gripped the banister and swung himself around, changing direction without losing speed.

"Jacob!" he called out, taking the first two steps.

He was about to take two more when the door behind him flew open, slamming the console table against the wall and breaking it into a thousand pieces. A wave of energy *whooshed* in and sent Greg staggering forward. He braced his fall with his hands and kept climbing on all fours, feet slipping.

He made the landing and ran toward the boy's room. "Jacob!"

Greg slammed the door open and ran in. His eyes inspected every corner of the room. No one. Not under the twin bed or behind the chest of drawers. Cursing under his breath, he rushed to the window and peered into the backyard where Jacob liked to chase bugs and climb the apple trees. Deep within the branches of one of the trees, a yellow splash of color caught Greg's eye.

He stood frozen, wondering what to do. He could open the window and order Jacob to use the back door into the kitchen where Portos and Perry could take him to safety. But what if he was safer in the tree? Veridan and his army were already inside, yelling orders, trampling, breaking things . . . climbing up the stairs.

Greg was still trying to decide what to do when Jacob jumped out of the tree and stared straight at him. The boy stood hesitantly. Greg gestured wildly, urging him to run away.

Jacob shook his head and ran toward the house instead, little fists pumping with determination.

"Dammit!" Greg turned to go after the boy, then froze.

Someone was standing at the threshold.

"Who do we have here?" the girl blocking the door asked.

Some leftover Keeper instinct gave Greg the necessary calm to assess his enemy without panicking. His eyes traveled the length of her body, drinking in her arresting figure. She was tall and athletic, even beyond Morphid norm. She stood with confidence, shoulders squared, gripping two long daggers. Black leather pants clung to her muscular thighs and knee high boots hugged her calves as if she'd been born wearing them. Her matching vest was also made of leather but appeared quite thicker—like some sort of armor—and was adorned with a coat of arms on its left breast. She had red hair pulled into a tight ponytail at the top of her head.

"Got your fill?" she asked, giving him a wicked smile and a look that made him suspect she knew exactly who he was.

He crouched, chest pumping up and down with anger.

"Brave, are you?" The girl asked. "No, stupid is more like it."

Casually, she twirled the daggers then, in one swift motion, holstered them behind her back. She looked around the room, her nose wrinkling as if she smelled something bad.

"Is this where you've been living?" She took two steps sideways and coolly peered behind the door. "I'm Florence Finely, by the way, the Regent Danata's High Warrior."

A shout followed by an explosion thundered from downstairs, shaking the planks under Greg's feet. He thought of Jacob running in and getting caught in the melee. He had no time to stand here listening to this conceited Morphid.

"I don't give a shit who you are," he said, then sprang toward the door.

He was fast, but not fast enough for the High Warrior, who effortlessly blocked his path and delivered a left hook straight into his gut. Greg folded over, gasping for breath.

Giving himself only a couple of seconds to recover, he went for Florence and grabbed her by the wrist. Gracefully, she twirled to the side and slipped out of his grip. He hated to hit a girl, but . . . Oh well.

He swung at her, throwing a punch that should have knocked her senseless, if it had hit its mark. Instead, she glided out of the way and elbow-jabbed him in the temple. Bells tolled inside his head.

Florence laughed. "You're wasting your time. *Maybe* if you were a proper Morphid, but you're nothing."

Greg saw red. So he wasn't a Keeper anymore, big deal. He had a cause, and it was greater than any of Danata's followers would ever possess. He was fighting for Sam. For the kind of love a being like Florence would never understand.

Damn it all to hell.

They were here to kill, and he wouldn't go down without a fight.

Resigned to die, he clenched his fists and charged.

***

A *whoosh* of air left Florence's mouth as her back hit the wall.

Pressing his advantage, Greg tried to bring her to the ground, but in some maneuver he couldn't fathom, the Warrior slipped from his grip and put him in a chokehold.

He'd barely had time to realize what had happened when Florence began ramming his head against the rickety dresser. Flashes of light burst in Greg's eyes as the world seemed to slide to one side.

Drunkenly, he fought to free himself, but it was impossible. The girl was strong. Too strong.

His head rammed into the dresser again. His brain and the contents of the drawers rattled. Something wet and warm slid down his brow. His vision blurred. His stomach twisted as his last meal made a slow climb into his throat.

As if aware of his impending sickness, Florence let him go.

Greg staggered back, crab-like, then fell on his rear. He placed his hands on either side of his spinning head. The room was a vortex threatening to swallow him whole.

"On the Regent's orders, you're coming with me," Florence announced.

Her words sounded garbled but, in the back of his mind, Greg understood their meaning. They would take him to Sam. Exactly what he wanted. If he'd known, he could have saved himself a huge headache, but he'd assumed they wanted him dead.

He groaned and wiped at the blood that blurred his eyes.

"Why she wants *you* is beyond me," Florence spat. "You're not even worth the air you breathe. Look at you. You're pathetic."

Greg bit back a nasty retort, hoping to appear properly subdued.

Chaos continued elsewhere in the house. Loud bangs and the sound of running feet echoed through the old walls. The crackle of magical energy added to the pandemonium. Smoke billowed out in the hall, its acrid smell clouding Greg's already addled head. There was a fire somewhere. Magic usually caused that.

"Greg!" Someone shouted from the hall.

Florence spun and faced the door, pulling her twin daggers from the holster at her back just as a disheveled Ashby and a sooty Perry stepped in, murder flashing in their eyes.

❦ Chapter 9 ❧
Ashby

Ashby was in shirtsleeves, the tie around his neck loose and crumpled. He'd lost his jacket at some point.

Greg was on the floor, bleeding profusely from a cut on his forehead, looking as if he'd ran into a boulder. But what could be expected after a spat against the High Warrior?

"Hello, Florence," Ashby greeted. "I had a feeling you were here, too."

Florence snarled and twirled her daggers.

"Me, too," Perry said. "Can't say I'm glad to see you, though." He stepped protectively to Ashby's side.

"Hello, *traitors*," Florence replied, inclining her head in mockery.

Greg struggled to his feet, looking as if the world were swaying around him. "Did you find Jacob?" he asked Perry.

Perry shook his head. "Sorry, mate."

"Damn." Greg looked conflicted as if he wanted to run out the door and stay right where he was at the same time.

"We'll find him, Greg. Don't worry," Ashby said, without taking his eyes off Florence.

They remained locked by each other's gazes for a moment, then something changed in the depth of Florence's eyes, and

Ashby knew she'd calculated her chances against Perry, the only one who stood a chance against her.

Before she made a move, he said, "You don't have to do this, Florence. You must know my mother is wrong. What she's done has no name."

"Save your words." Florence crouched lower, bending her knees. "I'm not a traitor."

Before Ashby could say anything else, she jumped into action, sliding forward and thrusting one of her daggers straight at his chest.

Flinching, Ashby managed to take a step backward, though his evasive movement would have meant nothing without Perry who whirled his hands in the air and released a shimmering shield that blocked the dagger's path mere millimeters from its target.

In a dance of her own creation, Florence spun, slashing toward Perry's neck with her second dagger. Lightning fast, the Sorcerer crossed his arms to block her. They glowed with a protective charm. Florence's weapon struck the magical barrier with force, sending sparks into the air.

Taking advantage of Florence's surprise, Ashby slammed a forearm against her wrist and sent one of her daggers flying across the room. The weapon twirled through the air and embedded itself a few inches from Greg's shoe.

Greg swallowed and drew his foot back.

Without missing a beat, Florence dropped a hand to the floor and kicked her legs up. Strong like a mule's kick, her booted feet slammed against Ashby's jaw, snapping his head back and sending him on a short flight across the room. The echoes of a loud crack resounded in his ears just as a wave of excruciating pain spread across his face like corrosive acid.

After what felt like a lifetime of pain, Ashby peeled his eyes open. Florence was stalking in his direction, dagger in hand. He struggled to a sitting position.

"Oh, no, you don't," Perry said behind Florence, slipping a hand to the amulet around his neck.

His lips rushed through an incantation. His body began to pulse with energy, and then he extended a hand toward the High Warrior. Green-colored power snaked from his fingers and wrapped around Florence's neck. In the next instant, her feet came off the floor. She kicked and gasped for air, eyes swiveling.

"I assume you got this?" Greg asked, inching toward the door as if he'd finally decided that staying here was a waste of time.

Perry nodded, his gaze locked with Florence's. "Yes. Go find Jacob."

Greg stumbled out of the room, holding his head.

Ashby struggled to his feet, wishing for special skills that could let him teach Florence a lesson. But never mind that. He could live vicariously through Perry.

๛ *Chapter 10* ๑
Greg

Greg had stayed with Ashby and Perry long enough to come to his sense. He couldn't leave Jacob to his own fate. Sam would never forgive him if he let anything happen to the boy. Besides, Perry had subdued Florence, so Greg's chances of going with her were gone.

Gradually regaining his balance after being used like a ramrod, he rushed toward the steps, ignoring the crashing sound that suddenly came from Jacob's bedroom.

They'll be all right. Perry has her under control, he told himself, resisting the urge to go back.

The staircase was filled with smoke, and the sounds of battle drifted upward. Without stopping to think about what waited past the haze, Greg pulled his t-shirt over his nose and took the steps one at a time.

Throat and eyes burning from the acrid smell of magical fire, he reached the bottom of the steps and tried to see past the thick, gray fog. He distinguished a few shapes in the hall and knew they were fighting only from the sound of their trampling feet and the scraping of metal against metal.

He stifled a cough and headed for the front door, hoping Jacob had been smart enough to stay outside. Skipping over fallen debris and crouching below the rising smoke, he stumbled outside.

Once on the gravel path, he inhaled deeply, blinking wildly. Cleaner air rushed into his lungs. His vision cleared gradually. Once he could see three feet past his nose, his eyes made a quick scan of the front yard and the field beyond.

No one. No wonder it was such chaos inside. The entire host of enemies had invaded the house.

Apprehension clawing at his heart, Greg tried to call for Jacob, but only a choked rasp made it past his raw throat.

Swallowing thickly, he tried again. "Jacob!" He took a few steps away from the house and called out once more. "Jacob." He searched for him behind the bushes and along the stone wall.

Nothing.

Turning back, Greg veered to one side of the house, feeling as if his world had gone from chaos to complete and utter disaster. He had failed to protect Sam, and now he was failing Jacob. Rounding the bend, he prayed the boy had hidden among the hedges there.

"Jacob," he called again, just as one of the side windows exploded, sending glass flying into the air. He ducked, arms over his head. Small shards rained on him, stinging like bees.

Sensing the hum of magic in the air, he scrambled away from the house. He'd barely taken two steps when red fire erupted through all the windows. The impact took him off his feet and sent him flying through the air. The back of his clothes ignited. Desperately, he rolled in the grass, until the biting heat was gone.

He sat up, panting. The blaze was consuming everything it touched, dissolving wood, melting rock, turning the house into molten rubble.

"Jacob," we said in an anxious whisper.

He spared a thought for Ashby and Perry, but it was Jacob his heart ached for. Greg stood. He had to find the boy, fire be damned. He took a step toward the house.

"Greg," a small voice called.

Greg whirled. A pale little face peeked through one of the hedges that lined the road. Relief washed over him.

"Oh, thank God."

Jacob left the safety of the bushes and ran in Greg's direction. Some sixth sense made Greg's skin crawl, but before he could decide what it was Jacob was there, wrapping his arms around his waist, pressing his tear-stricken face to his stomach.

"I was so scared," he said. "I thought you . . ."

"I'm okay," Greg said. "Are you hurt?"

Jacob shook his head.

"Good." Greg took one of the boy's hands and said, "Let's get out of here."

He pulled him back toward the bushes, planning to run as far away from the house as possible, but instead, found himself frozen on the spot before he even took the first step.

There would be no escape today.

Veridan had found them.

***

Greg pushed Jacob behind him, wishing he could make him disappear to a safe place, far from Veridan.

Eyes locked on Greg's, the High Sorcerer smirked with mocking satisfaction.

"I came just for you," Veridan said. "I wasn't needed. Not for this. Danata's Warriors are very efficient at their job, as you can see." He gestured toward the field where several of the MORF members were being manhandled by the Regent's army. "But I knew I would find you here, hiding like a coward."

Greg's eyes danced from left to right, his thoughts bouncing between escape alternatives. None seemed viable. He wiped a hand over his brow to clear the blood that hadn't stopped flowing since his run-in with the dresser.

"There's no way out of this one, little *Keeper*. You must surrender to me," Veridan said.

Greg blinked. Surrender to Veridan? What did that mean exactly?

Veridan curled a finger, beckoning.

Without Greg's immunity to magic, Veridan could have killed him already but, like Florence, the High Sorcerer seemed to be following Danata's orders. How obedient.

Going as a prisoner wasn't optimal, but it got him closer to Sam, which was what he wanted.

Slowly, Greg raised his hands. "Okay, I'll go with you. I won't fight you. Just let the boy go."

Veridan's mouth twisted in a dismissive gesture. He couldn't have cared less about Jacob.

"Go, Jacob. Hide!" Greg said as soon as he realized it was safe.

But the boy didn't move. He just stood there, looking up at Greg with huge blue eyes, his face ghostly pale. Tears spilled down his cheeks as he shook his head.

"I'll be fine, Jacob. Just do as I say."

"No," Jacob sobbed.

"I don't have time for this," Veridan said, lifting a hand in Jacob's direction and using his magic to push the boy out of the way. Greg hesitated and, for an instant, reached toward the boy's wind-milling hands, then decided it was better this way.

"It'll be fine," Greg told him.

"You should learn to listen to your elders," Veridan said as Jacob struggled on the spot, clawing at the invisible magic wall around him.

"Leave him alone," Greg growled. "He's just a child. I'm coming with you which is what you want." Greg took a step toward Veridan, blocking the Sorcerer's view of Jacob.

"Very well." Veridan pulled out a small flask from his tailored jacket and offered it to Greg. "You know how it works."

Greg took the flask and frowned at it. A transport potion, he figured. Or was it? For all he knew, it was poison. The Sorcerer had already tried to poison him once, via the same homeless man who'd attempted to drown Sam in an army-size pot of soup. His Keeper magic had saved him then, burning the poison out of his blood just in time to save Sam. Now, there would be nothing to save him.

"The hell with it," he said after a moment, then uncapped the flask and lifted it to his mouth.

But before the potion touched his lips a jolt of power hit his hand and sent the flask flying across the yard. Shimmering liquid splashed across the gray sky.

"Shit!" Greg shook his hand as it tingled with electricity.

Veridan cursed, got a hold of his amulet, and switched his stance to face Portos. The old Sorcerer had appeared behind Jacob, looking more dangerous than Greg could have imagined possible.

Without taking his eyes off Veridan, Portos flicked his wrist in Jacob's direction and released him from his invisible barrier. Staggering forward, the boy crashed into Greg and went back to clinging to his waist.

"Get back here, you two," Portos ordered.

"No, let go. Run and hide!" Greg fought against the boy's relentless little arms

Jacob had seen his father die at Veridan's hands. Of course, he wasn't about to abandon the only person he had left.

"We finally meet," Portos said, and straightaway, shot a bright ball of energy at the man who'd stolen his High Sorcerer job.

With a blinding display of sparks, the energy rebounded against Veridan's hastily-conjured shield and landed on the hedges, setting them on fire. Heat radiated in all directions. Greg and Jacob shrank back, their arms over their heads. Crouching, they ran toward Portos.

As Greg tried to usher Jacob out of harm's way, Perry suddenly shimmered into existence and, without hesitation, joined the battle. He stamped a foot on the ground and clapped his hands. The entire field rumbled, then rippled in a wave that traveled at a prodigious speed in Veridan's direction. The force hit the Sorcerer head on. His magical shield flickered, then blinked out.

Attracted by the renewed battle, a few of the Warriors down the field turned from their prisoners and rushed to Veridan's aid.

"We have to get out of here." Perry urged Greg and Jacob to hurry.

Greg picked up Jacob, cradling him to his chest, and ran. He was almost to Perry when something sprung from the ground and wrapped around his ankle. Pain shot up his leg as whatever had gotten a hold of him squeezed with bone-breaking force. Greg howled in pain.

Dropping to his knees, he set Jacob down. "Go!"

Jacob shook his head.

Greg pushed him. "God dammit, Jacob! Go with Perry."

A ferocious wind began twisting around them as balls of magic flew from one end of the field to the other. They ducked as a bright fireball whizzed past them.

"Get it in your head," Jacob screamed over the raging wind. "I'm not leaving you!" And with that, he dropped to one knee and began pulling at the giant, earthworm-like beast that encased Greg's ankle and was now climbing toward his knee.

"Are you two bollocks?" Perry demanded, pushing Jacob out of the way and laying a hand on Greg's ankle-biting attacker. Immediately, the moist, squishy worm withered into a sickening gray lump and dropped limp to the ground.

Jumping to his feet, Greg took a step away from Perry. "You go," he said to Perry. "I'm staying. Take Jacob with you. He won't listen."

"Don't be daft," Perry snarled. "Drink this!" He said, offering him a vial of transfer potion.

Greg took another step back.

The young Sorcerer opened his mouth to protest, but was interrupted.

"Hurry," Portos growled as his hands moved overhead, creating strange patterns that left trails of light in the air. "I can't hold them forever."

Wasting no time, Perry flung the vial at Greg, who snatched it from the air by mere reflex. The young Sorcerer began mouthing the transfer incantation while his eyes urged Greg to drink the potion.

"Please, drink it," Jacob begged.

Greg's fingers tightened around the vial. If he went with Perry nothing would change. He would remain the good-for-nothing ex-Keeper who didn't know when to shut up. Worse yet, what if they left England, further away from Sam? He would still be stuck in a hole where all emotions turned to anger. He stared at the vial, swaying on his feet and blinking away at the blood in his lashes.

"Please," Jacob said again.

Making up his mind, Greg waited until Perry finished the incantation, then pocketed the vial and backed away. "Sam needs me, Jacob."

"You daft bastard," Perry said, knowing it was too late. He was already becoming translucent as he placed his hand on Jacob's shoulder to let the boy absorb the transferring magic.

Greg smiled weakly, glad to know they would be safe.

"I said *not* going," Jacob growled, breaking out of Perry's hold.

Perry cursed as his spell took hold and tore him from the sleepy English village to who knew where.

"You idiots!" Portos growled. The old Sorcerer's knees were bending under the weight of Veridan's magic while a handful of Warriors furiously slashed at Portos's magical shield with swords, daggers, and all manner of weapons.

"Now what? You hardhead?" Greg demanded.

Jacob glowered. "Who're you calling hardhead?"

Out of nowhere, a young girl dressed in red robes materialized next to Veridan. Greg had never seen her but, judging by her sudden appearance, she had to be a Sorceress.

A foul curse word came from Portos.

At Veridan's command, the girl reached for the large pendant that hung around her neck and began an incantation.

"Get the Keeper," Veridan said, pointing a finger at Greg.

The girl's power expanded, tendrils of magic snaking like serpents through the air and piercing through Portos's defenses. Above them, it whirled at an immense speed and created what appeared to be the eye of a storm.

"No. Not the boy," Portos yelled, intensifying his attack until the entire sky turned a sickly shade of green.

Not the boy? Greg's eyes darted to Jacob.

With a *whoosh,* a vacuum opened above Greg and Jacob. It sucked in air like an inhaling giant. Their hair and the grass at their feet stood on end. Then there was a snap and the Warriors, Veridan, the Sorceress, and Jacob went up in smoke, leaving Portos and Greg in the middle of a charred field.

∞ Chapter 11 ∞
Ashby

Ashby's face felt like a throbbing heart. Everything between his temples pounded with viciousness. Inside, his nose burned and felt as if it had been stuffed with searing embers.

He had no idea where he was. Last he'd known, he'd been fighting Florence. Or at least helping distract her. Then, without warning, Perry had transferred him away from their battle, from the chaos. It had been Perry's task to protect him, but that was when he'd been the future Regent. Now that he was nobody, he didn't deserve this preferential treatment. He wanted to fight like the rest.

Wondering where Perry had dumped him, Ashby stood. He was indoors, in a dark room. That much he could tell. His legs trembled and the world tipped sideways. Resting his back against the wall, he squeezed his eyes shut and tried to will the nauseous headache away. It stayed right in place, pounding harder as if to mock him. He pinched his nose. It felt twice its normal size.

Definitely broken. Bloody Florence.

After a long moment, he opened his eyes and looked around. As his eyes finally adjusted to the darkness, objects began to take shape around him: tables, computer monitors, and was that a stack of mattresses? He couldn't be sure. Everything was blurry.

Where in the bloody hell?

Portos had evacuated Roanna at the first sign of trouble, then others had quickly followed. Had Perry taken him elsewhere? That made no sense.

Holding on to the wall, Ashby dragged his feet toward a narrow crack of light that suggested a door. He took short steps as the world spun around him. Claustrophobia getting the best of him, he staggered toward the door, yanked it open, and burst into a long hall. A lonely light bulb shone above him. He squinted at gray walls and a matching carpet that appeared as if it'd never been acquainted with a hoover.

The place was filthy and old and, for a moment, Ashby was glad his nose wasn't working properly. The place just looked . . . well . . . smelly.

Looking left and right, he tried to decide which way to go. Had Perry made a mistake? It was possible. The transfer hadn't happened under the best of circumstances. They'd been on the run from Florence after she'd pulled out a secret dagger and broke free, proving to be more than Perry could handle.

As he started to go left, a sound behind him stopped him in his tracks. Heart pounding, he glanced over his shoulder, expecting to find some squatter ready to slice him with a knife. But it was Mateo, standing at the end of the hall and peering at him with a mixture of perplexity and relief.

"Ashby!" He rushed to his side. "We were worried about you."

The man appraised Ashby in a strange way. He had helped Greg and Sam in New York and had turned out to be a friend of the family, but he made Ashby uncomfortable. He always seemed at the verge of saying something.

Ashby shook his head, unsure of what to say.

"Um, where are Portos and Perry?" Mateo asked. "Roanna is worried about them."

Ashby could barely tell up from down, much less the whereabouts of two meddlesome Sorcerers.

"What happened to your face?" Mateo asked with concern in his eyes. His caste was Caregiver, so he could probably tell Ashby was in a lot of pain.

"Florence," Ashby said in explanation.

"Who?"

"The High Warrior." God, he sounded like a nasally duck.

"Son, what possessed you to face the High Warrior?"

"Somebody had to."

Mateo shook his head. "Come with me. We've cleared one of the conference rooms. When Portos and Perry get back, they can straighten you out."

Ashby followed him. "What is this place?"

"Another MORF safehouse."

"Doesn't appear very safe to me," he said, looking around with a frown.

"It's an out-of-service hotel in America. Not very appealing, but safe nonetheless."

Mateo pushed past a set of double doors into a conference room that was packed to the gills with people. Half he recognized from their previous safe house, the other half he'd never met. Heads and eyes swiveled in his direction. The light from two portable lamps split their faces in sharp angles which made them look quite hostile.

"Oh, thank God you're safe!" Roanna exclaimed.

She rushed to his side, grabbed him by the shoulders, and turned him this way and that to examine his face. She grimaced, making Ashby wonder how bad the injury was. It felt horrible, but maybe a mirror would tell him it was worse. His nose was broken for sure, and from the way his vision kept shrinking and shrinking, he figured the swelling around his eyes was bad.

"Where are Portos and the others?" Uncle Bernard asked from behind Roanna. "Who brought you here?"

"Perry. He left me a few rooms down the hall then went back for Greg and Jacob."

"Oh, Fates! This is not good," Roanna said.

Uncle Bernard touched her forearm. "Don't worry. They'll be back any minute. They know how to take care of themselves." He turned back to Ashby. "What happened exactly?"

"Um," Ashby fought to organize his thoughts, "Greg . . . wouldn't leave without Jacob, so we went after him. Then we ran into Florence Finley—the High Warrior. We tried to subdue her after she pummeled Greg, but . . . well . . . she is who she is, and we had to run. Perry transferred us out of there after she tried to run us through with her daggers. And that's the last I remember."

Roanna paced, a hand on her forehead. "How did they find us?"

Ashby hid his face by pretending to look for somewhere to sit. He didn't want to bring up the pain he'd felt in his middle and the sensation of being watched until he had a chance to tell Portos about it.

"Sit here, mate." Joao, Mirante's son, pushed a rolling chair in Ashby's direction and helped him sit.

"Thank you," Ashby murmured and relaxed his entire weight into the squeaky piece of furniture.

"If we lose Portos and Perry . . ." Roanna let the words hang.

Ashby didn't even want to think about it. There were only two more Sorcerers in MORF's ranks, and neither of them as powerful as Portos and Perry. The caste wasn't as rare as Keepers, Rippers and Weavers, but it was rare enough. Without them, their rebellion against Danata wouldn't stand a chance.

Like a shadow peeling away from the wall, Mirante took a step forward and addressed all of those gathered around the scratched up conference table.

"Is everyone *else* accounted for?" she asked.

"No," Katsu said. "There are others missing. I should have been allowed to stay and fight. I would have confronted the High Warrior. But your Sorcerer," he pointed at Ashby, "snatched me away. I'm no good here. I'm a Warrior."

"Settle down, Katsu," Mirante ordered. "You weren't there to fight. Your visit had only one purpose, and that was decided by Portos and Roanna".

From her tone, it sounded like Mirante disapproved of said purpose. Ashby glanced from Roanna to the MORF commander. Something passed between them.

"Yes, well . . ." Katsu said with a dismissive shrug, "it's impossible to help those who won't be helped."

"Is there no one else who can go back and check on those who are missing?" someone with an American accent asked from the other side of the conference table.

The person was blocked by Roanna, but it had to be someone from this safe house since Ashby didn't recognize the voice.

Curious, he inclined his head to one side to get a look and found a small girl standing behind one of the portable lights.

"No, Finley," Mirante said. "Portos and Perry are the only MORF Sorcerers capable of performing transferring spells, and they are both *not here*."

Ashby frowned. What was a human girl doing here? Mirante didn't approve of Brooke already; she sure wouldn't like having a second "intruder" in the mix. Examining her closer, however, he noticed a certain resemblance between Finley and Calisto, Mirante's daughter. The same determined expression, the same tan skin and piercing green eyes—though Finley's hair was paradoxically blond and not dark. A human relative?

"How about Johnny?" the girl pressed in spite of Mirante's cutting tone. Whoever she was, the girl certainly felt comfortable interjecting her opinion.

"He's away at the moment," a man in his late thirties answered from the other side of the room.

Mirante waved a dismissive hand in Finley's direction, a cynical expression on her face. "*Quit being so useful*," she seemed to say.

"Well," Roanna said, "I guess the best we can do is wait and hope for the best. I trust they'll be here shortly." She failed to sound as optimistic as her words. Surely the plans they'd been working on this past week hinged heavily on Portos.

Roanna stepped closer to the table. "While we wait, we should get to know each other. Why don't we introduce ourselves. We'd planned on both groups coming together eventually, so this is not a bad outcome." She smiled. "Finley, why don't you begin?"

"Okay," the girl said, straightening her shoulders. "My name is Finley Mirante. I am Luana Mirante's niece, so these two here—" she hooked a finger in Calisto and Joao's direction "—are my cousins. I'm nineteen, and no, I haven't morphed yet, in case you're wondering. That's why I still look like this." Her tone was bitter and tired, as if she'd had to give this spiel several times.

Ashby blinked. Well, that explained things.

Most Morphid teenagers went through their metamorphosis between sixteen and eighteen years old, at the latest. Past that, it was a sign of trouble. Ashby had read about the condition in his studies, but had never met anyone who suffered from it. She was someone with no purpose. Someone not much different from him.

"You mean you're *Casteless*?" he blurted out without thinking.

Several around the table let out small gasps at the term.

"I . . . I mean . . ." Ashby cringed at a loss for words, then gave up.

Ashby met Finley's green, brooding gaze. There was hostility in her expression. He looked away, feeling like a total idiot.

Someone named Charles cleared his throat and introduced himself next. Then several other people Ashby couldn't concentrate on—not when his attention kept wandering back to Finley.

He tried to disguise his curiosity when she caught him staring more than once.

In spite of everything that had happened, he couldn't help but be surprised. He'd always thought Casteless Morphids were fiction, but again, he was proven wrong. Even after meeting

Keepers and Weavers, and being ripped from his Companion by his own mother.

What was wrong with the world? Or more precisely, what was wrong with Morphidkind? What did all this mean?

Throughout history—Portos kept reminding everyone—strange changes like this had been a portent of an upcoming jolt to their foundation and future. Did that mean Roanna would retake the Regency? Or did it mean something entirely different? The uncertainty scared him, made him wonder if Fate had decided that his people didn't deserve to go on—not after the mess they'd made.

Once more, Finley caught him staring. Abruptly, she pulled away from the wall and took a step toward the table.

"I'm not a circus animal," she said. "Stop staring at me."

Ashby stiffened. He opened his mouth to apologize, but no words came out. No one ever spoke to him in such bold tones—unless he counted Greg. He cleared his throat, resolved to say something, but Mirante spoke first.

"Finley, we don't have time for hostilities and tender feelings."

"Oh, so we're to disregard common courtesy?" the girl demanded.

"If it expedites things, yes," Mirante said in a firm tone.

Finley's eyes blazed in Ashby's direction. He composed his features, finally ready to apologize. But, before he could make amends, Finley stormed out of the room.

"Finley is very self-conscious about her condition," Charles explained as if to apologize for her behavior.

"Yes, well," Mirante said, "we all have reasons to be sensitive these days, but we don't have time to treat everyone with kids' gloves."

Roanna looked sideways at Mirante, lips pursed. She never seemed too pleased with the way her MORF commander conducted business, but never said anything—perhaps because the woman got results. At least that was what everyone said, though Ashby had yet to see any.

"When will they get back?" Uncle Bernard asked, glancing at his wristwatch.

He'd barely finished asking the question when three shapes materialized in the far corner of the room. Portos, Perry and Greg blinked at them, looking worse for wear. Ashby jumped to his feet, sending his world spinning again. Helplessly, he crashed back down onto the chair.

Greg followed suit, falling to his knees. The cut on the side of his face dripped blood that trailed to the soaked collar of his t-shirt. He swayed in place and, just before he face-planted on the floor, Perry took hold of his arm.

"Oh, thank the fates you're okay!" Roanna exclaimed.

Joao rushed to Greg's side to help settle him on the chair he'd just vacated.

"He looks like shite," Calisto said.

"You think?" her brother replied with a twist of his mouth.

"I'll tend to him." Portos knelt next to a half conscious Greg and pressed a hand to the side of his face.

Perry stepped aside, shaking his head and pulling at his hair. "Crazy bastard!" he mumbled.

"Portos, report," Mirante commanded.

But the Sorcerer ignored her, too busy to interrupt his incantation.

Seeing that her answers wouldn't come from the old Sorcerer, Mirante turned to Perry and demanded an explanation.

"Um," Perry cast around as if searching for an answer. He found it in a feeble Ashby. "I should probably tend to my charge before he passes out."

The young Sorcerer rushed to Ashby's side whose eyes kept crossing, making everything blurry.

"I think I'm concussed," Ashby mumbled.

"What?" Perry asked.

"Oh, for Fate's sake!" Mirante exclaimed in an angry voice. "Everyone get back in shape and report back here in an hour." With a huff, she spun on her heel and marched out of the room.

Several others abandoned the conference room, following Mirante. The air seemed to clear, but that didn't help Ashby feel less oppressed. He wanted to ask Perry if he was okay, but his tongue refused to move.

His consciousness was slipping away, and Ashby decided to let it.

"Hey, mate!" someone squeezed his hand.

Ashby opened his eyes.

Perry was kneeling next to him. "Let's take care of that, eh? Though, I don't know, it sort of gives you character."

"Character my arse," Ashby said. "Just fix me."

Perry placed his hand on Ashby's nose and murmured something under his breath. A cold tingle spread from his brow down to his upper lip, then seeped slowly into his sinuses and the back of his eyes. Even before Perry had been allowed to perform magic, he had used his power to heal Ashby from scrapes, bruises, and once even a nosebleed. But Ashby had never sustained an injury like this before and didn't expect the crippling pain that ensued as cartilage began to move inside his broken nose.

A hiss escaped through his clenched teeth as pain spread across his face. Tears spilled from the corners of his eyes of their own accord.

"What the hell?!" he exclaimed, wondering if Perry was having fun at his expense.

"Don't move," Perry ordered, breaking his incantation for a moment.

Ashby did his best to obey, hands clenching the armrests of the battered chair. After what felt like hours of torture, an audible crack issued from inside his skull and, finally, his face felt right again.

Perry pulled away. "All right, I think that's it."

"Bloody hell! Couldn't you have been gentler?"

"Gentler? Well, next time you want *gentle*, don't take on the High Warrior."

Ashby narrowed his eyes, pinching the bridge of his nose tentatively. "Yeah, sure. I'll keep in mind that I'm supposed to be worthless."

"Don't be daft! You know it's not your job. Besides, you're not . . . equipped for that sort of thing."

"I don't think—"

"Listen to your adviser," Portos interrupted, pulling away from Greg's slumped shape. "It's not your place to fight, and you well know it."

"Is that right?" Ashby coughed, then grimaced as congealed blood slid down the back of his throat from his newly-healed sinus cavities. He coughed again and said in a hoarse voice, "Then pray tell, what is my role? Because it seems to me I don't have one anymore."

"What in the devil makes you say that?" Portos said.

Ashby scoffed. "The fact that my mother will soon be deposed, and more specifically, the fact that I've been torn from my Companion who, by the way, also bears a Regent mark and will surely be favored by Roanna as her successor."

"You're jumping to conclusions, my boy," Portos said. "You would do best to leave predictions to others. You don't know what Fate will decide."

Ashby wanted to laugh. Given the circumstances *and* his luck, anyone would find it easy to predict that whatever was in store for him couldn't be good. Fate had turned its back on him. He had lost everything: his home, his Companion, the Regency and, somehow, he had the feeling Fate wasn't done with him.

Ashby stood abruptly from the chair. His stomach tumbled, and his knees shook. He hated the weakness that permeated through his very bones. He wished he could be strong, something other than a useless Regent without a crown.

Placing a hand on the scratched conference table, he steadied himself. He looked at Portos, wishing he could tell the old man exactly what he thought of Fate, but it was no use. The old Sorcerer was set in his ways, and whatever ideas he had about Fate were probably as immovable as mountains.

Tired of it all, Ashby turned and headed for the door. He didn't know exactly where he could hide in this place, but in an abandoned hotel, it shouldn't be hard to find a corner where he could lick his wounds. On his way out, he paused and glanced back at Greg. His shape still drooped on the chair, but his fists were clenched, white-knuckled and trembling. His eyes were squeezed shut as if he wanted to hide—same as Ashby.

That's when he remembered Jacob and realized he hadn't seen the boy. His eyes darted around the room, searching. Catching his eye, Perry gave him a stiff shake of his head. Something dark and ugly unfurled inside Ashby's chest.

"They took him," Perry said.

"But why? What could they possibly want with the boy?"

"*How* is the real question." Perry turned to Portos. "That was Rasha, wasn't it? What in the bloody hell did she morph into? She wasn't touching Jacob. How was she able to transfer him?"

Portos sighed and took a seat next to Greg. "A Traveler, maybe. I don't know. Could be anything these days."

"A Traveler?" Everyone turned to Greg, who seemed to have rejoined the living.

"Feeling better?" Portos rested a hand on Greg's shoulder.

Greg shrugged him off and waited for an explanation.

"A Traveler has only one power," Portos explained. "And that is being able to magically transport anyone, whether they're in contact with them or not. Rasha is August Dabworth's daughter. She was just a little girl last time I looked . . . and now . . ."

"If they hurt him . . ." Greg trailed off.

"They wouldn't," Ashby said. "They have no reason to."

He waited for Perry or Portos to back him up, but they just stared at the ground. Silence stretched between them, fueling the unspoken dread that nestled in their hearts. They all knew what Danata and Veridan were capable of.

"Are we finally going to do something?" Greg's question hung in the air.

It rung of accusation and stung like a hot barb.

❧ Chapter 12 ❧
Sam

Sam lay on her bed, shackled arms resting on her abdomen.

Breathing was a struggle. Her ribs hurt every time she inhaled, even if she kept her breaths shallow.

Feeling as if she might pass out from lack of oxygen, she sat up and let her feet dangle off the edge of the bed. Her tray with a bowl of dry oatmeal and a cup of water sat on the floor. She wasn't hungry, but the water was tempting. She licked her lips.

With considerable effort, she slid down until her bottom hit the floor, pulled the tray over, and picked up the cup of water. Awkwardly, she brought it to her lips and drank. She winced. *Damn!* Even swallowing hurt. She set the cup down and looked back at the bed, longingly. Why had she gotten up?

Pressing her elbows to her ribs, she lay on her side and rested her cheek on the cold stone floor, instead. She curled up, knees tucked up to her chest.

As she closed her eyes, a large fist swung in her direction. She coiled in tighter, as if it were more than just a memory.

"This is just a sample of what is to come if you don't do as the Regent orders," Simeon had said.

Would they come back and hit her again? She trembled at the thought.

Be brave. Don't crumble.

No matter the pain, the threats, she would stand strong. And not necessarily because she was brave and could withstand the physical pain, but because the anguish of watching Anima torn from her husband was far worse.

She closed her eyes, focused on the cold floor and hid behind her pain. It was dull and deep, but far safer than the monsters that lived in the castle.

Trying to ease herself to sleep, Sam imagined an empty canvas and began to fill it with pretty images, pushing away any dark colors that tried to creep in. Fluffy clouds paraded in front of a baby blue sky, serving as sheer curtains to a brilliant sun. To her relief, her mind began to drift, sleep blossoming like a sunflower in the center of the canvas.

A metallic clack startled her from her semi-awake state.

Her eyes shot open, and she jumped up like a spring. Her ribs screamed in pain, but adrenaline was already rushing through her veins.

Simeon pushed open the door and grinned at her, showing no teeth. It was a satisfied sort of smile, and it let Sam know more pain was waiting for her.

***

He pushed her out of the room and all the way until they reached the cell block. Before they got to Anima's cell, Sam stiffened.

"Want me to drag you by the hair?" Simeon asked. "You'll do as I say one way or the other. Best make it easy on yourself."

She planted her feet firmly on the ground.

"Have it your way," he said, grabbing a fistful of her hair and pulling her forward.

Sam stumbled, her scalp burning. Even if they forced her into the cell, they couldn't force her to weave. Except Simeon didn't haul her into Anima's cell, but the one across from it.

Sam staggered in as Simeon let her go. Her eyes roved around the empty cell and stopped at a thick metal bar protruding from the wall at over six feet from the floor. It gave her a bad feeling. She whirled and faced the guard, her chest pumping.

"You'll soon learn to do as you're told," Simeon said, massaging his knuckles. "I, for my part, wouldn't mind if you stay stubborn."

Sam had no idea where the courage to speak came from, but she said, "What? You get your kicks hitting people smaller than you, you sick bastard?"

The guard's right eye twitched. "Whatever it takes to keep my Regent happy," he said in an insinuating tone.

Just as he finished saying this, Danata walked into the cell. His grin fell, and he straightened to attention, looking as obedient as a trained dog.

"You were saying . . ." Sam prodded.

The guard growled at Sam. She smirked, even though she'd probably pay for it later.

"Ready to talk?" Danata asked.

Sam said nothing, just watched her from under a deep frown.

"All right, fine." Danata rolled her eyes and waved a hand at Simeon, looking tired.

The guard's eyes glinted. Grinning, he grabbed Sam by the wrists, lifted her arms, and hooked her manacles to the metal bar.

"How about now?" Danata asked.

Sam stood on tip toes, arms over her head, teeth clenched.

The guard got into position, squaring his feet and pulling a fist back. Sam closed her eyes.

"Or perhaps . . ." Danata's words lingered. The punch never came.

Sam let loose a trapped breath and opened her eyes.

"Perhaps, it's a bad idea to damage such a *precious* asset." Danata made a big show of pondering and scrutinizing Sam up and down as if she were a piece of furniture. "Perhaps, we can persuade you by other means." She smiled, a twinkle in her violet eyes.

The pleasure in the woman's expression sent a shiver down Sam's spine and made her heart speed up.

Danata pursed her lips. "Do I have your attention now? Simeon, fetch our new guest."

The guard straightened to attention, almost clicking his heels, then walked out. His steps echoed down the hall and were followed by a series of beeps. A door opened.

Greg!

Sam trembled with a sickening combination of fear and happiness. She didn't want Greg to be here, but she also wanted to see him.

"Move it!" Simeon said.

Greg whimpered. Oh, God. What had they done to him already?

Except it wasn't Greg that Simeon shoved into the cell.

It was worse. Way worse.

"Jacob," she managed in a strangled gulp.

When he saw her, his little face lit up. "Sam!"

The boy rushed away from the guard and crashed into her. Sam tiptoed backward, her manacles sliding back on the bar until she hit the wall. Her ribs smarted.

"Jacob." Sam wanted nothing more than to free her hands and hold him.

"Now, darling," Danata drawled, pulling Jacob away. "Let's see what you think about my *simple* request."

Lovingly, she wrapped her crimson-tipped fingers around Jacob's little neck and held him tight against her.

The boy's eyes widened as he swallowed a lump. Tears pooled in his eyes, but he didn't sob or make any kind of sound.

Except the terror in his blue eyes was enough to make Sam's spine turn to ice.

ೂ *Chapter 13* ೲ
Greg

Greg didn't deserve to be healed. If he'd been half aware of Portos's help, he would have pushed the Sorcerer away.

Again and again, Jacob's face flashed before him: his pale complexion, the smattering of freckles, the blue eyes that reflected nothing but innocence.

Now he was gone, and it was his fault. No one else's. He had failed to protect him, had practically handed him over to Veridan.

"Even they aren't as heartless as to hurt an innocent child," Portos had said when they gave Mirante a report of what had happened.

Greg wanted to trust the old Sorcerer's words, but every time he thought of Jacob dematerializing right in front of his eyes, he feared the worst.

He stood from the chair where he'd been sitting for the past two hours and began to pace the room they'd assigned him. The place was a dump, decorated with torn wallpaper and impregnated with a stale cigarette stench. The only "furniture" consisted of a stained mattress on the floor, a lamp with a bare bulb, and the chair he'd just vacated.

A knock on the door yanked Greg out of his dark thoughts.

"Come in." He expected Ashby and Perry, but his visitor surprised him.

"Hello, Greg," Katsu said. "I brought you something to eat."

The Warrior held out a paper bag as he looked around the room. "Where should I put this?"

Greg shrugged. "You can take it back, I'm not hungry."

"Even if you're not hungry, you should eat. If you want to be useful, you must keep your strength."

"I'm of no use to anyone. Ask Jacob."

"From what I understand, that was an unfortunate accident. Not your fault, really." Katsu placed the paper bag on the chair.

"Of course it was my fault. I was going to leave him behind. If I hadn't been so bent on going myself, he would be safe."

"Any situation can be twisted to fit our darkest thoughts. You should try to look at it from a different angle."

"It doesn't matter how I look at it. In the end, Jacob's still gone."

"And what are you going to do about it? Sit here and . . . pout?"

Anger fizzed in Greg's chest, but it was true. He'd been hiding in here for the last two hours, berating himself.

"Want to fight me again?" Katsu asked, gesturing toward Greg's clenched fists.

Greg held his tongue, trying to control his temper, trying to think before he acted. Because, if he only knew how to do that, he might prevent further disasters.

"I'm a Warrior," Katsu stated without arrogance. "And a good one, by the way. Very few people in this world can get the upper hand on me."

"Much less a fallen Keeper." Greg said. "Go on, say it. I know that's what you're thinking."

"No, that is not what I'm thinking. That is what you're thinking. You need to stop feeling sorry for yourself. Yes, your situation is bad, but all is not lost."

"Yes, I know," Greg said in a tired voice. "I need to wait. I need to be patient. Mirante will take care of it. Doesn't matter how much it hurts in the meantime. But Sam is alone with those monsters, and I can't understand why even her parents just sit here waiting, doing nothing."

"Because they know better and understand all that is at risk. Roanna is our rightful Regent, and she is capable of putting everyone's safety above her personal concerns. That is her duty, what her caste requires of her, her fate."

"Fuck Fate," Greg exclaimed.

Unable to control his fury any longer, he turned and punched the wall. His fist busted through the drywall, sending a lightning bolt of pain up his arm. He growled in frustration, wishing for so many things, especially the will to control his temper.

"You're still strong," Katsu pointed out, unfazed by the display. "Even though you've been severed from your integral, deep down you're still a Keeper. Some of your instincts are still there. You must feel them."

"Anger is all I feel," Greg admitted.

"Then you must harness that anger, use it to your advantage."

Greg turned and faced Katsu. The Warrior was standing leisurely, resting a shoulder on the wall. His black hair stood on end, shining under the light from the lamp. He was smirking as if he knew something Greg didn't.

"Why are you bothering with me?" Greg asked, feeling weary all of a sudden.

"You're finally asking the right questions." Katsu walked to the window and pulled the drapes aside.

Outside, it was twilight. There were a few bushes nearby, then a road, and after that, a line of pine trees. They were in Morrow, Georgia, a small town twenty-five minutes south of Atlanta. At least that's what Mirante had said during their meeting earlier, which made no difference to Greg. He still felt just as trapped as before.

After a moment staring out the window, Katsu finally answered, "Portos asked me to help you. That's why I'm here."

"Help me? How? What I need is a Weaver, and there is only one of them around."

"Are you always this mean?" Katsu asked.

Greg looked down at the worn carpet. It was dark blue with a pattern of red diamonds. Ugly, exactly the way he felt inside. It was true. He was being mean to everyone—even to this person he'd never met before.

He'd always been impulsive, with a temper that riled up easily, but in the last week he'd been downright awful to everyone.

Greg looked up again. Katsu was waiting patiently for an answer to what should have been a rhetorical question.

"This is the new me," Greg said with a shrug.

"Then I wish I'd met you before any of this happened."

"Trust me, me too."

"I can deal with it," Katsu said. "An assignment is an assignment. And for the moment, you're mine."

Greg narrowed his eyes, wondering what the old Sorcerer had in mind, and why exactly he'd gotten Greg a babysitter.

"Look, I can take care of myself. I'm sure there are better things you could be doing," Greg said.

"Oh, I'm not here to take care of you. I'm here to train you."

ℰ Chapter 14 ℛ
Ashby

Ashby walked out of the dilapidated room they'd assigned him and headed toward the lobby. The hotel had been part of a chain, one of those generic places with free breakfast, a shared exercise facility and an indoor pool. Nothing fancy, but certainly utilitarian.

Uncle Bernard had said they were in a small city outside of Atlanta, Georgia, an area where developers had expected community growth, except it had never materialized—hence the vacant hotel.

It was close to dinnertime, or well past it for him since his body was on Western European Summer Time. He figured he should be in bed, bracing himself for the jet lag, but the commotion of the day had left him restless and thoughts of his mother and what Portos said she had done plagued his mind. How much must she hate him to go as far as to break the bond that made her his mother.

It didn't help that many of the local MORF people seemed to be working, making him feel guilty for lying in bed.

Ashby had been told that dinner was served in the lobby, the area where the hotel used to serve its free continental breakfast. Dinner was in thirty minutes, but he didn't mind waiting. What he truly wanted was some tea or at least coffee.

"Ashby," someone called behind him.

He turned. It was Mateo, walking in his direction.

"Can I talk to you?"

"Um, sure."

Mateo stopped in front of him, his dark eyes searching Ashby's face for a long moment.

Feeling self-conscious, Ashby inclined his head as if to say "so what do you want to talk about?" Mateo smiled and pushed open the door to his left. It was the conference room where they'd been earlier.

Mateo invited him to sit. Ashby obliged, intrigued by the man's look of concern.

"Are you alright?" Mateo asked. "Portos told me what your mother did."

Ashby frowned but straightened his posture. What business did Portos have telling this man something so private? Something so embarrassing?

After Mirante ordered everyone to rest, Ashby had sought the old Sorcerer for a private conversation. He had explained the pain he'd experienced just moments before the attack, and how it'd left him feeling adrift and helpless, but more specifically watched or tracked.

Portos had paced for some time, rubbing his chin and muttering to himself, then, asking for Ashby's permission to perform a spell, found the answer to the riddle.

Danata had severed their filial bond and, by doing so, had discovered Ashby's location.

Despite telling himself it didn't matter, his mother had never really loved him, Ashby found that the knowledge hurt and left him feeling more unwanted than ever before. Still, he didn't need anyone's sympathy, especially not this man's.

"Look, I know you're a Caregiver," Ashby told Mateo, "but this is not something I would discuss with you. I'm sorry." He began to stand.

"My question has nothing to do with my caste." Mateo pinned him with his gaze, and Ashby found himself unable to leave his chair.

"My interest," Mateo continued, looking as if he was bracing for something, "is more personal."

"I don't understand." For some reason, his heart sped up.

"Ashby, I know Danata. I was her husband."

His heart stopped. "Are you saying that you . . ."

Mateo nodded.

"I was afraid to tell you," Mateo, his father, said. "I thought you might be upset, but after I learned what Danata did, I wanted to tell you that I'm not like her. That, even though I wasn't allowed to be with you, I always missed you and never, ever want to stop being your father."

Words had disappeared from the world and Ashby was speechless. Danata had never liked talking about his father, and often implied he was dead. But here he was, his eyes as black as his own, their shape and color exactly like what Ashby saw in the mirror every day.

"There is a bond between us that nothing will ever dissolve or break unless you wish it so," Mateo finished, then peered at Ashby, expectantly.

It took several beats for Ashby to regain the ability to speak. "Are you just saying what your caste is telling you I need to hear?" He couldn't keep the resentment from his voice, but how could he trust this stranger when even Ashby's own mother had betrayed him.

Mateo smiled softly, then stood. "You are my flesh and blood Ashby, but—as we well know—that doesn't guarantee trust." He paused and lifted his chin. "Trust is earned, and I will endeavor to obtain, then safeguard yours as long as I live. I leave you, now." He bowed his head. "I will see you around, son."

Ashby sat alone in the conference room for a long time, a strange feeling stirring in his chest.

He had a father.

A man who seemed honorable, someone who might be worth getting to know even. Did he want to?

Feeling lighter than he had a few moments ago, he got to his feet and left the conference room, a slight smile stretching his lips.

He continued on his earlier path and turned the corner into the lobby, expecting to find it empty, except the last person he wanted to see was there: Finley.

Bloody great.

He thought of turning around and going back to his room, but that would be cowardly and another slap in the face to the girl.

Instead, he straightened and walked firmly in her direction, determined to clear the air between them. He had no idea how long they'd be in this hotel, but if he didn't do something now, the situation might grow unbearably awkward.

"Good evening," Ashby said.

She was sitting at a square table, cross-legged on one of its four chairs, reading a book.

The girl looked up, startled, as if she'd been deep into her story, and Ashby had rudely pulled her out. When she realized who had interrupted her, the almost-innocent expression on her face quickly shifted to hostility.

Undeterred, Ashby asked, "May I sit?"

"No," Finley said and went back to reading her book.

Ashby knew it would be rude to sit without her permission, but the girl wasn't the epitome of manners herself. So he sat.

Finley glowered at him over the edge of her book and made as if to go.

"Please, don't leave. I wanted to apologize for . . . earlier. I didn't mean to stare. I assure you it wasn't out of malice."

Finley just kept staring over the edge of her book. Ashby shifted in his seat, wishing he could see her mouth. Her eyes were too brilliantly green and mesmerizing to make an objective assessment of her reaction to his apology. Was she smiling? Were her lips pressed into a harsh line? Or were they twisted in distaste?

He controlled the urge to reach out and push the book aside.

At last, Finley put it down. "Do you mean it?"

"Of course I mean it."

"I'm not a freak, you know."

"I can see that."

Finley held his gaze for a moment, then her shoulders slumped and she fell back on her chair. "I am a freak."

"Don't say that."

"It's easy for you to say. You've Morphed, and you're the Regent's nephew."

"Son."

"Nephew. Roanna's the Regent. Not Danata."

"Fair enough. Though being anyone's nephew doesn't mean anything."

"That's not true. Sometimes the people in our lives help define us."

Ashby thought for a moment. "You're probably right," Ashby said. "My mother feels like a permanent stain on my record. So in the end, I have more reasons than you to be considered a freak."

"Oh no, you will not steal my title."

"Your title?"

"Yeah," Finley thumbed the closed pages of her book, "for the last few years I've worn the badge proudly. No one alive can remember meeting a Casteless." She said the word with disdain.

"No one alive knows anyone who has been ripped AND whose companion chose someone else over them."

A knot formed in Ashby's throat. He averted his gaze and focused on the dusty floor. His face went hot from shame.

Surely, Finley and everyone in this place already knew what had happened to him, but he'd never said the words out loud to anyone.

He didn't know why he was telling her this—maybe to make her feel better about herself—though he'd never been the kind of person to do that. He had always been a self-centered bastard, born with a silver spoon up his ass, like Greg had once told him. At least until Sam changed things, rejecting him in spite of Fate's will.

"My own mother turned on me," Ashby said, unsure of where this honesty, this desire to tell it all was coming from. "She tore me from my Companion, destroyed my life, my fate, and more. Now, I don't know what I'm supposed to be. And from where I stand," he looked into Finley's bright green gaze, then quickly back down, "being Casteless sounds much better than this."

Ashby waited for Finley to say something, but she remained quiet. He peered in her direction, trying to decipher what she thought of him, but her expression was blank.

For a moment, her gaze traveled across his face as if its peaks and valleys would help her decipher him. After a short inspection, an expression finally settled on her tan features, and it was not pity, horror, or disgust as he expected, but a sort of surprised realization.

"You feel sorry for yourself?" she said in a half question.

"Is that so hard to believe?"

"It is. From the way people talk about you, and the way you carry yourself, I would have never suspected it."

"The way people talk about me?" he asked.

"Yes, I'm sorry, but people think you're an ass. I always like to form my own opinions, so I reserved judgment. But my first impression confirmed the gossip."

A biting retort rose to Ashby's lips. He didn't have to sit here and be insulted. He didn't owe Finley or anyone else any sort of explanation. He was courteous to everyone. What else did they want from him?

Ashby wanted to stand and walk away, but that would only prove her point. Instead, he looked down at his hands and interlaced his fingers, trying to look at himself from the outside in.

Finley wasn't the first one to point out his faults. Greg and Sam had made him aware of them, too.

Was he really an ass?

He shook his head, rejecting the idea. He'd been raised with manners, decency, dignity. His tutors had taught him etiquette, culture, discretion, and . . . and . . . everything, except how to be kind, humble, and all the things that, apparently, no amount of good manners could show.

Pride and righteousness served against him. He had been the future Regent, but now he was nothing, so his behavior couldn't be excused or tolerated.

Maybe, it was time to change, time to grow up, and understand that no one got everything they wanted, that his childhood had been an awful lie, an exercise in entitlement. No one owed him anything, especially when he gave nothing of himself.

Tears prickled in the back of his eyes. Would Sam have stayed by his side had he understood this earlier? Would there have been something for her to love?

He lifted his eyes from his intertwined fingers and found Finley looking at him, intently. He had no idea how long he'd been lost in his self-pity, how long she had been quiet, patiently waiting.

"Well, the reports are right," Ashby said. "I am an ass." He didn't go as far as admitting that he'd just realized the extent of his callousness. Still, this had to count for something. "But I'm working on it and hope to prove your first impression wrong."

Finley lifted an eyebrow. He focused on it as a distraction from the storm that was growing inside of him. The arch her brow formed was perfect, so was its thickness and color—the exact shade of her blond hair. It was either perfectly plucked or a feat of nature.

"You have pretty eyebrows," he blurted out without thinking.

Finley frowned, then said, "Thank you. I was beginning to think no one ever noticed."

Ashby smiled. "I won't claim to always be this perceptive."

They smiled nervously at each other.

"Um . . . so where are your cousins, Calisto and Joao?" Ashby asked to make conversation.

"Mirante sent them away. She said they'd caused enough trouble already. They didn't want to leave, but . . ." She shrugged. "My aunt thinks you lot are a bad influence on them."

"That we are," Ashby admitted.

"Um, if you were here to get something to eat . . ."

She pointed at a few people who had just walked in carrying several plastic bags. The smell of greasy food wafted through the air as they began unpacking and setting Styrofoam containers on the counter along the far wall.

"Looks like Chinese food," Finley said, wrinkling her nose. "Again."

As if a dinner bell had rung, people filed in and, immediately, began filling plastic plates, dropping noodles and rice onto the counter and fighting over small packets of soy sauce.

"I hope you like Chinese," Finley said. "There are only three restaurants within reasonable driving distance, so we eat it a lot."

Ashby was about to say that he'd never had American Chinese food—something to subtly suggest nothing so cheap had ever crossed his lips—but managed to bite his tongue.

Don't be an ass. He cleared his throat. "Yeah, I . . . I love it," he said, getting up and offering a hand to Finley, inviting her to join him at the line.

She stared at his fingers. Ashby anticipated a refusal, but then she smiled, took his hand, and assured him the egg rolls weren't too bad.

He smiled in return. Apparently, being nice every once in a while did pay off.

ℰ Chapter 15 ℛ
Sam

Simeon glanced at Sam and wrapped his big hand around Jacob's throat, making him fight for breath and drowning his cries to mere gasps.

His face was turning red, and his pupils began overtaking the blue of his widened eyes. Sam held his gaze from her perch, arms hooked to the bar overhead.

"Let him go, you monsters," she spat.

Danata put on a regretful expression and turned to Jacob. "Whatever happens now, dear, it won't be my fault. You're in Samantha's hands, not mine . . . or his." She gave a dismissive flick of the eyes toward Simeon. "One word from your hero and everything will be all right."

She pressed a hand to the side of Jacob's face and caressed his cheek. He did his best to turn away, but Simeon held him in place. Danata inclined her head to one side and smiled sweetly at Jacob, though her eyes brimmed with malice. Sam thought of Ashby then, and wondered how many times this witch had talked to him in the same manner. Had he been able to see through the mask?

"Don't touch me," Jacob said in a hoarse voice.

"I don't want to hurt you, little boy," Danata said, "but there's something Samantha needs to do for me. It is very important to the Regency, to Morphidkind. But she refuses to help. As the Regent, I can't allow that."

Jacob croaked something in response.

Danata gestured to the guard to ease his chokehold.

Jacob took a deep, desperate breath, then said, "But you're not the Regent."

Danata's mouth twisted. "Whoever has been stuffing lies into that empty head of yours?"

"I'm not stupid. I understand what's going on," Jacob said. "Your days are numbered. Fate doesn't want you here and you know it or you wouldn't be threatening me. I'm only ten and you don't even know me."

Danata flicked a hand at Simeon, and he tightened the chokehold again.

"I see he has been brainwashed." Danata straightened, attempting to hide her anger behind a casual tone. She faced Sam again. "I was hoping we could avoid all this unpleasantness, but obviously I'm wasting my time. So let me speak plainly to avoid any misunderstandings. If you don't weave Anima and her husband as many times as I tell you to, the boy will pay for it."

Tears slid out of the corner of Jacob's eyes. Sam's bottom lip trembled, impotence filling her heart.

"What do you say, *Weaver*?" Danata asked. "Do you follow your instincts? Or do you become the reason a little boy dies today?"

"Don't listen to her, Sam," Jacob rasped.

He tried to deepen his voice, but the fear was painted on his face as clearly as his innocence. In spite of that, his words made Sam realize he was the bravest person in the cell.

"I'm losing patience," Danata snapped, grabbing a handful of Jacob's hair and wrenching his head back.

A whimper escaped through the boy's half-opened mouth. Danata put a long fingernail under his eye and pushed down, revealing the pink part of his lower eyelid.

"Such beautiful blue eyes," she said. "It would be a shame if something happened to them. I wonder, do they remind you of somebody?"

Jacob cried out. Blood seeped from under the half-moon of the Regents nail. She pressed harder.

"Stop!" Sam said. "I'll do it. But you have to let Jacob go."

Anima and her husband had at least been happy for a time, but Jacob was an innocent child who had already been through so much. Sam didn't want him to suffer anymore.

"You're in no position to make demands, dear. The boy isn't going anywhere. He will stay right here, in case you decide to change your wise decision."

***

A moment later, Sam stumbled into Anima's cell as Simeon shoved her in. The Seer was sitting on her cot as despondent and wretched as before. Her eyes were lost and vacant, no life shining from within. She was still like a picture inside a frame, a snippet of film from a movie, cut out and left to slowly rot away.

Simeon moved closer, yanked Sam's hands up, and undid the manacles. Again, she was tempted to reach for her own vinculum, but she managed to stay in control.

Danata stepped next to Sam and looked at her expectantly.

Sam peered around the room. "Where is her husband?"

"He doesn't need to be in here," Danata answer. "Go ahead. Or do we need to bring the boy in?"

Jacob had stayed in the other cell, crying quietly. Sam hated to think of him alone in that bleak space, but that was a thousand times preferable to having him witness this.

Sam stepped closer to Anima. The woman's empty gaze remained fixed on some spot on the wall. Tears stood in Sam's eyes as she reached for Anima's twice-broken vinculum.

Her fingers played over the ribbon of light, moving dexterously over its ethereal surface. For a moment, she imagined herself a pianist and almost heard beautiful music as each torn strand weaved itself back together. The brightness of the pale link slowly increased, creating a breathtaking display of shimmering color, like the wings of a firefly or the surface of a lake kissed by the sun. The tears spilled down Sam's cheeks at the beauty and horror of it, a newly-made bond already doomed to the ripping.

Anima came to her senses with a gasp. She blinked and panted, a hand pressed to her chest. It took her a few agonizing minutes to recover and recall the wicked game she was being forced to play. Eyes wavering, she looked from Danata to Sam and back again.

"I'm sorry," Sam said in a weak breath.

Anima let out a shuddering inhale, then gave Sam a simple nod of understanding.

Without a word, Danata stepped forward and, unceremoniously, stuck her hand in front of the Seer. "Show me," she demanded.

Anima stared at the Regent's hand with indifference, then turned her face aside, saying nothing—though her refusal was clear.

Hand twisted into a claw, Danata grabbed the woman's face, and turned it in her direction. "Show me!" she shouted.

Anima held the Regent's gaze without blinking.

"I will rip you again," Danata threatened.

Even as the Regent dug polished fingernails into Anima's face, the old woman lifted her chin in defiance.

"You should hear your husband scream," Danata said. "You might think yourself brave, but he suffers like a helpless child."

Tears filled the Seer's eyes.

"The next time I rip you might be his last."

Anima swallowed thickly and jerked her face out of Danata's grip. The Regent allowed it and stepped back, wiping her hand on her gown.

"What makes you think that more suffering will make me change my mind?" Anima quietly asked. "Your cruelty can't change anything."

Danata kept a composed expression, but the reddening of her face betrayed her anger.

"My death, and even my husband's, would be a relief." Anima looked at her hands and turned them over. "I don't even recognize myself. These hands don't belong to me. You stole my youth, stole my happiness. Years gone. What is a little more pain before death comes?"

Danata laughed. "A little? You won't say that next time, if there is a next time."

The Regent lifted her hands in the air and, in one jerk, ripped the vinculum Sam had so carefully woven together.

Anima shrieked in agony and, in the other cell, so did her husband.

Sam shrank away, her shoulders caving in, her head going down in shame until Simeon grabbed her from behind and pushed her toward Anima once more.

"Do it again," he growled in her ear, "or I'll get the boy and all this screaming will be nothing compared to what you'll hear from him."

"I can't. I can't. I can't." Sam shook her head, pushing against the guard.

She couldn't be responsible for this horror. She couldn't let Danata get away with this. This was worse than torture. It was hell. She knew it well. She'd endured it twice.

"Get the boy," Danata ordered.

The man hurried away and came back with Jacob in tow. He pushed him into the room and forced him to his knees. The boy looked up, eyes red from crying, face disfigured by terror.

He had been safe and, now, he was back into the middle of this nightmare because she couldn't be strong.

Before Sam could think twice about what was happening, the guard kicked Jacob in the ribs and sent him sliding across the floor. Jacob cried out and curled up into a ball, holding his side. He moaned and twisted, struggling to breathe.

"No, stop!" Sam jumped between the guard and the boy. "I'm sorry, Jacob. I'm sorry." She made as if to kneel by his side, but Simeon pulled her by the hair and yanked her down to the floor, while Danata watched with detachment.

"Get out of the way," he growled, as he prepared to kick Jacob a second time.

Quickly, Sam scrambled back to her feet, tackled him low, and pushed him off balance. The guard staggered back, but managed to stay on his feet. With a grunt, he righted himself and went from Sam, murder on his face.

"Stop! I'll do it. I'll do it," she pleaded desperately.

Hands up in the air, she stepped closer to Anima and got a hold of her vinculum. Danata held a hand up, ordering Simeon to stand down.

Tears overflowing her eyes, Sam began to weave, all the while aware of the battered boy at her feet. Her indecision had caused this. She couldn't afford to be weak, not if this was the price to pay. For all his impulsiveness, Greg never hesitated. He made a decision and pushed full steam ahead. How she wished he was here!

Anima's closed eyes sprang open and filled with the panic that had abandoned her the moment Danata *ripped* her. She gasped for air as if she'd been drowning, legs and arms thrashing.

"What did you do?" Danata demanded.

"Nothing," Sam said.

After a drawn out moment, Anima went still and stared up at the ceiling, panting. Finally, she blinked and turned to look at them, her suffering almost palpable.

Shame washed over Sam. She was responsible for this pain: Anima's and Jacob's alike. But she had to focus on the boy. She could only travel one path, and Sam had chosen him.

"Sit her up," Danata order the guard. The tall man stepped forward, grabbed Anima by her dirty top and pulled her to a sitting position.

As soon as he let her go, Anima began to slide sideways along the wall, but she managed to brace herself with a limp arm. Her chest rose and fell. Her watery eyes drifted toward Danata with a mixture of hatred and pity—two things that had no business lingering together.

"How about now?" Danata asked Anima. "Ready to do as I say? Or will you continue to refuse me?"

The Seer swallowed thickly, then opened her mouth as if to speak. Her lower lip trembled, but she didn't say anything. Instead her attention turned to Sam, scrutinizing her features for a moment. Sam held her gaze, though she wanted to hide from the judgment Anima had every right to pass on her.

Except no judgment came. No harsh words. No recriminations. Instead, she noted Jacob on the floor as if to let Sam know she understood.

Anima licked her lips. "Don't worry about me," she said. "I *know*."

"Quiet!" Danata yelled.

Anima ignored the command. "Do what you must to make sure she doesn't win."

Danata slapped Anima across the face, then ripped her again.

"Weave her!" Danata ordered.

"It's too much," Sam said. "She'll die."

Danata's response was a quick glance in Jacob's direction. The boy whimpered and curled himself tighter.

It was all the warning Sam needed.

Keeping her face as steady as possible, Sam got to work, her fingers weaving at a steady pace, Anima's words ringing in her ears.

Don't worry about me.

She had barely finished her task when Danata ripped the vinculum again, without giving Anima a moment to recover.

The Seer's screams echoed inside Sam's head as the woman's body contorted, back arching, blood seeping from the corner of her mouth as she bit herself. She groaned for several minutes before finally going quiet.

"Again," Danata said.

Sam didn't hesitate this time. She just did as she was told, making sure Danata didn't look in Jacob's direction again.

After several iterations of the same, Sam lost count of how many times her fingers weaved through the strands of Anima's vinculum.

She remembered the first time she had used her skill and how she'd reveled in the experience. Giving back what had been taken was something beautiful, something worth doing. It had felt majestic, the healing, the bonding of two Integrals who were meant to be together.

It had felt like Fate.

But this . . .

With Jacob curled up on the floor, and Danata and her evil guard watching over the spectacle with glee in their eyes, Sam began to wonder if her skill was a curse, a tool Fate had created to exert some wicked plan against Morphidkind.

For the tenth or twelfth time, Sam stepped to the side as she finished connecting the last thread. Wearily, she waited for the Regent to tear it apart once more.

Except this time Danata just watched the Seer as she painfully and slowly came back to her senses, her body shaking with tremors, her mouth spilling a tendril of pink saliva, her hollow cheeks shining with tears and sweat.

Through her half open mouth, Anima breathed in small gasps, eyes rolling behind closed lids.

She's dying, Sam thought. Her heart hammered with fear and guilt.

"She can't take any more of this," Sam murmured, realizing for the first time that the husband's screams had ceased.

Oh, God.

As if she'd read her thoughts, Danata said, "It seems your husband has gone quiet."

A low moan sounded in the back of Anima's throat. She was trying to speak, but maybe it was too late.

"You're ready now, it seems," Danata said, squatting next to the cot and placing a hand in front of Anima's face.

The Seer took in the Regent's cruel face and then her waiting hand. For a moment, she didn't move, but slowly, something changed in her eyes. Sam's stomach clenched, making it harder to breathe.

Anima had finally broken.

The Seer was ready to give Danata what she wanted.

Anima's hand twitched, then inched toward Danata's.

The Regent smiled, her regal face relaxing with satisfaction. "A good decision, Anima. I might even leave you this way."

The news brought no joy to Anima's face. If anything, it seemed to crack her open, forcing a tear to spill from her already-wavering eyes. Still, she pressed her fingers to the back of Danata's hand.

At contact, the Regent's face twisted in disgust and, for a beat, it seemed as if she would pull away. Instead, she turned her hand over and clasped Anima's frail fingers tightly.

Gradually, the Regent's gaze acquired a faraway quality, as if she were being transported to another world. Her pupils grew, covering her violet irises and spilling onto the white of her eyes.

Sam's heart thumped at the sight of that inhuman gaze. More than ever, Danata looked like a creature spawned from the depths of hell. In contrast, the Seer's eyes glowed like tiny, radiant suns capable of swallowing Danata's darkness along with the rest of the world.

For who knows how long, the two women remained immobile, then a wavering light began to pour from Anima's eyes. It moved like two lazy snakes weaving through the air, carrying what Danata wanted—something toxic, if Sam had to guess.

Sam's heart froze with dread. What knowledge would the broken, old woman give the Regent? What tool to kill everyone's hope?

She couldn't allow this, not even if it meant Jacob's life and her own. There were others to consider, other besides those she loved.

She shook her head.

An unexpected battle of wills unleashed like a storm inside of Sam—her human side against the Morphid half that made her a Weaver and a Regent, a protector and leader of her kind.

Sam shut herself to her hardwired instincts and, making a split-second decision, launched in Danata's direction. Except Simeon was as fast as her decision making and captured her, wrapping an arm around her waist.

Kicking and clawing, Sam reached out, trying to snatch a handful of Danata's hair. But it was already too late. The snaking tendrils had already reached her eyes and turned their black, glassy surfaces into mirrors.

Shimmering colors played in the silvery surface for no more than a few seconds, then the wisps of light retreated back into Anima's eyes. In an instant, her gaze returned to normal and so did Danata's.

The Regent yanked Sam's hand away, as if repelled, and pressed it to her chest.

Tears rolled down the outside corners of Danata's eyes. Something Sam could never have imagined possible.

Anima spoke then, her voice barely a rasp. "That is all I will ever give you. Your own son will be your doom."

෨ Chapter 16 ౪
Greg

"Climb down," Katsu said, pointing toward the empty hotel pool.

"Is this a joke?"

Yesterday, when the Warrior had said he was going to train him and asked to be followed here, the claim had sounded far-fetched, now it seemed completely ridiculous.

"Just play along," Katsu said.

Greg frowned, but went with the flow, descending the rusted ladder and jumping the rest of the way when the rungs ran out.

Numbers shaped from black tiles indicated the deep end was eight feet tall. Greg judged it was probably three times that long and wondered if inhaling any of the flaking, blue paint that covered the walls would be bad for his lungs.

He chuckled to himself.

I'm literally and figuratively in a hole.

"What's so funny?" Katsu asked.

"Nothing. So . . . what's this all about?"

Katsu stood a few paces in front of him, two swords strapped to his back, handles sticking from each side of his head like horns. He smiled knowingly as if he held a secret no one knew.

Greg had no real skills to speak of, unless bouncing a basketball counted. So sword training would take forever, which was probably Portos's intention.

"Listen, I humored you!" Greg swept a hand in a circle to demonstrate how far he'd come. "So, go ahead, waste my time a little more, and then tell Portos I did what he wanted."

Katsu sighed. "You have so much to learn. Patience, for instance."

"Dude, we're the same age, so stop trying to sound like Obi-Wan."

"You are rash to act and make judgments. You need to learn to control that," Katsu insisted.

"Spare me and get to the point."

"As you wish." Katsu inclined his head and, wrapping his left hand around his right fist, inclined his head in a respectful bow.

If the Warrior hadn't been so stern-looking, Greg would have thought Katsu was mocking him. But no, the dude was serious. Straightening, Katsu pulled one of the swords from the scabbard at his back. A metallic *zing* echoed in the hollow space. He examined the weapon, turning it this way and that, gently resting the blade on the fingers of his opposite hand. It was long and seemed wickedly sharp.

"This one is for you." Katsu offered the sword with deference, as if he were relinquishing some religious relic.

Greg stared at it skeptically but, after a moment's consideration, he wrapped his hand around the hilt and lifted it. To his surprise, he found the grip comfortable, even if the weapon was heavier than he'd expected. It was beautiful too, the blade carved with intricate patterns. He lowered it, watched the light reflect off its too-shiny surface, and wondered why they'd trust him with such a weapon.

"It feels good, doesn't it?" Katsu asked, removing the scabbard and setting it next to Greg.

He met Katsu's inquisitive eyes and shrugged.

It was a nice sword, no doubt, but what could it accomplish? And why give it to him? Why not a gun? Something to shoot Danata right between the eyes. That would surely kill her faster than this. Ripper or not. He said nothing, though, since Katsu was still smiling like the mouse that ate the cheese.

Pulling out the second sword, Katsu slashed it left and right, cutting the air with a whistle. He struck a pose, the Japanese-style blade erect before him, splitting his face in two halves with its shadow. Where the sword Katsu had given him seemed like a medieval weapon from a King Arthur movie, Katsu's reminded him of old Samurai films he and his dad had watched years ago.

"You look . . . great," Greg ventured, trying not to sound sarcastic. "And it probably works for you, being a Warrior and all. But I have no sword skills. I've never handled a gun, but I'm sure it would be a heck of a lot faster to learn than this." He tilted the sword in his hand.

"What good is a bullet against magic?" Katsu asked.

"Same as a sword, I suppose."

"Ordinary swords, perhaps, but these swords—" Katsu stopped abruptly, his gaze darting above Greg's head.

Greg turned to find Perry standing at the edge of the pool, his head cocked to one side as he regarded them, making Greg feel like a fish in a bowl.

"Good place to practice," the Sorcerer said, taking the ladder, then jumping down to meet them.

"If you don't mind, Katsu and I are busy," Greg said. He was still mad at Perry for not helping him get to Sam.

"Actually," Katsu said, "he's here to help us."

"Is he going to magically teach me how to wield this thing?"

"No, we don't have to teach you that," Katsu said.

"Then what the hell are we doing here?" Greg asked with a frown.

"Just shut up and listen," Katsu said, losing his temper.

Greg was taken aback. Katsu's tone was always even and gentle, but he had turned on a dime.

Perry rolled his eyes and headed toward the shallow end of the pool.

"Why don't we just give him a little demonstration?" Perry said once he'd reached a higher vantage point.

"Yes, please! He's exhaustingly negative, and I'm getting tired of it."

Greg laughed. "Sorry for disrupting your zen."

"I used to help Veridan and Portos train Danata's Warriors—Florence among them," Perry said, unbuttoning his shirt. "Now, I wish I hadn't."

He cast the shirt aside, rolled his shoulders, then threw a few punches in the air, feet moving as if he were a boxer. His snake amulet hung at his breastbone, swaying like a pendulum.

"Training Warriors is always a good workout," he said. "I'm kind of looking forward to this."

He grinned sideways and, without preamble, made a strange pattern in the air, his hands moving faster than the eye could see.

Teeth bare, he pulled back his arm and pitched a green ball of energy straight at Katsu's head. The projectile moved at a prodigious speed. Greg jumped back, surprised. He opened his mouth to warn the Warrior, but Katsu was already angling his sword and, with a quick flick of the blade, easily deflected the attack.

"No warning?" Katsu asked. "I would call that cheating,"

"It's not cheating when you're fighting the best Warrior in the world," Perry replied.

"Very generous of you to grant that title to me. I trust you don't do it in mockery."

"No, at all. Portos told me about you. I understand you morphed prematurely, and have been training for over seven years. I believe that's longer, at least by a year, than the High Warrior herself."

Mid-sentence, Perry rolled to one side, hands whirling. As he came around, he aimed at Katsu's chest and released a huge orb of energy that sped along, leaving a trail like a comet bent on destruction.

Greg took a step back, squinting at the singeing heat, while Katsu stepped forward, a smile on his face.

A pang of envy twisted in Greg's chest. He'd felt that confident just days before, fearless of magic, invincible. And now . . .

The scorching ball rushed toward Katsu. Greg expected him to shield against the magic the way he'd done before, but instead, Katsu threw his sword up in the air.

Greg's heart froze.

The sword reached its apex, then came down, tip first. Katsu clapped his hands together as it descended, and caught it, trapping the naked blade between his palms.

Perry cursed, took a knee, and pressed his hands to the bottom of the pool, an incantation fast at his lips.

The magic struck Katsu's praying hands. Eyes blazing, the Warrior growled as green energy crackled up and down the blade and across his shuddering body. Then he separated his hands, caught the hilt, and pointed the sword at Perry.

"Shit!" Perry's face fell. More spell words dashed out of his lips.

Rising from the ground, a shield began to form around him, the sides of a sphere racing to meet at the top. But they never closed. Perry wasn't fast enough and his own magic returned, hit the would-be barrier and consumed it with an explosion that sent him sprawling on his back. Perry's body seized once, then he moaned and went still.

Greg released an oath and took a step toward the Sorcerer. "What the hell did you just do? Mirante's going to kill us!"

Katsu shrugged, unfazed.

"Perry?" Greg murmured, getting closer. "Is he even breathing?"

As Greg took another step, Perry jolted to a sitting position, a string of foul curses spewing from his mouth.

"Bloody hell, that hurt." His hair was standing on end and his bare chest was red, but otherwise he seemed fine.

Katsu laughed. "Just what you deserve."

"You weren't supposed to do that!" Perry complained.

"What kind of a demonstration would that have been?" Katsu turned to Greg. "Ready to *really* listen now?"

℘ Chapter 17 ℃
Ashby

Ashby knocked on Perry's door, but got no answer. He waited a few seconds, then headed for the common area, hoping to find him there.

He wasn't there either. Instead, he found Finley, sitting at the same table as yesterday, reading a new book, a faint smile on her lips. Ashby observed her, unnoticed. She was playing with her hair, twisting it around her index finger. The gesture was feminine and absent.

He wondered if she would ever morph, and if she did, what would be her caste. He couldn't pretend to know her, but something told him she would get mad at him for pondering her fate. As they talked further through dinner, she'd acted as if never morphing would be okay, as if it were unimportant—like never learning how to drive since one could take the tube—and let's not forget walking. It was clearly a defense mechanism. Just a few months back, it would have been impossible for Ashby to relate, but now . . .

He wondered how long before she gave up and went to live among humans. She could pass for normal among them, so why live with the stigma? The idea had become a distinct possibility for Ashby, himself. So why not for her?

Except something in her fierce, green eyes told him she would never do something like that. She appeared to be made of something stern, something he wished was part of his backbone.

He tore his eyes away from her and shook his head. Had he learned nothing the last time she caught him staring?

Ashby looked back over his shoulder, wondering where to look for Perry next. An idea had started forming in Ashby's mind, and he wanted to discuss it with his friend.

"Looking for someone?" Finley asked from her place at the table.

Ashby's head snapped back. Had she noticed him watching her?

"Um, yes. For Perry." He walked closer to Finley, peering at her book, suddenly curious about her literary interests.

She closed the book and placed an arm over the cover. "I saw him about an hour ago. He went that way." She hooked her thumb over her shoulder.

Ashby frowned at the dim hall.

"The pool is that way," Finley said.

"There's a pool?"

"Just a hole in the ground, now. The gym is also in that direction, though there's no equipment. Vending and ice machines used to be there, too. They'd sure come in handy now."

Had Perry sneaked out to go see Brooke? He'd been ordered not to, but it wasn't as if he ever listened to anyone. Or perhaps he'd found a new female interest among the MORF rebels. Ashby shook his head, doubtful. Perry had always enjoyed a variety of female companions, but he seemed to have formed a real attachment to Brooke.

"Why are you shaking your head?" Finley asked sliding her book off the table and placing it on her lap.

"Nothing, just wondering about Perry's tendency to . . . get into trouble with members of the opposite sex."

Finley nodded. "He does strike me like that kind of guy."

"Why? Did he try something with you?"

"Oh, no." Finley's eyes fell to her lap, cheeks growing red. She seemed embarrassed for a moment, but her expression quickly turned serious.

Ashby fidgeted, worried that he'd offended her. "Sorry, I hope I didn't—"

"No, no." She stood, moving the book behind her back. "I'd better leave."

"Please, don't leave on my account. *I* will go. I have to find Perry, anyway."

"Sure." She seemed disappointed, which was confusing since she was the one who had wanted to leave in the first place.

"Um, want to come with me?" Ashby asked. "To look for Perry, I mean."

Finley's eyes roved around the room as if trying to find an excuse to say no. She probably liked being alone, and he kept intruding.

"Um, never mind." He smiled and took a backward step. "I can tell you want to leave."

"No, I'll come with you. I'm curious to see what Perry's up to. Maybe he's practicing. Portos and the others go in there sometimes. Inside the pool, I mean."

Finley put her book on the table, cover down, and joined him. They started down the hall.

"What are you reading?" Ashby asked point-blank.

"Just whatever."

Ashby was tempted to rush back to take a peek, but that was childish. This was only his third conversation with Finley, and he was still trying to make up for the first.

"I used to read quite a bit when I was small," Ashby said, attempting to break the awkwardness between them. "Lately, I haven't had much time for it, but I miss it. I used to enjoy . . . "

Ashby stopped. Saying that his favorite subject was philosophy would probably sound pretentious, even if it was true. He enjoyed other things as well, so he should probably lead with those.

"Um, science fiction about other worlds. Strange stuff, really." He smiled, finding that it felt good to share something of himself that wasn't part of his perfect Regent persona.

"I would've never guessed," Finley said a smile in her voice. "I pictured you more like the—oh, I don't know—scholarly type, studying philosophy and geology and stuff like that."

"And that would be bad?" Ashby asked, not knowing whether to feel insulted or not. "I like many things, you know." He added trying not to sound defensive.

"Oh, no, it wouldn't be bad. I guess I just imagined you sort of . . . one-dimensional. But I guess I was wrong." She smiled up at him, her cheeks coloring.

He was surprised to see how beautiful her tan skin looked when she flushed.

Beautiful? The thought left him feeling confused.

"I was . . . um . . . reading a stupid human romance novel," Finley admitted.

Ashby raised his eyebrows, not sure what to think of that admission. Morphids had no room for romance novels. They were all filled with drama, break-ups, cheating—things that didn't belong in their world. Companions were fated to faithfully share their futures.

"Please don't tell my aunt," Finley blurted out.

"I don't see why I should mention it to her. Why should she care, anyway?"

"She thinks it's pathetic," Finley said, hiding her face.

"Well, it's just fiction. You just have to suspend reality more with romance novels, that's all." He chuckled to himself.

"That sounds a heck of a lot like something she told me once," Finley said, her voice wavering.

Was she going to cry? Ashby tried to catch her eye, but she stared at the ground. His jaw worked up and down as he tried to figure out what to say.

"I'm . . . sorry. I don't know what . . . I . . ."

"You don't have to apologize." Finley rushed forward, headed for a double, metal door with the word "pool" painted on it.

He followed, scratching his head. Was he being an insensitive idiot again? The way he had been with Sam and Greg and everyone he'd ever met?

"Finley, wait!"

She ignored him and pushed past the door. Ashby caught it before it slammed on his face and walked in.

An unusual scene greeted him: Perry sprawled at the bottom of the empty pool, his hair on end, a hand over his reddened chest, and Katsu and Greg hovering over him.

"What in bloody hell is going on?" Ashby asked.

Katsu and Greg looked up, smiling. They were both holding swords.

"We're training," Perry said with a groan that sounded a bit exaggerated.

"Training for what? And why didn't you tell me? I might have joined in."

"Portos didn't mention anything about training you," Katsu said. "Greg, I think it's your turn." The Warrior gestured toward Greg's sword.

"My turn?" Greg echoed. He lifted the weapon, examining it. "Is this sword just like yours?

Perry stumbled to his feet. "Aren't you a bloody genius? Of course it's like his. It was forged with magic by a *traitorous* Sorcerer. That's the only reason this little Warrior was able to stop my attacks. But if this is how it's going to be, I'm not training anymore. I didn't come here to get clobbered."

"Sorry, I didn't realize you were so delicate," Katsu said, wearing a twisted smile.

Perry didn't take the bait, for once, and just narrowed his eyes at the Warrior.

Greg held the sword, reverently. "So it can withstand any kind of magic? From any Sorcerer?"

"Probably," Katsu said. "It was forged by my great grandfather—not a traitorous Sorcerer, by the way." He gave Perry a derisive glance. "If you wield it properly, you may as well be immune to magic."

Realization dawned on Greg's face, and a certain something he'd lost when he was ripped from Sam seemed to return.

Perhaps it was confidence, hope or just relief to find out he didn't have to be useless anymore.

Ashby's chest tightened. Why hadn't Portos offered *him* a sword? Why had they left him with nothing?

He bit his lower lip, doing his best to stop the questions from pouring out and spilling to the bottom of the pool. Questions he didn't really need to ask because he knew the answers.

He was rubbish. To everyone. His mother, Sam, and Portos included.

Anger rose within him, but he fought it down. He was resigned already, wasn't he? He'd come to the realization that the things he once had would never return. Loss after loss after loss, Fate had made it clear that his initial casting had been a mistake.

It had all been written, and there was nothing he could have done to change it. So none of it had been his fault.

Not my fault.

"Are you okay?" Finley asked, pressing a hand to his forearm.

"Uh, sure. I'm fine." He smiled weakly.

Not my fault.

Fate's fault.

Why hadn't he realized this earlier?

His manner, his upbringing, his clueless pomposity hadn't been the reason. Sam would have never loved him properly, no matter what.

And didn't he deserve more than that?

Before, he'd thought he'd made peace with his situation, but judging by the weightlessness he now felt, it was clear he hadn't. He exhaled, feeling lighter than he had in a long time.

His smile stretched further. "Yeah, I'm fine," he said. "I'm truly fine."

ℰↃ *Chapter 18* ℂ℞
Sam

Your own son will be your doom, Anima had said, and now Danata sat on the floor looking dazed.

The guard had let go of Sam and was now tending to Danata. Unnoticed, Sam gestured to Jacob not to move, then inched closer to the old Seer and knelt next to the cot. Her hand trembled over Anima's face. She wanted to smooth a lock of hair off her forehead, but she was afraid to touch her. The woman was so still that Sam feared she'd died.

How would death feel through her fingers?

Taking a deep breath, Sam smoothed the graying piece of hair back. Tears filled her eyes.

This is my fault.

Gently, she caressed Anima's forehead.

"I'm sorry," Sam whispered. "Please forgive me."

Slowly, Anima's eyes opened and found Sam's. A muscle near her mouth twitched, and Sam imagined the Seer wanted to curse her. However, a weak smile formed on the woman's lips instead.

"This was my purpose," Anima said in a broken, barely intelligible voice. "Do not fret. Now remember yours . . . remember the homeless. Remember them."

Anima winced, let out a small cough, then went utterly still.

"What . . . what are you doing?" Danata asked.

Sam turned back. The Regent was shaking herself, getting back to her feet with Simeon's help.

"What did she tell you?" Danata demanded. She'd dried her tears, but red blotches dotted her face.

"She didn't say anything," Sam lied. "She's dead, you murderous bitch."

"No, she's not." Danata took a step toward Anima's body, denial stamped on her features. It only took her a second to see the truth etched on the Seer's vacant face.

Panting like a bull, she whirled back, took a hold of Sam's hair again, and pulled her to her feet. Sam's scalp burned as strands of hair tore from their roots.

With no intention of being abused this way, Sam reached for the Regent's face, claws out, but before she managed to unleash her own ire, a searing pain shot down her spine, igniting her every nerve as if lightning had struck her.

For a moment, she thought Simeon had tasered her, but then realized that Danata had taken hold of one of her broken vinculums and was ripping it further, tearing small pieces of the already frayed bond.

All ability to fight fled Sam's body as pain spread like wildfire to her arms and legs. She went limp and dropped to the floor. With more strength than Sam would have given her credit for, the Regent dragged her to the cell across the hall.

"My Regent, I can do that," Simeon offered.

Danata didn't answer, but continued to drag Sam into the cell, the guard staying well-away.

"Your usefulness has considerably diminished," Danata growled, throwing her to the floor.

Too limp to brace her fall, Sam collapsed face first on the stone floor. Pain sizzled under her every pore. Her spine arched. Her eyes swiveled into the back of her head.

"But you'll still be useful, damn you! If only one last time." Danata's words crackled in Sam's ears as the Regent turned and walked out, her heels pounding like hammer blows. "Lock her in. No food. Only water."

Simeon snapped Sam's manacles back on, then the door closed, a click following as the lock automatically engaged.

The room spun.

Sam's skin burned as if the pain in her heart were trying to escape. In her feverish suffering, she thought of Jacob in the next cell, hurting because she had dared come into his life. She thought of Greg wherever he was, torn from her, perhaps not even aware of the world around him. She thought of the parents she'd never met. Of Ashby, who she'd disappointed even though she'd been fated to love him. She thought of all those homeless Morphids Anima had reminded her of, those people who no one but Sam could heal.

She had let down so many. People she'd probably never see again. She didn't understand what being a Morphid meant. She hadn't been raised to believe in Fate or trust its purpose. And no matter how hard she racked her brain, she couldn't figure out why Fate would allow this to happen.

Why had she grown in ignorance of who she really was? Why had she been raised by two people who didn't love her? Why—when she'd finally found a breath of happiness, a reason for being—was it all taken away? And for what? For this?

Sam crawled to the cot that sat against the wall, rested bent elbows on its edge and laid her head between them. Her manacled hands hovered uncomfortably above her head, and she wished she could press her knuckles into her temples until the misery that weighed on her squeezed out.

She sobbed like a child, like she hadn't in quite some time, at least since she'd met Greg and learned she could be loved. She despaired, convinced that he would have been better off without her.

Physical pain soaked through her bones, mixing with her emotional anguish and erasing all hope of the simple life she'd always dreamed of.

She was a Morphid and Fate had planned this for her. And now, she'd come to the end of the line. Loneliness sidled next to her, an enemy that pretended to be a friend. She cried for a long time, feeling as if the tears would never run out.

But slowly, a certain calm came to her. She imagined Greg standing over her, smoothing her hair, and telling her everything would be all right. His gentle words took away the pain and slay the loneliness, making sure it would never return. His handsome face smiled down at her, blue eyes sparkling with assurances. She nearly smiled to herself. Instead, she sniffled and ran a hand over her face, dispelling the last of her tears.

She opened her eyes slowly, wishing to find Greg sitting next to her, his strong hands ready to pull her into a tight hug. But what she found surprised her nearly as much as if he'd actually been there.

Afraid to break the spell, she glanced around the room, holding her breath.

Tendrils of light were whirling around her, soothingly touching her, delivering comfort and warmth.

Her torn vinculums had stretched and separated into thinner strands, translucent filaments blanketing her like hundreds of comforting arms.

Shining brightly, they arched around Sam, assuring her she was not alone.

๛ Chapter 19 ๛
Greg

Portos had wanted to give Greg a fighting chance. Really?

Rather surprising, considering that Greg had thought the Sorcerer wanted to sweep him under the rug. Still, he didn't see what good this sword or any other could serve in *his* hands.

Greg's gaze went back and forth between Perry and Katsu. "Magically forged or not, I don't know how to wield it. I've never even touched a sword before."

"That's because you didn't need to," Katsu said. "Now, you do."

"Yeah, that and ten-thousand hours of practice to become an expert. And while we're at it, a billion dollars would be nice." Greg peered around the dilapidated pool as if searching for the money.

"I'll have to agree with Greg," Ashby said, sitting at the edge of the pool, feet dangling. "It would at least take months, and he doesn't have that kind of patience." He smirked.

Greg flipped him the bird.

"It won't take as long as you think," Katsu said. "Even though you're not a Keeper anymore, your body is still built for battle. Certain innate abilities remain. At least that's what Portos thinks."

Greg cocked his head, his interest more than piqued.

"What he's saying," Perry intervened, "is that a Keeper without his immunity to magic is still as good as a Warrior."

"Hey!" Katsu exclaimed indignantly. "I didn't say that. I could beat him with a blindfold on."

"All my quids are on Katsu," Ashby piped in.

"Wise man." Katsu pointed at Ashby, then turned to Greg. "What I'm saying is that you're strong, agile, and keen enough to wield the sword to good purpose. Don't get me wrong, it's still a great risk, but you can become useful in the battle . . . when it comes. Plus it can cut through magical shields, if you manage to get close enough."

Strong. Agile. Keen.

Greg's gaze shifted to the sword in his hand, feeling the truth of Katsu's words. He lifted the weapon and traced an arc in the air, testing it out. Maybe it would work, and he wouldn't mind being able to cut through protective shields.

He took a step back and crouched into a fighting stance. "Let's give it a try then."

Katsu smiled and looked him up and down, considering. Then, with a few taps on Greg's arms and shoulders, the Warrior corrected his fighting stance and hold on the sword.

"Good," Katsu said, then turned to Perry. "This is your chance. If you hold a grudge against this man, make your magic mean and fast."

The Sorcerer rubbed his hands and smiled. "Someone's gotta pay for this." He pointed at his battered, reddened chest.

"Um, this doesn't seem very wise," Finley said, peering down at them, concern in her eyes.

"Probably not," Ashby said. "It involves Greg and Perry. Two troublemakers, if I ever met any."

"From what I hear, they aren't the only troublemakers around here," she said.

Ashby gave Finley a raised eyebrow. She was smirking at him, though not in disapproval. Ashby smiled back.

"His mother would agree," Perry offered.

"That evil woman?" Finley said. "Forgive me for saying that but—"

"No need to apologize." Ashby waved a hand and turned his attention back toward the impending fight.

Taking this as an invitation, Perry whirled his hands and released his initial attack.

Greg's first thought was that the approaching green orb didn't look impressive, nowhere near to what the Sorcerer had used on Katsu.

His second was that he was screwed.

Magic hit his right shoulder, crackling and sending him flying against the concrete pool wall. The sword fell out of his hand and hit the concrete with a metallic clatter as he cradled his arm and shifted to one side.

"Son of a bitch!" he cursed. "It hurts."

It felt as if a giant wasp had stung him.

"Sorry," Perry said, sounding anything but sorry. "Just so you know, I'm too powerful to cast weaker magic than that. It's simply not possible."

"I think all that means is that you have no control." Greg sat up, holding is arm.

Goading Perry was a terrible idea, but the cocky Sorcerer had a knack for getting under his skin.

Greg stood and shook his arm.

He could take this pain and much more just to save Sam's pinky finger. For the whole of her, he would gladly die.

Picking up the sword and squaring his shoulders, he said, "Again."

ᔆᗡ *Chapter 20* ᗉᗋ
Ashby

"This is horrible," Finley said, pressing a hand to her mouth.

"Oh, he'll be fine," Ashby said. "Perry wouldn't really hurt him."

Or would he? He considered Perry's intent expression.

"How many people will die?" Finley asked in a quiet tone.

Die? He turned to Finley and found her worried expression had grown deeper.

"I never met my parents," she said. "I grew up among all these people. Each one of them taught me different things. I didn't even go to school. Yanci taught me how to read and write. Homero taught me math. Others filled in wherever needed. When I was ready, I took a test online and got my high school diploma. It was easy. You might think it's sad, but I wouldn't change a thing. These people are my family, everything I have—the only ones who understand me and know I don't need a caste to be someone."

Ashby listened, watching her expression intently, the way her mouth curved slightly with fondness and her eyes seemed to sparkle with warm memories. What she described sounded a lot like what he'd gone through with his tutors, but in reality, it was quite different. She loved these people, her family as she'd said.

Guilt washed over Ashby.

All of this was his mother's fault. People—including those Finley loved—would suffer because of Danata's whims.

It was wrong, unfair and, not to mention, devastating for Morphidkind and its already-low numbers.

They didn't need war, but peace.

A Regent who could give them confidence in a world that didn't and couldn't understand what they were.

He'd had plans before, ideas to help his people. He'd hoped to be the Regent they required, but that chance was gone now. He would never be able to make a difference now.

Unless . . .

The idea that had been tickling the back of his mind sprang to life. It wouldn't be easy, and everyone would hate him for it, but what else could he do?

"Don't worry about your family, Finley. They will be fine," Ashby said.

But she wasn't paying attention to him anymore. Instead, she seemed mesmerized by the battle below.

"It's like someone lit a fire under him," Finley said as Greg took a stance once more and got ready for another magical volley from Perry.

"Indeed," Ashby said, considering Greg with new eyes.

৪৹ Chapter 21 ৹৪
Sam

Omar escorted Sam along a hall she'd never crossed before. Simeon had the day off, apparently. That, or he had someone else to torture.

"Where are you taking me?" Sam asked.

"The Regent's office," he answered.

"What for?"

"How should I know?"

"I want to see Jacob," Sam said in a pleading voice. Omar was the least bad of the two, so it was worth a try.

The guard huffed. "Ask the Regent."

"You could take me to him."

"You must think me mad."

"Could you at least tell me how he's doing?" Sam asked.

"I've no idea."

Tears prickled in the back of her eyes. "You people have no hearts."

"Be quiet," Omar said, though not without a hint of guilt in his voice. He might not have a heart, but he did seem to have a conscience—albeit a very small one.

"Could you make sure he—"

"Be quiet, I said."

She lowered her head and focused on the corridor ahead. A couple of minutes later, they reached a carved wooden door that opened into a wide open area occupied by two rows of desks on each side.

Sam stopped as many pairs of eyes turned and locked on her. The murmur of voices died slowly as Omar gave her a small shove.

State-of-the-art computers topped every desk, looking entirely out of place in the ancient castle. To the right, a wall made entirely of glass let in light from outside, making Sam want to press her cheek to its surface and be kissed by the sun. A plush runner rug extended for about 40 feet, marking the way straight into what Sam assumed was Danata's office.

Danata's staff—fingers frozen over their keyboards and phones—appraised her, giving her manacled hands a careful examination. Did they know who she was? What their Regent was doing to her? Well, if they didn't, she would remedy that.

"My name is Sam Gibson," she said out loud. "In case you don't know, I was Ashby Rothblade's Companion, but—"

A jab to her back made her stumble.

"You don't know how to keep mum, do you? That big mouth of yours is going to get you killed." Omar grabbed her by the arm and hustled her to the end of the hall.

"Ah, that hurts." She tried to extricate her arm, but it seemed Omar had had enough of her.

"You bunch of cowards!" Sam shouted over her shoulder.

"Dammit!" The guard shoved her into an office through a fogged glass door.

Sam blinked at the office occupant, a shiver traveling down her back.

The guard bowed slightly, stepped out, and closed the door, making Sam feel as trapped as a mouse in a venomous snake's cage.

"I trust you rested, after your . . . exhausting task," Danata said from behind a massive wooden desk. She lifted a crystal glass in her direction, making its amber-colored liquid swirl and sparkle under the overhead lights.

"Sit, Samantha." Danata gestured with her glass toward a chair.

"I'd rather stand," Sam planted her feet firmly.

"Suit yourself."

"What do you want? Nothing good I'm sure," Sam said.

"Good for someone," Danata replied. "There's a whole world out there, dear. You must learn not to be so selfish."

"Cute."

"Despite what you may think, I'm a good Regent, Samantha. I focus on the whole, not the individual. I want progress for our kind, and I will not tolerate those who oppose me. I was chosen by Fate to do this, to weed out the bad seeds that undermine our traditions."

"And what does the Council think about that?" Sam asked.

Danata waved a hand in the air, looking tired. "I won't discuss politics with a snotty *American* girl. Your accent and tone grates on my nerves."

Sam frowned.

"You know, my sister has always been a sentimental fool," Danata said. "And I trust she will think you are special. Maybe it's a good thing she has never met you and has likely grown to idolize you. If I know her well, she's created some ideal of you in her mind and believes you're worth saving. I suspect she will have no trouble relinquishing the Regency and turning herself in, all in exchange for her worthless daughter.

"You should know that I don't intend to go easy on her. I made that mistake before. I harbored a few useless sensibilities. But I've grown. I know better now. Weakness breeds contempt. I was weak when I spared you and Ashby. Now instead of being grateful, he hates me and has turned on me. I shall not err in that manner again. If I ever had a heart, it has since withered away.

"Still, I'll give you one more chance to be useful. Tell me where MORF hides, and I promise you, their deaths will be painless."

Danata raised her eyebrows, waiting for an answer.

"I don't know what you're talking about. Even your Sorcerer told you so. Don't you trust your own people?" Sam asked, holding her gaze.

Danata ignored the jab. "Lying will not help you or your mother. You were with Mateo Espina. He is a MORF sympathizer and kept you hidden in New York." Danata's violet eyes drilled into Sam's.

"Ashby's father, you mean?"

Danata's face twisted, and there was a flash of hurt in the expression, but she hid it quickly. "And you expect me to believe that's all he shared with you?"

"I don't know anything about MORF," Sam said between clenched teeth. "And even if I did, I wouldn't tell you."

"Alright, have it your way." Danata gave a dismissive sweep with her hand. "You will die as soon as you serve your purpose anyway, and so will everyone you've ever known or even heard of. In the meantime, enjoy our *hospitality*."

ഇ Chapter 22 ര
Greg

Katsu, Ashby, and Finley had left, but Greg convinced Perry to practice a little longer. As exhausted as he was, he didn't want to rest until he got the hang of the sword.

"I think we should up the stakes," Greg said.

Up to now, Perry had hurled strong magic, but nothing life threatening, and maybe that was the problem, maybe Greg needed a real threat to speed up his progress.

Perry shrugged, apparently okay with the suggestion. Clearly, the Sorcerer didn't care if Greg ended up like a tater tot.

"Ready or not," Perry said, shooting another ball of magic at Greg.

Energy rushed forward, barely giving him time to square his shoulders and lift the sword. As Katsu had instructed, Greg tried to present the sword's broad side, grasping it lightly at the hilt.

Once more, he wasn't fast or accurate enough, and Perry's magic hit the blade at an angle. Green electricity crackled down Greg's arms, traveling past his elbows and shoulders, then meeting with a snap inside his chest.

Once more, his arms flailed, relinquishing the sword as the electric shock caused him to stiffen. His vocal cords seemed to hum of their own accord, issuing an involuntary moan. His rigid hands flew to his neck as a choking sensation clawed its way from his chest. Heat climbed toward his face. He screamed, this time quite willingly. His skin sizzled. His eyelashes burned to a crisp. Twitching, he fell, head hitting the concrete floor with a crack.

Surprised he was still alive, Greg groaned and curled up on his side, fighting the whimper that threatened to escape his lips. Through the ringing in his hears, he heard Perry laughing like a bully on a playground.

The bastard was having a field day.

"Are you sure you don't want to go back to baby magic?" Perry asked.

Greg opened one eye, wincing at the lingering pain. Perry loomed over him, hands at his waist and a crooked grin on his face.

Refusing Perry's hand, Greg struggled to his feet. His head throbbed, but he managed to stand without holding on to the wall. He examined his t-shirt and ran a hand over his face, expecting to find scald marks, blisters, soot, something. But there were no traces of the blow. Moreover, the pain was quickly dissipating.

"See," Perry said, "I'm still going easy on you."

The Sorcerer looked smug. Greg's determination redoubled. The damage had felt real, even if it wasn't, and the threat of intense pain might give him the motivation he needed to learn as quickly as possible.

"Let's do it again," Greg said, reaching for the sword.

Perry shrugged as if saying have-it-your-way and took his place. Greg waited for the onslaught, but Perry just stood there, looking bored. That was until he gave a small wave and incandescent magic shot from his fingertips, surprising Greg.

Again he was too late, and Perry's power hit the sword at an angle and sliced in two like an orange, the remnants striking Greg's shoulders.

He dropped, head curling toward his bent knees. He clenched his teeth as pain seared through his every muscle. A groan past through his clenched teeth, even as he tried to hold it back.

He almost cursed Perry's mother, but he managed to control his fury. Whatever pain he felt, whatever he had to go through to learn to wield this sword was worth it. For Sam.

When the pain subsided, he jumped to his feet, sword poised and ready. "Again."

Perry rolled his eyes and released another attack.

For the next hour, the same scene played out over and over. Magic and failure. Pain and stubbornness. The right angle at which to hold the sword remained impossible to attain. Fatigue and anger deteriorated things further, making Greg fear that his fighting instincts weren't good enough.

"Why don't we take a break?" Perry said, "Let's continue when Katsu can join us again."

"I don't need a break, or Katsu," Greg said, still too stubborn to concede, in spite of his repeated failures.

"Well, I do." Perry ran a hand through his hair and headed toward the metal ladder.

"Just a few more times."

The Sorcerer ignored him and started to climb.

"Hold on." Greg reached out and grabbed his wrist.

Perry glanced at Greg's hand.

He let go and lowered his head. "Please. If not for me, for Sam."

Perry sighed and jumped off the ladder. "Fine, just a few more times. But there's no point if you're frustrated when you should be *focused*."

"I'll focus. Promise."

They began again.

Maybe if Katsu were here things would go better, but he was tired of waiting for everyone else to make Sam a priority.

Focus.

He held the sword—tip pointing to the ground—and flexed his knees. With a deep breath, he filled his lungs to the brim and put his entire attention on Perry's hands. Relaxing his shoulders, Greg tried to clear his mind of everything, including Sam. It wasn't easy, but he managed to focus on nothing else but Perry and the sword.

This time, when magic poured from the Sorcerer's fingers, Greg's vision tunneled. Unlike before, he didn't hear the hissing sound of the magic burning through the air; he only saw the bright beam slicing the space in two, promising pain as it rushed in his direction. More clearly than ever, Greg tracked its trail and velocity, seeing it almost in slow motion. With nothing else to weigh him down, no thoughts to get in the way, his nature took over, and he acted purely on instinct. Moving a fraction of an inch to the right, he repositioned the sword, hoping to create an angle that was perfectly perpendicular to Perry's magic.

He clenched his teeth, preparing himself for the pain. Instead, the glowing spell hit the sword with a pop and a sizzle, then slowly dissipated, traveling up and down the length of the blade until it shrank to a pinprick of light and disappeared with a final *zing*.

His jaw dropped open. He turned the sword this way and that, incredulously, as if he would find the magic, hidden on the other side of the blade. Greg lowered the weapon and stared at his hands in surprise.

"I did it," he murmured. A smile twitched on his lips, but he suppressed it almost immediately.

"Yes, you did," Perry said with a heavy note of relief. "Now, definitely time for a break. Stop on a high note, you know."

Greg shook his head. "No, this is nothing. It'll take more than this to stop Veridan."

"Give yourself a break, mate. You're new at this."

"You agreed to do it a few more times," Greg said.

"Bloody hell. My amulet is nearly depleted," Perry said, rolling his eyes, but immediately giving Greg what he asked for: another volley of powerful magic.

Pain started to acquire a façade: Perry's face.

But Greg learned to love it.

ℰℴ Chapter 23 ℭℛ
Greg

For the first time in a long time, a genuine smile spread across Greg's lips.

"Did you have to do that?" Perry asked, running a hand through his brown hair. "I mean, you could have been grateful for my help."

"Like you didn't enjoy hitting me who knows how many times," Greg replied.

They were walking down the hall, away from the dilapidated pool. Sweat soaked their shirts, and their feet dragged over the dusty carpet. Greg rubbed his biceps, enjoying the ache the exercise had left in them. Perry mussed his singed hair, which was considerably shorter after Greg managed to return two of his magical attacks.

"I have to admit," Perry said, "I wasn't sure this crazy scheme would work. I'd only ever seen Warriors use magical swords like that, but I guess I'd never met a Keeper."

Greg didn't correct him. He wasn't a Keeper anymore, but after the intense practice session and what he had been able to do, he'd started to feel a little like his old self.

As they passed the conference room where Mirante subjected them to her ranting monologues, a few people walked out. Greg frowned. Had they missed a meeting while they practiced? The gatherings were pretty useless, but he hated to miss any potential news.

He stopped and peered inside. Across the conference table, Ashby and Mirante talked in hushed tones, intent on each other. Greg tried to listen in, made curious by their secretive demeanor.

As if sensing him, Ashby stopped, eyes darting toward the door. Mirante followed his gaze and seemed to freeze for an instant, then turned back to Ashby.

"Please don't waste my time. I have many things to do, which you kids don't seem to understand."

She walked around the conference table and exited the room without a glance wasted on Greg or Perry.

"Had a meeting?" Greg asked, stepping into the conference room.

Ashby came around to meet them. "We did."

"What about?"

"Same old. *We are busy finalizing our plan. We need to be patient,*" he parroted in a shrill impersonation of Mirante. "Glad at least *someone* has a purpose." He looked them up and down, wrinkling his nose at their grubby appearances. He smirked as Perry fluffed his hair self-consciously.

"I take it you're getting better," Ashby observed.

"I think I am." Greg was unable to leave the satisfaction out of his voice.

"Well, I don't know about you, but I'm hungry," Perry turned and walked away. "I'm going to see what meager food I can scavenge at this hour."

Greg followed along. They'd missed lunch, a bad idea after how hard they'd worked.

They found the dining area empty—not even Finley, who seemed to spend a considerable amount of time reading at one of the tables, was there.

Like destitute children, they raided the cabinets and found bottled water, and a few bags of chips and chocolate chip cookies. Greg settled for a bag of Bugles, not because they were his favorite but because it was the largest bag. Perry chose two packets of cookies and, on second thought, a third one. He looked as if he wanted more, but after debating for a moment, he shut the cabinet door close—whether for concern over his girlish figure or the many hungry mouths that came in and out of this place, Greg didn't know.

"Not hungry?" Greg asked Ashby, noticing his empty hands as they sat at one of the tables.

Ashby shook his head. Greg almost expected him to say he couldn't stomach American junk food—he'd turned up his nose at pizza once, after all—but his mind seemed to be elsewhere.

"You alright, mate?" Perry tore open one of his cookie packets and offered one to Ashby. "Want a cookie to make it all better?"

Ashby huffed as if doubtful a cookie could make anything better, then took one anyway.

"Did Mirante chew your ass up again?" Greg asked after popping a few Bugles into his mouth.

"You know her," was Ashby's only response.

"Yeah, frustrating as hell," Greg said. "If she at least told us how long it'll take her to make a freakin' decision."

"Just being safe, *kids*," Perry said, imitating Mirante and crushing his water bottle.

"It's easy for them," Greg said in a near growl. "They're safe from Danata in their little private conferences and planning sessions." He made a fist on top of the table, barely containing the desire to smack it down. "Mirante only cares about taking back the Regency. But who gives a shit about that?"

"Sorry to disappoint you, but most of the people around here," Perry twirled a finger in the air, "do."

"Including you two, right?" Greg said.

"Apparently." Perry shrugged apologetically, his gaze darting toward Ashby.

"Having second thoughts yet?" Greg asked, sensing something was up with Ashby.

"I don't know. Maybe." Ashby sighed and shook his head. "They *are* taking too long. They should have an action plan by now. But this is getting ridiculous."

"Did Mirante say something?" Perry asked, furrowing his brow.

"Mirante never says anything, unless it's an order."

"She's just trying to keep us entertained and out of the way. Especially me." Greg pointed at his chest. "This training is great, and it's given me a way to fight, but how long will it go on?" Greg leaned forward and lowered his voice. "We have to act. You can't be okay with sitting here doing nothing while Sam *and* Jacob . . ." he trailed off, unable to say more. "Plus, the longer Mirante and Roanna wait, the longer Veridan and Danata have to prepare."

"It's only been two weeks," Perry said. "I know it seems MORF is dragging their feet, but this is not a simple matter. There's a lot at stake, more than just Sam." He looked over at

Ashby as if he were just a mouth piece, repeating what he'd been told to say.

"Right?" Perry pressed when Ashby said nothing.

Ashby rubbed his chin, narrowing his eyes at his Sorcerer.

Something was definitely up and Greg intended to find out what it was.

☙ *Chapter 24* ❧
Ashby

Ashby had no idea if Perry would agree with his plan, but there was no time for second-guessing. He'd made a decision, and he would stick with it, no matter the consequences. He was done waiting, done letting things happen to him. It was time to be the wind behind his own sails.

"Maybe I agreed with Mirante before," Ashby said cautiously, "but now I'm not so sure."

Greg's eyes opened wide, wider than Ashby had ever seen them. "Are you serious? Are you finally willing to do something?"

"Maybe," Ashby said, avoiding Greg's intense gaze, focusing on his intertwined fingers on the table and trying to sound vague. "Maybe if we can come up with a plan that makes sense . . ." He let the words hang in the air.

Practically vibrating with expectation, Greg pushed to the edge of his chair.

"We can think of something," Greg said.

"Wait, have you gone mad?" Perry asked.

Ashby shrugged. "Not mad. I'd just be going back home. That's all." He hated to keep Perry in the dark, but it would be easier this way.

"Going back home? You're mum will probably bite your head off the moment she sees you," Perry said.

"A possibility, but she might also welcome me back."

Perry burst out laughing, then stopped abruptly. "Welcome you back? Yeah, you've lost your mind. Not to be mean, but she severed your filial bond. She wants nothing to do with you."

"Perhaps."

"What are you on?" Perry asked. "I know she's always had a soft spot for you, mate, but she literally . . ." Perry made scissor motions with his fingers. "*Twice!*"

"She'll at least grant me an audience, if only to gloat. Don't you think?" Ashby asked.

"If only to bring the guillotine back into fashion, you mean."

"What exactly are you planning?" Greg narrowed his eyes at him. "You must have something in mind, other than just waltzing in and being welcomed like the prodigal son."

Ashby shook his head. "I don't know what I'm thinking. Going back and pretending I regret what happened seems like the most straightforward way. I guess I'm just thinking out loud. Besides, what else can I do? It's not like I can challenge her Warriors."

"Is there no way we can get into the castle without being detected?" Greg asked. "I don't know . . . it sounds stupid, but maybe some secret passage or someone who can help us from the inside."

"Clearly, you have seen too many movies," Perry scoffed. "Nobody would give us that kind of help. Everyone remains loyal to the Regent, if they know what's good for them."

"So no magic trick up your sleeve, oh wondrous Sorcerer?" Greg mocked.

"Shut up, Greg. You don't know what you're talking about."

"Perry," Ashby said in a sobering tone, "I would like us to think about this, to really consider every possibility. How can we get into Rothblade castle, since she won't grant me an audience?"

"This is mad." Perry shook his head. "Suicide, I say. So just leave me out of it."

"You don't have a choice," Ashby said. "You have to do what I say. You swore an oath."

Perry stood abruptly, his chair tipping over and falling to the floor.

"Does that even mean anything anymore?" Perry asked.

The words felt like daggers to Ashby's heart. Here was definite proof that he'd lost everything. Even Perry thought nothing of him now that the Regency had slipped through his fingers.

Ashby got to his feet very slowly, making sure his chair didn't tip. He did not break eye contact with Perry, but held his gaze, an implicit challenge burning in his eyes.

"So I guess I was wrong," Ashby said. "I *have* lost it all. I'm nothing now, though I suppose that doesn't bode well for you."

"That's unfair," Perry said. "You're not thinking straight. All I'm trying to do is keep you alive."

"Is that so?"

Perry licked his lips and inhaled deeply. "I'm not being disloyal. I'm your friend and, more than that, your subject. I didn't give my oath lightly. But that oath didn't mean I would let you do stupid things. And this *is* stupid. The stupidest thing you've ever come up with, actually. And there's been a number of them."

"That never stopped you," Ashby said.

"That's because you never listen."

"We can at least think about it. Can you promise to do that much? Maybe there's a way, and we just have to consider every possibility to find it."

Perry looked down at the floor, his gaze searching the carpet as if the gaudy pattern held the answer. After a long moment, he frowned and looked up.

"What is it?" Ashby asked.

Perry thrust his chin toward the large planter behind Ashby. The tip of a gym shoe was sticking out from behind one of its corners.

"Shit," Greg said under his breath, getting to his feet as if ready for a fight.

Perry walked around the planter and leaned down.

"Hey! Get your hands off me," a small voice said.

Perry lifted the eavesdropper off the floor and pushed her into the open.

Finley staggered forward, arms wind-milling to keep her balance. She looked up at them, her eyes big and round like a cat's.

"Um, I was just," she hooked a finger over her shoulder pointing toward the planter, "reading. I didn't—"

"Don't even try," Perry said. "Bugger, what are we going to do now?"

✤ Chapter 25 ✤
Greg

"Hey, it's not what you think," Greg said, taking a step in Finley's direction.

Her eyes opened wide. She retreated, holding her hands up. "Whatever. I don't care what you do." But the panicked expression on her face told Greg otherwise.

Faster than Greg had ever seen Ashby move, he grabbed Finley's arm, spun her around, and pressed a hand over her mouth, wrapping an arm around her waist to keep her secure. Frantically, he looked about the dining area.

Finley wiggled and kicked, but she was small, and no match for a full-fledged Morphid.

"We need to talk," Ashby said, lifting Finley off her feet as if she were a child. Half-carrying her, he rushed out of the room and headed in the direction of the pool.

Perry and Greg exchanged a confused glance and followed them. At the end of the hall, Ashby kicked the metal door open and released Finley with a curse. She sprang away from him and twirled to face him, a feral cat with her claws out.

Ashby shook his hand, hissing in pain. "You bit me!"

"You kidnapped me!" Finley said.

"I didn't kidnapp you. Don't be ridiculous."

Greg closed the door to the pool area, hoping no one could hear the two screaming. "Why don't we just calm down and talk this through."

"Talk what through?" Finley asked. "The fact that you are planning to betray MORF?"

"We're not betraying anyone. We were just discussing . . . possibilities," Ashby said, rubbing his bitten finger.

"Yeah, possibilities that go against my aunt's orders."

"Look," Greg said, "I didn't sign up to be anyone's soldier. I don't have to follow Mirante's orders."

"And why would you? You're just a bunch of selfish brats who only care about yourselves."

"You know nothing about me," Greg said. "This is about Sam and Jacob and no one else."

"Finley," Ashby said in a pacifying tone, "do you know what my mother is capable of?"

"Of course, I do."

"Then you can imagine the torture our friends must be going through."

"You . . . you don't know that for a fact. They might just be in a cell with boredom as their only punishment."

Ashby's face twisted in a disappointed expression. "I never thought you'd be this callous."

"I'm not callous," Finley protested, pressing a hand to her stomach as if the thought made her sick.

"Then, like us, you *wouldn't* hang the life of a loved one on a supposition. Like us, you *would* risk everything to save them."

"Not everything." Finley shook her head. "Not *everyone*." A drop of sweat slid down the side of her face. She wiped it off, panting, anger getting the best of her.

"We won't risk anyone but ourselves," Ashby said.

Finley's gaze jumped from Ashby to Perry, then to Greg. "You don't know what ripples your intervention will cause. It was your actions that put Sam in this situation in the first place. You led Veridan to her."

"Gee, thanks for reminding us," Perry put in.

"I prefer action to inaction," Greg said. "And may I also remind *you* that I am Sam's Keeper. My sole purpose is to protect her."

"A grand job you did." Her hands trembled at her side.

Greg wanted to hate this stranger for her recriminations, but he couldn't. She seemed too fragile and lost for that. Still, if she went to Mirante and told her what she'd overheard, they were screwed. The MORF commander would likely lock them up for good.

"Please, Finley," Ashby said, using a damn-good reasoning tone, "help us. We may be able to come up with a way to save our friends. I know you've never met them, but I'm sure that if you did, you would feel exactly the same way we do."

"Help you?!" she asked in a shrill, incredulous voice. She opened her mouth to say more, but she coughed instead, her small body shaking with the force of the spasms. She shook her head and, after a moment, managed to rasp, "No, I won't help you. I trust my people. They will do what is best for *everyone*."

Ashby stepped closer to Finley. "Okay, don't help us then, but don't tell anyone about what you overheard. We don't really have a plan. We were just . . . I don't know . . . hypothesizing." He forced a laugh. "What hope would we have, after all? Right, mates?"

"Yeah, right," Greg and Perry echoed.

Finley snorted. "What? Do you think I'm four or something? No, I won't tell anyone, I'll tell *everyone*, so we can all watch our backs in case you decide to stab us."

Ashby growled in frustration. "You can't do that. You'll ruin everything. You'll—"

Greg jumped forward and caught Finley right before she collapsed to the floor.

"Bloody hell!" Perry exclaimed. "What's the matter with her?"

"Man, she just got all worked up." Greg gingerly pressed a couple of fingers to her forehead. She felt really warm. He frowned. "Can we really kidnap her now? 'Cause if we don't, she'll get us in a shit-load of trouble when she wakes up."

Perry knelt next to the girl, pushed her eyelids back to look at her pupils, then took her pulse. "I don't think she'll be waking anytime soon."

Ashby and Greg exchanged panicked glances.

"No, she's not dead, you idiots," Perry said, rolling his eyes. "She's morphing."

∽ Chapter 26 ∾
Veridan

"Do we have to do this, now?" Danata asked her ridiculous secretary, Vitorio Carso Pestile.

Veridan understood her frustration, but in this, he would support Vitorio all the way. The Conscription Ball was the perfect opportunity to get all the Council members in one place. Now that he had all the energy he thought he needed.

"I know it's a stressful time," Vitorio said, nervously adjusting his tie, "but this is one of our most important traditions, integral to the Council. We cannot cancel it, my Regent."

"I'm afraid I agree with him," Veridan said in a sorrowful tone, as if it pained him to give her this advice.

Danata left her high back chair and poured herself a full glass of potion. Her hand shook as she lifted the drink to her lips. Vitorio waited, looking as if he'd rather bury his head in a sandy dune in the middle of a distant desert.

"We are at risk of losing more than our traditions," the Regent said between sips of potion. "This ball will be nothing but a distraction and a waste of time."

"We have word of at least two newly morphed council members, my Regent," Vitorio pleaded. "It is possible there are others, especially in these critical times. We would send the wrong message if we do not receive them."

"We don't have to host a ridiculous ball to receive them," Danata said. "Let them come whenever they want—for all the good they will do."

Vitorio looked appalled at the Regent's comment.

Veridan cleared his throat. "You are right, Regent. A ball is not required, but you should consider that canceling the event may send the wrong message. It might suggest that you are afraid, that MORF has managed to shake the foundation of your most dignified institution."

"Afraid?" Danata laughed and finished the last of her potion, throwing back her head.

"Rumors of your sister's return are already abound," Veridan continued. "And those who remember her weak reign need a reminder of why you are a better choice than her, no matter the circumstances of Roanna's disappearance." Veridan knew that bringing up Danata's sister was always a good way to get the Regent agitated, and he wasn't wrong.

"Fine!" she said, throwing a hand up in the air. "Have your useless ball. As usual, the High Sorcerer will be in charge of security which, given the circumstances, will need to be tighter than normal. Veridan, spare no resources, magical or otherwise. There would be no worse way to show weakness than to have something go wrong during the Conscription."

Vitorio bowed, an expression of relief on his face. "I will set the preparations in motion, my Regent." He scurried out of the room, clearly relieved of the fact that he had a party to organize rather than a party to cancel. He would have been in charge of writing and distributing the unsettling communiqué to the new council members, and if there was something Vitorio feared, it was angry, Fate-chosen leaders.

"I'm tired of all these stupid traditions. Remind me to slowly dismantle them." Danata sat back down, looking truly exhausted. "I have real problems to deal with. This is ridiculous."

Veridan twiddled his thumbs behind his back, thinking about Danata's order for redoubled security.

The Regent exhaled in a clear effort to let her frustrations over the ball dissipate. "Any luck making contact with my sister?"

"Not yet, but I wouldn't worry. The message will get to her."

"I suppose." She shook her head, rolling her eyes toward the ceiling. "I can't wait to sweep this matter under the rug."

Veridan often wondered if that was true, if Danata and her volatile personality didn't thrive under these chaotic circumstances. Or maybe it was his own tainted perspective that made it seem this way since, for him, there was no better Danata than a highly eruptive one.

౸ Chapter 27 ಌ
Sam

"C'mon, c'mon."

Sam squeezed her fists together, trying to focus. She was in her cell, kneeling in front of the cot, attempting to control her tattered vinculums. Her Weaver instincts were afire, urging her to try again. She knew better than to ignore them.

She'd been at it for the last hour with no result, but she wasn't about to give up.

Lowering her head between her manacled hands, she tried to recall the feelings that had driven her to despair. Sam let her mind wander.

As hard as it was, she thought of what she'd done to Anima— as if the Seer's suffering under Danata's cruel reign hadn't been enough.

And what about all the homeless Morphids in New York? What if Sam never got a chance to restore what they'd lost? What if she died in this place and her last deed was helping Danata kill an innocent woman whose only sin was guarding knowledge of the future from the one person who needed it the least?

At least Anima had fought, in her own way. And what had Sam done? Nothing. Just waited to be rescued, except no one had come.

Tears broke free in spite of her effort to keep them back. Mad at herself, she pulled away from the cot, swatting at her face. Hating her weakness, she jumped to her feet. Another tear tickled her cheek and she slapped it away.

But it wasn't a tear.

Sam froze, staring at the luminous threads of lights that floated before her.

A cold shiver walked up her spine. Her vinculums seemed to have a mind of their own, hovering above her and offering comfort with their easy undulating movements.

Trembling and afraid of breaking the spell, Sam gently raised a hand to one of the strands. When her fingers were but a fraction of an inch away, she stopped as if she were about to pet a skittish cat.

After a breathless moment, she realized she should have control over them. They were part of her, too.

Maybe it wasn't a strictly physical connection of nerves, synapses, and sinew, but it was just as real. She could feel it, the same way she felt air filling her lungs. The way she felt pain when she recalled Ashby's black eyes filling with disappointment the day she crushed his heart. The way sorrow expanded inside her chest every time she thought of Greg. The way anger seized her when she imagined Jacob huddled in a corner, crying and trembling in fear.

Come.

The broken strand came to her, the skittish cat giving her a chance. It slowly wrapped around her finger like a vine finally surrounding a waiting trellis.

Sam gasped at the cool, soothing touch.

Don't be angry, it seemed to say. Jacob is all right. Nothing will happen to him.

And you know that how? Sam asked, anger flaring once more at the thought.

More broken strands came to soothe her. She imagined Greg—and maybe even Ashby—offering comfort. After all, these were the bonds she'd shared with them.

Slowly, tendrils of light travel up her arms until they were caressing her face. It should have been strange, creepy even, but it just . . . made sense.

She enjoyed the comfort for a long moment, then pulled away. As if obeying some silent command from within, the tendrils retreated.

"What now?" she asked out loud.

The vinculums weaved themselves back together into two thick ribbons and bobbed at eye level as if waiting for instructions.

Sam frowned. There was no one else to soothe. She had cried enough and somewhere along the way she'd regained the strength she'd lost while Greg had been there to protect her.

"So what good are you now?"

The vinculums dipped down as if they were lowering their heads in embarrassment. But that was ridiculous. An idea occurred to her. Sam's eyes shifted to the door. The vinculums twisted as if following her gaze. She took a big breath and held it, imaging crazy possibilities.

Hesitantly, she approached the door and stared at the smooth, metal surface. There was no handle, no keyhole, nothing to give anyone purchase. But maybe that didn't matter—not to thin strands of light, anyway.

She put her hunch to the test.

ℰ Chapter 28 ℃
Veridan

The nebula whirled around Veridan. He was inside the inky ocean of despairing souls. Walking with steady steps, he ignored the sniveling souls crying in a dark corner or wailing like banshees, trying to be heard outside of their prison.

He dismissed the paths he'd explored before, and walked down a tarry slope, his shoes making sucking sounds. Shadows loomed all around him, bringing to mind the hundreds of Morphids he'd delivered to Danata for her ripping pleasure.

Maybe they suffered in some ethereal way that could hardly be compared to physical pain, but that suffering didn't matter—not when their sacrifice would mean the redemption and rejuvenation of Morphidkind, a superior race that never should have to take a bow to the likes of humans.

A crumbling ruin lay at the bottom of the slope. This was his fourth time in as many days searching the nebula, and he hadn't come this way yet. Massive gray rocks littered the tarry ground—the fallen pieces of what in one of these souls' memories must have been a grandiose structure.

The things the minds in here conjured were at times bizarre and illogical, but Veridan had stopped wondering what they all meant, and decided his surrounding were nothing more than the broken dreams of broken people, creatures who were too weak and irrelevant to amount to more than this.

He stopped and surveyed the area. It was as good a place as any to try to open a passage. He'd failed to do it several times before, but he told himself it was because he hadn't found the right place, and not because the nebula didn't have enough energy yet. Ashby's filial bond had to be enough.

Lifting his amulet—which he'd been holding tightly in his fist, the chain wrapped around his wrist—he let the practiced incantation flow from his lips.

He was almost done with the spell when a dark shadow rose from behind a fallen pillar. The figure rippled like liquid obsidian and lurched in his direction.

Alerted by his sharp senses, Veridan jumped back. He held out the amulet and, on instinct, called on a bright ball of flames to surround his hand like a torch.

"Keep back," Veridan ordered.

The advancing figure came to an abrupt halt, hands held out like claws.

"You . . ." the figure groaned in a deep voice.

Veridan took another step back, glancing over his shoulder, imagining more tortured figures ready to receive him into a smothering embrace. No one was behind him, however, and his eyes quickly snapped back to his unexpected attacker.

The *thing* before him held as few Morphid features as a mannequin. It was nothing but bare extremities and a round, featureless head, as if the memory of what it had once been was incomplete. Only the newest or strongest victims seemed to retain this shape, stubbornly holding on to the past. But this—the bold acknowledgment of Veridan's presence, the single word that seemed to imply recognition—this was new.

Maybe his recent, repeated trips into their gloom were to blame for it. He hadn't given the specters long enough to forget him.

Either way, it didn't matter. He had no time for their sudden jolts of remembered humanity. They were a means to an end, and he would not allow them to become obstacles.

Back in control of himself, Veridan stepped forward, firmly holding the red flame before him. The dark shape cowered, pressing an arm to its eyeless face.

"Go!" Veridan commanded, his voice deep and charged with authority.

The shape cowered further, slowly getting smaller until it dissolved into the ground, melting into viscous tar with an echoing cry.

Veridan held the fire in his hand for several minutes, shining its warm light behind every fallen stone. The nebula had gone completely quiet. The underlying whimpering and sniveling he'd grown used to was gone, as if everyone was intent on escaping his notice.

The absolute adherence to his command should have pleased him. Instead, it unnerved him.

Hanging the amulet about his neck, he rested both hands on it and decided that, for the moment, he would relinquish this task.

Best not to press his luck.

So, with a nod, he issued the spell that transferred him back to his alcove. Once in his room, he assured himself that he still had time—even if he didn't have patience.

❧ Chapter 29 ☙
Perry

"Well, that was some timely metamorphosis," Perry said, throwing his head back against the wall. He was sitting on Greg's mattress which rested on the floor. He kicked off his shoes and felt very much like taking a nap.

After Finley passed out by the pool, Ashby had carried her to the conference room while Perry tried to find Mirante. Since the MORF commander or anyone of import had been unavailable, they'd left her with Mateo, who didn't ask any questions and told Ashby not to worry because he knew exactly what needed to be done. If Perry had read things right, the secret was out of the bag, and Ashby knew Mateo was his father, which was a good thing.

Perry had been more than glad to wash his hands of Finley, but Ashby had looked oddly concerned and he still did.

"I suppose it was timely," Ashby said. He sat on the floor next to the hazy window, claiming he needed sunlight. Now, his blond hair glowed with the rays that seeped between the dusty curtains.

"This means we have two weeks before she can tell anyone what she overheard," Greg said as he popped the tab off an infernal drink called root beer. He was also sitting on the floor, near the foot of the mattress and directly across from Perry.

"There abouts," Perry agreed.

"Should be plenty of time for us to do something." Greg took a swig of his fizzy drink. "Any ideas yet?"

It hadn't been an hour since they'd talked, but Perry had already thought of something. It was so obvious he was surprised it hadn't occurred to Ashby first.

"As a matter of fact," he said, "I *do* have an idea."

Both Ashby and Greg sat straighter.

"Ah, what would you two do without me?" Perry gave them a lopsided smile.

"Well, don't just sit there looking like you swallowed a peacock. Spit it out!" Greg placed the drink down on the floor and gave him his full attention.

"The Conscription Ball," he said triumphantly.

"The what?" Greg frowned.

"Conscription Ball," Ashby repeated in a near whisper. "It's coming up." He checked the date on his wristwatch. "I should have thought of that."

"What the hell is a *Conscription Ball*?" Greg asked. "It doesn't sound fun."

"That's what I've always said!" Perry exclaimed. "But no one ever listens to me." He gave Ashby a meaningful look.

Ashby glowered at him, then turned to Greg to explain.

"It's a old name. It probably should be changed, but it's a tradition, and we try to leave those alone."

"Sure, mate," Perry put in. They'd had this argument more times than he cared to remember, and he wasn't about to have it again.

"Every year," Ashby continued, "The Council and the Regency host a ball at Rothblade Castle. Anyone who has morphed into a council member since the last ball is invited to attend and is welcomed into the ruling Morphid circle."

"Sounds boring," Greg said.

"You have no idea,," Perry said, remembering the times he'd had to stand by Portos, acting the part and *behaving like a proper retinue member to the future Regent* . . . blah, blah, blah.

Greg stood and began pacing at the foot of the mattress. "So you think we might be able to get into the castle during the ball? And will they still have it under the circumstances?"

"My mother is no fan. She might try to cancel it." Ashby said, frowning.

"The Council won't let her." Perry had already considered the possibility, and he'd concluded that no one in the Council would allow its cancellation. "They're sticklers for tradition, and I'm sure they'll consider the current *circumstances* too critical to snub new council members. They'll probably be wondering if those newly morphed individuals have any answers *handed down by Fate*." He added the last part with a subtle dose of mockery.

"And so they might," Ashby said. "Sorcerers don't understand *calls*." He told Greg. "They don't experience them, therefore they assume they are lies."

"Are you serious? You shoot . . . stuff from your hands and pack amulets with magic, and you don't believe in the pull and push of Morphid instincts?"

Perry shrugged. He had no interest in compulsory calls of the sort, though a call from Brooke and her tight, hot body had more power over him than he liked to admit.

"You might be right. The Council might deem the ball indispensable," Ashby said after some thought.

"How can we be sure?" Greg asked.

Ashby thought for a moment, tapping his temple as he sometimes did.

"Do you think Mateo might be able to find out?" Perry asked. "His family still has connections with the Regency and the Council."

"He might." Ashby nodded. "I will ask him?"

Perry exchanged a knowing glance with Greg. It seemed that Ashby was starting to trust his not-so-secret father. Good.

"What about getting past the guards *and* Veridan's security?" Ashby said, turning to Perry for ideas.

"Doesn't sound easy. They'd be on the lookout for us," Greg said.

"Wise observation, genius," Perry said. "That's the part we need to brainstorm. But the gates will be open to let the guests in, and that's one less obstacle to overcome."

Greg leaned down and picked up his soda can. "How do you get through? Is there an invitation?"

Ashby nodded. "Yes, unless you're a new council member in which case a staff on your mark is your invitation."

"Awesome," Greg said sarcastically. "Seems like all we need is a new caste. Oh, and a new face. Should be easy."

Perry sighed. "Where is Hermione when you need her? Could use one of those transfiguration potions."

Neither Greg nor Ashby appreciated his joke. Brooke would have. She loved teasing him with such references.

Maybe he would talk these blokes into visiting her. Fresh air might help them brainstorm.

❧ *Chapter 30* ❧
Sam

Sam became pure instinct, her body pulsating with an otherworldly sensation she'd never experienced before. She'd pressed her forehead to the door, eyes closed.

Concentrating, she pictured the hall outside and imagined herself there. In response, her manacles came loose and fell to her feet. She stared in surprise, then watched the vinculums slip under the door after undoing her bonds.

In her mind, the image of the hall morphed into a clear picture of perfect dimensions and detail. She saw the cracks in the walls, the scuff marks on the floor, the red LED light shining on the security device next to her door.

She was *seeing*. Truly.

Like a bug with antennae, she had feelers.

Was it a dream? The lack of guards outside made her wonder. Wouldn't they leave someone there to watch her?

She felt a nudge from her instincts. Sam obeyed, taking a deep breath and relaxing. Her view of the hall changed as her vinculums shifted. The security device on the wall came into focus.

Without hesitation, the frayed strands of her links went behind the edges of the small black box and, like live wires, played over the microchips and tiny electrical inputs. A tingle went over her body as she tampered with the device. Her teeth went on edge, and she was about to pull away when there was a buzz and the door opened with a click.

Sam held her breath, afraid that someone—a guard beyond the confines of the hall—had heard. After a moment, she pulled the door open and stuck her head out, her vinculums eagerly floating above her.

Heart drumming, she stepped outside of her cell. Her sneakers scrapped the stone floor, making a sound. She cringed and watched the end of the hall with unblinking eyes. Nothing.

After kicking off her shoes into the cell, Sam tiptoed to Jacob's cell and pressed an ear to the door.

Silence.

She resisted the urge to call out for him. It wouldn't do to get him agitated, especially when she had no clue of what to do next. With a small prayer for the boy, Sam pressed her hand to the door.

You'll be alright, she reassured herself.

Pushing away, Sam moved along, her socked feet growing cold against the floor. As she reached the staircase, she rested her back against the wall and took a shuddering breath. Her first thought was to peek into the stairwell, then she realized she didn't have to.

Her vinculums could be her eyes, and no one other than Danata would be able to spot them. Moreover, the Regent would have to be looking for them to realize they were even there.

Fast and confident, her vinculums turned the corner and gave her a clear view of the stairs. No one.

She climbed the winding steps, silent as a mouse, an ear cocked for the sound of approaching footsteps. But the place sounded dead. Was it nighttime?

The heavy wooden door at the top of the stairs was shut. She sat on the last step, closed her eyes, and waited for her heart to settle down.

"Go on," she mouthed once her breathing steadied.

Like obedient soldiers, her vinculums slipped under the door and gave her a clear picture of what laid outside.

A man was keeping guard—if what he was doing could be called that. He sat slumped on a chair, his head thrown back as he snored. He wore a crumpled white shirt and his dress jacket was draped over the back of the chair. His wristwatch read 1:17 A.M. A gun was strapped to his torso, secure inside a leather holster.

Great!

Sam examined the door after assessing the guard. There was no security device, only a heavy latch that was probably a couple of centuries old.

As quietly as she'd made it up the steps, Sam headed back down and, this time, didn't hesitate to call for Jacob. At first, there was no answer, but after a moment, the boy's sweet voice whispered back.

"Sam, is that you?"

"Yes, I'm coming in."

Sam's vinculums made quick work of the security box, then she pushed the door open. Jacob stood against the back wall, looking terrified, as if he was expecting someone other than Sam to walk in.

Slowly, the boy's panicked expression crumbled into a grimace that was a combination of relief and anguish. He pushed away from the wall and met Sam in the middle of the cell where they clutched each other and sobbed without tears, because they'd all been spent.

"How did you get out?" Jacob asked when he seemed able to form words.

"I can do *things*. But it doesn't matter, right now. Look, I don't know if we can escape—there's a guard at the top of the stairs—but I'll try to come up with a plan. Okay?"

Jacob nodded, looking uncertain.

She pulled him into an embrace, once more. "I just wanted to let you know it will be okay. You're not alone."

"I know," Jacob said, and those two words gave Sam more comfort than anything else he could have said.

"I love you, Jacob." She didn't know what made her say that, but it felt right to do so.

"I love you, too."

Sam pulled away, fumbling for ideas of what to do next.

"Don't go yet!" He held her tight.

"I'm not." She squeezed him reassuringly and pulled him toward the cot. They sat, Sam's back pressed to the wall, Jacob's head on her lap. She caressed his hair, mind turning.

Before long, Jacob fell asleep. Sam's heart seemed to exhale, as if all along it had been holding its breath, waiting for something terrible to happen. Her shoulders slumped. Her eyelids drooped. Here, sharing Jacob's warmth, was the safest she'd felt in a while.

I'll make it up to you, Jacob, she thought as she drifted to sleep.

♔ Chapter 31 ♕
Ashby

The afternoon sun was bright, but several degrees cooler than it had been in Georgia, inside their derelict hotel. Ashby welcomed the breeze that blew on him, pushing his hair back and cooling his warm forehead.

They were in West Lafayette, Indiana, Sam's hometown.

Perry had transferred them there, and now they stood under a tree in front of West Lafayette High School, waiting for classes to let out. Perry was eager to see Brooke and wanted to surprise her, while Ashby had just wanted to get out of that depressing hotel.

"So did Mateo say the Conscription Ball is on?" Perry asked.

Ashby nodded. "He made a couple of phone calls for me, got two affirmatives."

"Well, changing someone's face is not that hard . . . if one knows the correct spell," Perry said, continuing the conversation.

"And do you . . . . know the spell?" Greg asked.

Perry shrugged. "I read it once, but I don't remember it. If I could get my hands on that book again, my idea would work. I could change Ashby's face and his mark . . . remove the Regent part, you know. They would have to let him in."

"Could we make that permanent?" Ashby asked with a drop of sarcasm, fully aware that truly changing one's caste was impossible. Many throughout history had tried. And failed.

Perry rolled his eyes. "It doesn't have to be permanent, and I do know a spell that can alter a mark for a few hours, which is more than we would need."

"Too bad it won't really help since you can't get rid of his ugly mug," Greg said with a grin.

Ashby smirked, something he would have been unable to do just a few weeks ago. Greg had started as a rival, but their relationship was changing.

"I assumed the book you're referring to is in Rothblade Castle?" Greg asked.

Perry nodded. "The High Sorcerer's library."

A deep crease parted Greg's forehead as he seemed to ponder something.

"What?" Ashby asked.

"My parents know a couple of Sorcerers. I wonder if they could help."

Both Perry and Ashby perked up.

"My dad mentioned them a few times when I was little."

"Who are they? What are their names?" Perry asked.

"I don't know. They're very secretive. Like my parents."

"Hmm." Ashby exchanged a looked with Perry. "Dissidents?"

"Probably," Perry said. "A handful of Sorcerers did make themselves scarce after your mum became Regent." He scratched his head, cocking it to one side.

"Let me find out." Greg stepped away to one side, pulling out his cell phone, and dialed. "Hi, Mom." He moved away from the tree and lowered his voice.

Perry turned toward the school. "Could be promising."

A bell sounded in the distance, but Ashby barely noticed it. He was lost in thought, his decision and the possible consequences weighing heavily on his mind.

A sharp squeal pulled him back into the moment.

"Perry!" Brooke was jogging across the parking lot, her brown hair swinging from side to side.

To Ashby's surprise, Perry rushed to meet her, lifting her off the ground and twirling her around with uncharacteristic excitement. Ashby frowned, watching them hug and kiss as they went about in circles.

"Stare much?" Greg stepped up next to him, pocketing his cell.

Ashby turned away, blinking. "Guess I do. Perry just acts strangely around Brooke. That's all."

"And by *strangely* you mean *in love*?"

"Perry? In love?" Ashby paused and looked back at the Sorcerer. "Nah, it can't be? Can it?"

"That's what it looks like to me."

"But . . . Singulars don't fall in love."

"Keepers are Singulars," Greg murmured.

"But Brooke's human." It was impossible, unheard of.

"We're not that different."

Ashby felt strange inside, as if someone had pulled the rug from under him to reveal a hole into an unknown void.

"Perhaps things are changing," he said, something he would have never admitted before. "I used to believe Fate was immutable, but maybe it just takes time. Like tectonic plates or evolution."

Greg nodded. "It rings of truth."

They were lost in thought when Perry and Brooke walked up hand in hand, smiling like a couple of idiots.

"Thanks for not being a jackass and letting him come!" Brooke smacked a kiss on Ashby's cheek.

"Wait? Weren't you supposed to," Ashby placed the tip of one finger to his temple, "erase her memories?"

"Ooops!" Brooke pressed a hand across her mouth, her eyes moving from side to side.

"I wasn't going to risk erasing *me*," Perry said. "I altered her memories substantially during Sam's metamorphosis. There's only so much you can get away with before causing damage."

Ashby put his hands up. "Fine by me. It wasn't *my* order."

"Hey, Brooke." Greg leaned forward and gave her a hug.

"Greg!" Brooke returned the hug. "How are you holding up?"

"Better."

"Oh?"

"Let's get out of here, Perry," Greg said, looking around the parking lot at all the homebound students, "see if that plan of yours will work."

"Where to?" Perry asked.

"New Orleans."

◦ Chapter 32 ◦
Greg

It felt odd standing in front of his old house, the small two-bedroom colonial with its red door and modest front yard. Greg remembered almost collapsing on the lawn the day he morphed, and Mom finding him in the foyer halfway turned into goo. It seemed like forever ago since he argued with her over the benefits of being a Singular and having no Integral. She'd worried he would never find love. How wrong they'd both been.

"Well?" Perry asked.

Greg shook himself. "Sorry." He crossed the walkway and mounted the stairs to the front porch. "Mom said she would leave work and be home early," he added, wondering whether to knock or not.

The door sprang open, freeing him of his indecision.

"Greg!"

Mom pulled him into a hug before he had a chance to say anything. At first, his arms hung limp at his sides, but as the surprise passed, he embraced her, letting her warmth comfort him. Her blond hair smelled like home.

She pulled away and drank him in, a satisfied smile on her beautiful face. "So handsome!" she said, pressing a hand to his cheek as if he were a little boy.

"Mom, these are Perry, Brooke and Ashby." He moved aside to introduce them.

"Call me Erica," she said, shaking their hands.

After greeting each other, they went in and followed Greg's Mom into the kitchen. A large pot was on the stove, and the table was set for seven people, one extra chair squeezed in one corner.

Greg gave his mother a questioning look.

"We have to wait for your father and Jules. I imagine you'll all be hungry by then."

"That's great, Erica. Thank you," Brooke said approvingly. "Lunch at school was terrible today."

Ashby stepped forward. "Mrs. Papilio, what can you tell us about Jules? Do you think he can help us?"

"She," Mom corrected. "Jules is a Sorceress."

"My apologies." Ashby inclined his head.

She waved a hand to indicate the formality wasn't necessary, then walked to the stove. "I don't know exactly what you need—Greg didn't say—but she knows a lot, was apprentice to someone important, though I don't know who." She uncovered the pot, stuck a spoon in, then took a taste. She nodded approvingly.

Greg caught the scent of something familiar. "Is that étouffée?"

"Yes, honey. Your favorite." She turned, spoon in hand, and beamed at Greg. He gave her a huge smile, touched by her relentless cheeriness.

While they waited at the kitchen table, she kept them entertained with talk about the neighbors, her job, and endless offers of iced tea. Greg didn't miss the fact that she didn't ask any questions about Sam or why they'd come, which he appreciated.

"Greg, your mom is adorable," Brooke said, "and so pretty!"

"Thank you, honey. You're pretty, too."

Greg glanced at his watch. They'd been waiting an hour already.

"Um, maybe we should eat." Mom didn't wait for them to agree and laid out dinner on the kitchen island.

Following Greg's example, they all spooned a layer of white rice into the bottom of their bowls, and topped it with a generous serving of crawfish étouffée. They gave him a sideways glance when Greg dusted filé over his stew. Only Perry did the same, curious about the thickening agent.

Sighs of pleasure and surprise went around the table as they ate.

"This is good!" Brooke mumbled after stuffing a spoonful into her mouth. "What do you call it again?"

They were almost done with their dinner when the front door opened. Greg jumped to his feet and rushed out of the kitchen. Dad was in the foyer, setting down his briefcase. He straightened and turned. Their eyes locked. A smile spread across Greg's face. He walked to his father and stopped a couple of paces away.

"It's good to see you," Dad said, extending a hand.

They shook hands, squeezing hard and lingering. Greg fought the impulse to hug him. He wasn't a little kid anymore, but he hadn't seen him in a while. The awkward moment stretched until Greg's mother skirted around them.

"Where is Jules?" she asked, peeking into the living room. After a short perusal, she turned around, frowning.

"She didn't want to come," Dad said.

"What? Why not?" Ashby stepped into the hall, too. The space was starting to feel quite cramped.

"These are Greg's friends," Mom said. "Ashby, Perry, and Brooke."

"Ashby *Rothblade*?" Dad asked as they shook hands.

Was his father star-struck by the Regent's son? No. There was something else in his eyes. Distrust?

"At your service," Ashby replied.

Dad's eyes lingered on Ashby's face before moving to Perry and Brooke.

Greg hardly let them greet each other. "Will your friend not help us?"

"Let's go in the living room, and I'll explain," Dad said.

Greg exchanged a cautious glance with his mother. She shrugged and shook her head.

All four sat at the edge of the large sofa, Greg's parents across the glass coffee table.

"Are you the Sorcerer?" Dad asked, singling Perry out.

"That's me," Perry said.

"And you need this spell to help Sam?"

"Yes." Perry eyes danced between Greg and Ashby. "Greg explained, didn't he?"

"Yes, he told me over the phone, but I want to hear it from you."

"Um, okay." Perry scratched his head.

"Why the interrogation?" Greg interrupted. "I already explained—"

Dad held up a hand, never breaking eye contact with Perry.

"Well," Perry continued, "we have a plan to rescue Sam. It involves getting into the heavily guarded and magically protected Rothblade Castle. Our plan is to change our faces and marks to gain passage into the Conscription Ball. The castle is too heavily fortified to enter otherwise."

"Who are your parents?" Greg's father asked.

"What does that have to do with anything?" Greg demanded. "This is ridiculous."

"It's okay, Greg," Perry said, sounding magnanimous, an odd tone for him. "His friend probably put him up to it, am I right?"

Dad nodded.

Perry smiled. "She must not part easily with spells. Some Sorcerers hoard them like gold."

"Hoard them?" Dad said. "Don't you mean protect them?"

"Nick, what is the matter?" Greg's mom asked. "If Jules isn't willing to help just tell us."

Dad jumped to his feet, nearly crashing with the coffee table. "The Regent, her family, and her Sorcerers are hardly the kind of people who need help."

"Nick!" Mom's face turned red. "It is our son who needs help."

Dad stared at the floor for a moment, his jaw muscles jumping. He slipped a hand into his pants pocket and fingered something inside.

"Sir," Ashby said, "I would not be surprised if past grievances exist between Jules and my mother, but I assure you, Perry and I are no longer associated with Danata Rothblade."

"Is that right?" He asked, sounding dubious.

"It *is* so. She finds my betrayal so abominable that she made sure to severe *all* our ties, and I honestly couldn't care less."

"*All* ties?" Dad asked as if he understood exactly what Ashby meant. But since when did he know about filial bonds and vinculums? It's not like it was common knowledge. What the hell was going on?

Dad was silent for a moment, his eyes dancing from side to side, as if weighing the situation. The humming of the AC seemed to grow louder as they waited.

"Sheesh, I couldn't cut the tension with a chainsaw," Brooke whispered.

"Veridan severed it?" Dad asked.

Huh? Greg had never mentioned Veridan to his father. Something wasn't right.

In his pocket, Dad's hand moved again.

Everyone tensed. Perry's hand jumped to his amulet. Greg pushed closer to the edge of the sofa.

Dad held Perry's gaze with an expression that seemed to say *"don't do anything stupid."*

Slowly, he pulled out a stone, set it on the coffee table, and said, "If you're worth your *stones* as a Sorcerer, you will know what to do with this."

And before anyone had a chance to say or do anything, Greg's father disappeared into thin air.

ಏ Chapter 33 ಞ
Veridan

Veridan tossed on his bed, unable to sleep. He knew he needed to wait, needed to give the nebula's inhabitants time to forget he'd been there, lest they tried to attack him again—except an eerie feeling told him there wasn't much time left to act.

With a groan of frustration, he got out of bed and dressed. After securely tying his polished shoes, he checked his amulet to ensure it held enough energy. Inside the nebula, its vast energy was all he needed to power his spells, but if he succeeded in his plan, he'd be on his own.

Satisfied, he rushed into his alcove. The nebula waited, floating and throbbing as it always did.

Wasting no time, he issued the spell and plunged into its darkness.

Walking firmly and keeping his eyes wide open, he made his way back to the dilapidated structure where he'd encountered the obsidian figure. He inspected the area, checking behind every massive stone, making sure none of the *ripped* souls lay in wait.

Once sure he was alone, Veridan issued the second spell, intoning each word with care. When he finished, there was no sign of a portal anywhere, but he'd learned too many spells in his lifetime to be discouraged by this.

He repeated the incantation again.

And again.

And again.

Something sparkled against the tarry backdrop of the nebula. His heart picked up its pace as what looked like tiny stars hovered in mid-air, going out then bursting back to life. It was nothing like a portal, just a scattering of light, but that was all the proof he needed. His grandfather's books had been right—with enough energy it was possible to go back.

Veridan redoubled his efforts. More careful with the incantation, he enunciated every word with the same cadence and emphasis every time. The shimmering lights grew brighter and more numerous with every new iteration of the spell.

Sweat trickled down his forehead, and he was glad the nebula allowed him limitless power.

Veridan's focus didn't waver and soon the sparkling lights started to expand, moving away from each other and forming a wide circle. The shape hung at ground level, like a circus master's ring of fire, waiting for a giant lion to leap through it.

I will be that lion, Veridan thought, giving himself in to the incantation.

His words rose, a growing crescendo in which he poured all his dreams, hopes and desires. This was what he'd worked for all these years, and nothing could stop him now.

Nothing.

A pinprick of light appeared in the middle of the circle. It came into life like a firefly, intermittent and tenuous. But without warning, it burst like a supernova that expanded until it reached the outer ring, sizzling on contact and releasing blinding light that nearly dropped him to his knees.

He covered his face with a forearm, tears spilling down from a combination of joy and the piercing light. Blinking, he stared at the ground from under his arm. For a moment, he feared he would have to enter the portal blindly, but gradually the brightness diminished until he was able to look into it.

Cautiously, he approached the portal, a hand over his brow. Within the circle, something like a veil of silk rippled and shimmered in subtle rainbow colors.

Heart hammering with expectation, he extended a hand to the gossamer surface until his fingertips made contact. The light undulated at his touch, sending a cold shock up his arm that was almost pleasant.

He smiled, feeling the way a proud parent might feel at the first touch from his child.

"At last," he whispered.

Veridan was so enthralled by the magnitude of his creation— the nebula, the portal—that he barely noticed when a shadow peeled away from the dark surface of one of the rocks, and launched at him.

He had a split second to understand the threat and decide on his only course of action. There was only one choice, a path he was bound to take regardless of the danger.

Embracing his self-made destiny, Veridan stepped into the portal and was quickly swallowed by the cold light and the unknown world he'd sought for a lifetime.

ℰ Chapter 34 ℂ
Sam

Sam's dreams weaved with reality to form a vivid nightmare.

Greg was hurt, covered in blood and on his knees. She tried to reach him, but her legs were heavy, filled with lead. After an eternity, she got close, very close, but not enough to touch him.

She stretched her arms out. He did the same. Mere inches separated their fingertips.

"Greg!" she called out desperately.

Then his eyes rolled into the back of his head, and he *thudded* to the ground.

Sam woke up with a start, heart in her throat, a scream at the edge of her lips, the *thud* of Greg's body ringing in her ears.

A warning flared in her mind, telling her the sound wasn't part of the dream.

"Jacob! Jacob! Wake up!" she hissed.

The boy was still asleep on her lap. He sprang up, wide-eyed.

"We fell asleep. Someone's coming." She got to her feet and whispered over her shoulder. "Close the door behind me as gently as you can."

Sam rushed out without a backward glance, trusting Jacob to do as she'd instructed.

She slid into her cell on socked feet and scrambled for the door. She resisted the urge to slam it closed, and instead, eased it until the electronic lock engaged with a click. Next, she dropped to her knees by her discarded manacles, and got them on even as her hands trembled and the bar between the cuffs took great effort to engage.

Just as the door beeped, she slipped into her cot, facing the wall, and pretended to be asleep. At the familiar sound of someone sliding a metal food tray into the cell, she rolled over, blinking blearily at the guard. He glowered at her, then looked around the cell as if expecting to find something suspicious. After a quick inspection, he left, satisfied that everything was in order.

Sam sat up and buried her face into sweaty hands.

"Stupid stupid stupid," she mumbled. If they had caught her, the small advantage she'd gained would have been taken away.

After her heartbeat returned to normal and her limbs stopped buzzing with adrenaline, she ate her breakfast, quickly stuffing a dry piece of toast into her mouth and washing it down with water. Danata hadn't been lying when she said she would enjoy her hospitality, though she forgot to add the word "meager" in front of it.

When she was done, Sam decided it was time to test the limits of what her vinculums could do.

"Okay," she said, placing the disposable water cup at the edge of the cot. She sat crosslegged in front of it and directed her links to knock it down.

One of the tendrils approached tentatively and tapped the cup. It wobbled a little or so she thought.

She rolled her shoulders which were stiff from sleeping propped up against the wall and focused, trusting the instinct that told her she could do more than weakly tap the cup. She had tampered with the electricity in the lock, after all. The cup was more substantial, sure, but it had to be possible.

At the thought, energy hummed through her.

Sam blinked in surprise and squirmed on the spot as a chill when up her spine. She commanded her vinculums to wait even as they lashed in front of her eyes, electrified. Something was building within her, and she had a feeling patience would pay off.

When her entire body felt ablaze with harnessed power, Sam let go. Her vinculums pulled back, and for a moment, she thought her instincts had led her astray, but they hadn't.

Tendrils of light lashed out like whips, crackling and spitting sparks. They struck the cup, sent it flying against the wall, then lashed at it again and again, keeping it from falling as she ripped it to shreds.

Torn to small ribbons of plastic that attached to the base, the cup fell back on the cot, barely recognizable.

Sam found that she was on her feet, her body stiff and shaking from tension. Her chest pumped in and out, feeling strangely empty after releasing the power that had pulsed within her.

Hands trembling, she picked up the battered cup and examined it. Each shred was long and thin, the edges straight and smooth as if a pair of scissors had cut them.

She placed the waste on the tray and sat on the cot, considering this new power. Last night, it had seemed to have no possibilities, but now . . .

This could change everything.

Sam let her imagination fly.

෨ *Chapter 35* ෬
Perry

Perry's brain fought to understand what had happened. Greg's father had disappeared mid-blink. But how? The man was a plain Companion, nothing else.

Greg's mum was standing where her husband had been just a second ago, looking struck.

"Nick?!" She spun in a circle, as if she expected him to reappear in the same abrupt fashion.

"What the hell?!" Brooke exclaimed. "What just happened?"

"Where is he, Greg?!" his mum asked, her cerulean eyes turning to Perry accusingly. He shook his head and put his hands up.

Greg frowned and opened his mouth to say something, but closed it again. His gaze fell on the rock on the table, then went to Perry.

"That . . . that wasn't Dad," he said, almost like a soft question.

"What do you mean?" his mum asked, a silver line of tears pooling in her eyes.

"That was Jules." Greg's voice sounded more certain this time. "That was the Sorceress. It had to be. She must have been using the spell we want to make herself look like Dad."

"Where is Nick then?" Greg's mum demanded, oblivious to everything else.

Greg didn't answer. Instead, he picked up the rock and thrust it into Perry's hands. "What is it?"

"But Nick," Greg's mum seized her son's arm and pulled him. "Where is he?!"

"Mom, I'm sure he's fine. This Jules person is a friend, right? Just calm down and we'll figure this out." Greg turned back to Perry. "So?"

Perry examined the stone, turning it around. The thing would have been as plain as any rock found by the side of the road, if not for its shape.

"It's an orthotope," Perry said.

"A what?" Brooke asked.

"This is not the time to play smart, Perry," Ashby said.

"What's an ortho . . . whatever?" Greg asked.

"It's a rectangular cuboid," Ashby said. "A 3D rectangle, in other words," he explained further when met with frowns.

"I can see that much," Greg said, narrowing his eyes at Perry.

"I'm not playing smart," Perry said. "It's just what we call it. Though I didn't know that's what orthotope meant." He scratched his head.

"Please explain. This is all Chinese to me," Greg said.

"I think it would be easier if I show you." He put his hand out, the way he always did when they were transferring somewhere.

They all stared at his hand until Brooke placed hers on top and said, "this gets more interesting by the minute."

Ashby's hand joined next.

Greg looked at his mum.

"Take me with you," she said.

"Sorry, Mom. I think it would be safer if you stay."

"No, Greg. Don't you dare."

But Greg laid his hand on top of the pile and nodded at Perry.

Squeezing the orthotope tightly, Perry closed his eyes and spoke the spell Portos had drilled into his head and made him practice during countless lessons.

"This spell you will *learn, Young Cocky Sir,"* Portos had said. *"I don't care how long it takes you. If you don't, you can forget about learning transferring spells."*

Portos had never taught Perry how to use magic to transfer himself or others to a different location. Transferring was difficult and dangerous. So instead, the old man insisted on teaching him how to make perfect transferring potions and extract accurate destinations from pre-programmed orthotopes. Tired of the stalling tactics and eager to help Ashby find his Integral, Perry learned transferring spells on his own, sneaking books from the High Sorcerer's library at Rothblade Castle. A dangerous prospect since a poorly trained Sorcerer could easily transport himself into the pit of a volcano or a vat of boiling water in an electric plant.

That's why, as training aids for their apprentices, experienced Sorcerers recorded exact and safe coordinates into orthotopes. Their own brand of magic became part of the stones which made them particularly hard to read, harder even than the transferring spells themselves, although not risky, like getting one's skin peeled off the bone by scorching lava.

Regardless of the difficulty, Portos had succeeded in teaching Perry how to read the tricky stones, so in a matter of seconds, he deciphered the destination and took them away from Greg's house, feeling but a twinge of regret at leaving Greg's mum behind.

It was only when they blinked out of existence that Perry bothered to wonder if following after a crafty Sorceress was a good idea.

Then, an instant later, he realized it definitely was not.

The moment they reappeared in a dark, unidentifiable place, someone yanked Perry's amulet from his neck, and a shimmering rope wrapped around his torso, pinning his arms into place.

"Bloody hell!" he exclaimed, flopping to the floor like a fish.

Was this a *suppressing lasso*? If it was, his magic was restrained, and he was as useless as a Companion.

Greg, Brooke and Ashby knelt around him, their faces skeletal in the glow of his restraint.

"Dammit! Where is a sword when you need one?" Greg said.

"A sword?" Brooke asked. "God, I feel like I've missed so much."

"Never mind." Greg looked around and called out, "Jules! Show your face!"

"Are you okay?" Ashby stared warily at the lasso. "Does it hurt?"

"No, but she took my amulet, and I can't use magic with this thing around me. God, I'm so stupid!"

"Yes, you are," a chilling voice echoed throughout the dark space.

"That's enough of this game," Greg said.

Laughter echoed. The darkness melted away, slowly revealing a wood-paneled study flanked by floor-to-ceiling bookshelves and lamps in every corner.

"Cool," Perry said, watching the darkness crawl under the Persian rugs and into the gilded air-vents that adorned the polished hardwood floors. Conjuring darkness was not an easy thing to learn. Perry's mouth watered at the prospect of acquiring the particular skill.

"Are you kids okay?" A man that looked just like Greg stepped out of the receding shadows.

"Dad!"

"Son!" The man, Nick, pulled Greg into a tight hug. He even thumped his back and chuckled in relief. "It's so good to see you."

"Me, too, Dad."

Nick pulled away from Greg. "Jules, they're pale as ghosts. You promised not to go too far."

"I did not," someone protested in a British accent.

Perry craned his neck back and stared into a pair of worn, leather shoes. He assumed they belonged to Jules, though they didn't look particularly feminine. Other than the shoes, the only other thing Perry could see was the bottom of the chair the Sorceress occupied, which was upholstered in ochre fabric with a pattern of small smoking pipes weaved with golden thread.

"Ma'am," Ashby said, "I kindly request that you release my friend."

"Outstanding manners, Mr. Rothblade, but they won't buy you anything here. Your *friend* will remain restrained."

"It's obvious that manners are of no use to you," Ashby snarled. "This is no way to treat a guest."

"I would've assumed you were used to this. It's your mother's way, after all."

Ashby's eyes narrowed, and his upper lip trembled.

Uh-oh, a sign he was about to lose the very manners her had demanded.

Ashby opened his mouth to speak, but Greg, of all people, put a hand on his shoulder and attempted to get the situation under control.

"Let's back up a little and remember why we're here," he said. "Jules . . . may I call you that?" Greg waited and must have received non-verbal confirmation because he continued. "I assume my father explained our situation and told you what we're after."

Silence again.

"So you know we didn't come here looking for a fight," Greg continued. "We need help, and if you can offer it, I would be tremendously grateful. The Regent has my Integral. I was supposed to protect her, and I failed her. But I'm not the only one who needs her back. There are hundreds of people who could use her help. She's a Weaver, and she can undo what Danata Rothblade has done. I sense you understand what I mean."

Perry cursed inwardly, wishing he could see the Sorceress' reaction. His hands were starting to go numb. The lasso was too tight around him. They needed to talk some sense into the crazy woman before he lost his digits.

"Nick might have mentioned these details," Jules said, nonchalantly. "But one can never be too safe when dealing with the Rothblades."

"You led us here," Greg said. "Why would you do that unless you'd already decided we *are* safe?"

Um, good point.

"Oh," Jules stood, "just for a bit of fun. Can you blame me? The life of a dissident can be so boring."

Now, Perry could see the woman's chin, and a mean eye peering down at him as if he were dirt on her rug. She snapped her fingers, and Perry's restraints disappeared. His arms were limp at his sides, and the tips of his fingers tingled as blood rushed into them.

Perry clambered to his feet, rubbing life back into his arms. "Some way to have fun," he complained.

His gaze locked with the Sorceress'. She gave him a raised eyebrow and an expression that made Perry feel as if he actually ranked lower than dirt on the rug. He frowned, a strange feeling tickling the back of his mind. The woman looked familiar, though just vaguely. She had chin-length, gray hair and green eyes. Had he met her at Rothblade Castle at some point? Did she used to work for Danata or something?

"Do I know you from somewhere?" he asked, unable to stop himself.

Jules had begun to turn away, but she turned back and gave him a second, appraising look. She frowned and cocked her head to one side as if searching her memory. Something seemed to pass over her features. Her eyes widened, and she stood still for a moment, as if holding her breath.

Then she spun around and walked to a small, roll-top desk in the corner. She opened the hatch and pulled something out of one of the many small drawers. She held it up and stared at it, her chin trembling. After a moment, she looked back at Perry and stretched out a piece of paper in his direction.

Perry took it, a hollow feeling expanding in his stomach.

"What is this?"

Jules said nothing.

He inhaled, afraid of what he had in his hand. It was a photograph, old and creased, just a harmless piece of paper. There were three people in the photo, a couple and a little boy of about six. They stood in front of the Eiffel Tower, smiling from ear to ear. The boy stood in the middle, holding his parents' hands, his feet swinging in the air.

"Who . . . who are they?" he asked, though the hollow feeling in his middle had grown so big there seemed to be only one answer to his question.

"I'm pretty sure they're your parents," Jules said.

ဆ *Chapter 36* ଔ
Perry

Perry's hands went limp. The picture dropped to the floor. Jules picked it up and put it back in the drawer.

"What do you mean?" Ashby asked. "How would you know about Perry's parents?"

Just what Perry wanted to ask, but his mouth had gone dry, and Jules's words were echoing in his ears, emphasizing a message which carried the disturbing ring of truth.

"Perry? That's what they call you?" Jules shook her head. "Your name is Quintin, Quintin Addington."

Perry swayed on his feet. The sound of the name was pleasant and horrible at the same time.

"I don't know why I didn't notice it right away," Jules continued. "You look so much like Maggie."

Maggie Maggie Maggie. The name was like a hammer hitting a barrier inside Perry's mind. He wanted to demand an explanation, but he seemed to have lost the ability to speak. Good thing Ashby was there.

"Please, explain what you mean," his friend demanded.

But the Sorceress had lost all her initial bustle and was now as silent as Perry. She eased back onto her armchair, shaking her head at the floor, knees trembling as she sat.

"She got what she wanted," she said after a few long beats. Her eyes lost in some faraway memory.

"Who do you mean?" Ashby insisted.

"Your mother!" Jules said in a near growl. "That indecent person who dares call herself our Regent. That's who I mean. Maggie was my daughter. She disappeared thirteen years ago along with her husband and my *grandson*." At the word, she looked at Perry and blinked as if she expected him to disappear.

"Are you saying that Perry . . ." Ashby looked back and forth between them, then lost his speech too.

"I'm sure there is a memory spell on you," Jules said. "You were old enough to remember when they took you. Our family has unerringly produced Sorcerers in every generation. Danata was counting on you Morphing into one. No doubt about it. She needed someone for her heir." Jules looked toward Ashby with palpable hatred. "And you did morph into a Sorcerer, and a powerful one, it seems." Her voice broke, and she shook her head as if to hide her emotions, but the effort was useless. There were unshed tears in her eyes, wavering and reflecting the light of the lamp at her side.

Silence saturated the room. No one said anything for a long time, and the only thing that seemed to break the spell was Brooke taking a step closer to Perry and intertwining her fingers with his.

"I could remove the spell," Jules said, "if you want."

Perry shook his head, and it was as much a response to the Sorceress as a sign of his internal conflict. If someone had tampered with his mind, it had been to do more than just erase memories. They had also implanted a fake childhood, along with fake parents who had died before he turned three. Maybe at some point he should have questioned those memories, but he never had. There had never been a reason to do so. He'd been happy at Rothblade Castle. He'd been happy growing alongside Ashby, his friend, his brother. Why would he ever question such a thing?

Perry wanted to refute Jules, to tell her it was impossible. He wasn't her grandson or related to her, even remotely. But he *was* the boy in the picture. He remembered his own face at that age. And why would this woman have a photograph of him? And why would the woman in the photo look so much like him? Why, if it wasn't all true?

"We . . . are . . . here for a different reason," Perry said, his words halting and fragile.

"I think this news is a shock to everyone," Ashby said in his most diplomatic voice. "Especially Perry. It will take some time to process." He looked apologetically at Perry, as if he was to blame for what his mother had done.

Perry nodded, grateful that his friend was here. He had no idea how else he would have been able to keep himself under control.

"I understand," Jules said in a gentle voice that seemed to surprise even Greg's father, the person who knew her best. She didn't look like the kind of woman who could sound mellow. She looked tough and weathered by many years of suffering.

"I apologize for my antics," she continued. "I've never had any reason to expect anything other than subterfuge. And I have always acted accordingly. None have ever gotten the best of me after Danata. I knew she was responsible for whatever happened to Maggie," she turned to Perry, "and to you, but I was never able to prove it. So when Nick told me about your missing friend and I understood what Danata's caste is, those old wounds reopened, and I planned to take her son, the way she took everything from me. That's why I led you here. I'm sorry."

She looked genuinely regretful, and Perry could feel nothing but pain for the old woman.

"To make it up to you, I will give you what you need. Please, follow me."

Jules left through a heavy oak door in the back of the study. They all exchanged uneasy glances and waited for Perry to make the decision to follow.

Brooke pressed a cheek to his chest and hugged his waist with one arm. He rested his nose on her hair and inhaled her strawberry shampoo. His heart grew quiet and calm. He felt something deep for her, and that knowledge made everything else appear small and inconsequential. It also gave him strength.

"Let's do this," he said, and began walking with Brooke by his side, her hand tightly in his, their steps in unison. He could even feel her heartbeat in his palm. It, too, was in perfect unison with his.

ℬ Chapter 37 ℭ
Veridan

After stepping into the portal, its blinding light died, abruptly disintegrating into deep darkness. Unbalanced by what felt like a physical assault, Veridan fell to his knees. He screwed his eyes, then blinked, desperate to see his surroundings.

His other senses overcompensated and threatened to drown him in a myriad of stimuli. The smell of wet earth and sharp pine filled his nostrils. An incessant chirping overpowered any other sounds but for the pounding of his heart. His fingers curled into claws, digging into what felt like mud.

By degrees, his vision adjusted. He was on all four in a clearing of wet land, surrounded by ferns, thorny bushes, and huge shadows. For a moment too long, he stayed frozen, telling himself he wasn't being a coward, rationalizing that his senses needed to become accustomed to the onslaught.

One muddy hand moved to his amulet as he reassured himself there was nothing to be afraid of. He was a Sorcerer and no matter where he went his caste had to be one of the most powerful.

Veridan rose to his knees and looked up. Legs trembling, he stood, head thrown back. Straight overhead, he could see a patch of night sky, and the small corner of what looked like a blue moon. The top of the trees scratched the purple-hued sky, almost reaching the stars.

Slowly, his gaze dropped, following the length of one tree for what felt like an entire minute until reaching its base. He marveled at the massive girth of its trunk. He took a few steps back in the hopes of understanding its magnitude, but it did no good. The trunk was at least as wide as a bus, but Veridan had a feeling it prove much larger in the daylight. There weren't trees this large in London, not to mention a blue moon.

A smile spread across his lips.

He'd done it.

He was in Nymphalia.

Veridan turned his attention to the chirping that still filled his ears. With his senses back to normal, the sound didn't seem as loud. Still, he wondered if the bugs responsible for the horrible din were as large as the trees. The idea made him grimace. He pushed it aside.

He stepped out of the mud, the soles of his shoes making a sucking sound. Once on dryer ground, he stamped his feet to dislodge the larger chunks. His pants were ruined, but he refrained from using a spell to clean them. It would be foolish risking his amulet's energy at a moment like this.

Lowering his gaze, he searched the ground for two stones that would fit in his palm. He found two jagged ones with bits that sparkled as he held them to the moonlight. Gripping them tightly, he spoke an incantation and felt them change until they became a perfect pair of orthotopes. He'd learned a long time ago to always make a back-up, as Fate seemed to have a wicked sense of humor against those who were unprepared.

Now, he would be able to return to this very spot from anywhere inside the nebula.

Pushing ferns and bushes aside, Veridan eased his way out of the clearing, following nothing but an instinctive sense of direction. He walked through the strange forest for ten minutes, passing several of the massive trees and catching hints of wildlife—scuttling sounds in the underbrush and the wingbeat of what might have been an owl. The night was crisp, the air the cleanest he had ever smelled.

When he began to think the forest had no end, he spotted something ahead.

He rushed forward, abandoning the care that had guided him thus far. Tripping over a large tree root, he stumbled onto a cliff's edge. The supple ground under his shoes abruptly changed to rock.

Veridan held his breath as he peered over the edge of the cliff to a large valley below. He inched closer, skirting around a boulder that he'd barely noticed in his awe. He drank in the scene below, his chest tightening with a feeling that had, long ago, become a stranger to him.

Happiness.

A city sprawled before him—something pulled out of a fairytale, the jewel of his dreams. It was no crude human city, infected by pollution and made garish by millions of neon lights in all the colors of the rainbow.

No. What lay before him was nothing like that.

Veridan couldn't believe his eyes, the pristine layout of the streets, the soft warm lights that illuminated every window, the abundance of trees, fountains, and cobblestone roads. But what stole his breath most completely was the magnificent palace that sat in the middle of the city like a precious jewel in the center of a perfect amulet.

Veridan trembled with delight. His expectations hadn't been wrong. Morphids had built this place and it seemed like they lived as diligent masters of their own land—unlike humans who destroyed everything in the name of progress and in their mad race to overpopulate every place they inhabited with their most inferior specimens.

He stepped away from the cliff's edge, his heart swelling with a strange pride. He wished we could transfer down into the city this very moment, but he had to become familiar with this realm before being able to do that.

But no matter. He was closer than he had ever been.

He was contemplating what to do next when a movement caught his eye. The boulder he'd skirted just a few minutes ago had moved.

Veridan stepped back and took hold of his amulet.

Something squirmed inside the large boulder. A sigh escaped from its depths. Veridan looked closer, never blinking, never releasing his amulet, and discovered that what he'd mistaken for a boulder was a person wrapped in a gray blanket.

The person rolled over. A pair of dirty, bare feet and a head of matted hair stretched out from under their covering. It was a man, old and decrepit-looking. He blinked and yawned. Then, with a start, got to a sitting position, curled his legs in and hugged them. He cowered, avoiding eye contact and murmuring under his breath.

"Please please please . . ." he pleaded, speaking something that wasn't English, but that Veridan could understand, nonetheless.

"Don't hurt me. Please please please. I don't bother anyone. I stay away. I stay away."

Veridan's lip curled in disgust. "Pathetic creature," he said and was surprised by the foreign, yet familiar, words he'd spoken.

"Yes yes yes. Pathetic. Filthy. Casteless."

Casteless?!

The Sorcerer took another step back.

"Spare me, your Eminence. I will retreat further from Alas. I will not soil your sacred city."

The man's words raised a thousand questions in Veridan's mind, which weren't wise to ask until he understood this place, its inhabitants, and its politics better.

"Leave." Veridan made a dismissive gesture with his hand.

The man didn't wait to be told twice. He gathered his dirty blanket and woven bag he'd been using as a pillow, and disappeared into the brush.

When the rustling of the man's retreat ended, Veridan walked closer to the cliff's edge and, creating a flame on the palm of his hand, found a path by which to descend.

A two-hour hike would take him within the city limits. He was tired and coming back later might prove a better decision, but Veridan couldn't leave now. He had waited too long for this, and it was now within his reach.

He began the journey down the side of the mountain. Nothing would stop him now.

ഇ Chapter 38 ര
Sam

For the next couple of days, Sam practiced using her powers to exhaustion. Her main focus had been to increase her reach to be able to spy better and, perhaps, find a way to escape. So far, she'd barely accomplished the former goal and was sorely disappointed in the latter.

Though, through cracks in the wall, she'd been able to reach outside the confines of the cell block, she'd been unable to extend her tendrils any further than the labyrinthine halls in the general vicinity, catching glimpses of an ornamental suit of armor, the guard's boots, and nothing else.

Now, she was pacing, waiting for her dinner to arrive, waiting for the courage to try the plan that had been swirling in her mind after she concluded her feelers had reached their limit.

When, at last, steps echoed outside her cell and the door opened, she sat at the edge of her cot, looking hungrily at the tray. The guard gave her and the room a quick once over, then left with little more than a huff.

Sam knelt by the tray and ate her toast and drank her water. Her stomach twisted, hoping for more. Toast and water for a wanna-be chef. What torture.

Damn it, if she ever got out of here, she would cook herself the richest pasta bowl she could concoct.

After sipping the last of her water, she pushed her back against the wall and focused on keeping track of time as best she could. She estimated that dinner was brought down around 8 P.M., so she planned to wait four hours before setting to work.

When she started to nod off, Sam jumped to her feet and paced, counting the seconds.

"One-Mississippi. Two-Mississippi. Three Mississippi."

They trickled into minutes and refused to become hours.

Yet, she waited, staying in her cell. Manacles on.

At last, she slipped off her restraints and left the cell, closing the door behind. She tiptoed in front of Jacob's door. There was a twinge of guilty as she passed by, but she didn't want him to worry while she did this. She would see him later to share what she found out.

At the top of the stairs, she slipped under the door—she'd started to feel as if it was her consciousness doing all of this, not the vinculums—and confirmed a guard was outside. Unlike the one the other night, this one stood at attention, a gun at his hip, eyes wide open.

Sam cursed under her breath.

What now?

Sneaking out was going to be risky enough with a sleepy guard outside, but this?

She pulled back and sat on the top step, considering. An idea occurred to her that immediately sent her heart into a rapid patter.

Making up her mind, she went back downstairs and to the end of the hall. There, she let her longest vinculum slip in through the tiny crack in the wall—one she'd been using to spy the halls above. She rose through a thick layer of old stone and mortar. The hall she reached was empty besides the suit of armor and a few dim sconces.

Light bounced off the armor's polished surface. The dude cut a massive figure with large shoulder plates, a slitted helmet, a long spear, and a hatchet-looking thing.

Sam moved closer to examine the platform it stood on. She hadn't paid close attention to it before, but now she examined it from every angle and saw that the plated armor was not attached to the wooden pedestal by any visible screws.

Tentatively, she pushed on the armor, testing for any give. There was none. She pushed harder. The helmet rattled a bit, but that was all. Sam frowned. Would it prove too heavy to move?

Well, that wasn't an option, was it?

She took a deep breath, pulled her vinculum back, and then, with all her energy, lashed it at the armor like a whip. She felt faint for a moment, but forced herself into alertness. Slowing her breaths, she watched the hollow knight tip and balance on one leg, rattling slightly. It stood suspended, neither falling nor returning to its original position.

Allowing herself a small smile, she pressed her vinculum to the helmet for one final push.

One. Two beats.

The armor crashed to the stone floor. Sam imagined its thunderous clatter like a dozen frying pans thrown by an angry chef.

Adrenaline jetting into her veins, she ran back up the stairs, taking the steps two at a time. Her vinculums went ahead of her, wriggling under the door before she even reached the top step.

The guard had abandoned his post and was nowhere in sight.

The suit of armor was just around the corner, and he might not stay away too long. She had to hurry.

Without wasting another moment, she wrapped her vinculums around the heavy metal latch and slid it out of the way. The door swung open in her direction. Heart in her throat, she stepped through the doorway, into the hall, then quickly closed the door, leaving the latch in the exact same position.

Fists pumping, she ran in the opposite direction of the armor and around the corner of a different hall. As soon as she turned, she stopped and pressed her back to wall.

She had no idea how she would get back into the cell, but that wasn't the pressing matter at the moment. Right now, she had to focus on making her escape count.

She had to find at least one clue or idea of how to truly escape with Jacob. And that meant not being discovered.

ஐ *Chapter 39* ෬
Greg

By the time they got back to the hotel, Greg was exhausted. The whole ordeal with Perry's grandmother—Greg still couldn't believe that turn of events—had been draining, even for him. And he didn't want to think how it was for Perry himself, especially after he'd had to say goodbye to Brooke again.

Now, the Sorcerer was sitting on Greg's mattress in the same spot as before. He was uncharacteristically quiet, drawn into himself like a turtle with its head inside its shell.

Ashby was standing by the window, lost in some faraway thought, also dead quiet.

Restless, Greg pulled out his sword from the scabbard and practiced a few defensive moves, relishing the weight of the weapon in his hands.

Jules had taught Perry the transformation spell, and he had learned it in no time. No one had been surprised, least of all his grandmother. She'd only smiled proudly, her eyes full of some sort of yearning that Perry seemed oblivious to.

Now, all they had to do was wait a couple of days for the Conscription Ball, and they would be inside of Rothblade Castle, rescuing Sam and Jacob.

In the meantime, he would practice with the sword until not a drop of Perry's magic could get past him. Ashby had assured him that even though Greg would be unable to bring the weapon to the ball, there was one in the castle that they could easily fetch once there—a display piece of some kind. This made Greg uneasy, but nothing was going to stop him from getting into Danata's lair.

After a while, he put away the sword and turned to Perry. The Sorcerer looked depressed, sitting like a limp scarecrow without a backbone.

Greg had just opened his mouth to say something when a commotion sounded outside the room. Ashby and Perry snapped out of their stupor and looked toward the door.

"What's going on?" Greg slung the sword across his back and opened the door.

A few people passed in front of his door, craning their necks and murmuring, an air of surprise and disbelief in their expressions.

With his usual authoritative way, Ashby grabbed someone by the arm and asked, "What is this all about?"

"It's Finley. They're saying she's come out of her cocoon already!"

Ashby let the guy go and exchanged a heavy glance with Greg.

"Oh, shit! Poor girl," Perry exclaimed behind them. He held both hands up and waved them repeatedly as if fending something off. "I don't want to see that."

Ashby went pale and pressed a hand to his stomach as if he was about to be sick. One day was not enough time for a proper metamorphosis. The changes required at least two weeks. Something had gone wrong for Finley and, whether she was still alive or not, it wouldn't be pretty.

"Hey," Greg pressed a hand to the crook of Ashby's elbow. "Are you okay?"

He had stepped out of the room and was looking down the hall at the retreating rubberneckers.

Perry pushed past Greg and joined Ashby. "What's the matter?"

"She didn't deserve that," Ashby said.

"No one does, mate."

"She was a nice girl. What if we . . . ?"

"What if we *what*?" Perry asked.

"We upset her. Maybe the stress—"

"Oh, crap!" A thought occurred to Greg. "What if she's . . . fine."

He had no idea what *fine* could mean for someone whose metamorphosis had failed, but what if she could still remember what happened and told everyone about their plan.

"What if she . . ." But he didn't finish. Instead, he rushed down the hall and followed the line of people toward Finley's room.

He pushed his way past the mass of bodies that crowded the narrow hall. He ignored their protests and kept at it until he reached the door and heard Mirante ordering everyone to clear out.

"There's nothing here to see. Everyone out!" she growled.

People protested in quiet mumbles and reluctantly started to back out of the room.

"She looks all in one piece," someone murmured in awe.

"How is that possible?"

"How long was she in stasis?"

"Hardly twenty-four hours."

"Yeah, no more than that."

When everyone had walked past Greg, he swallowed and took a quiet step into the room. He peeked around the corner and saw Finley on the bed, her arms around her chest, holding tightly to a white sheet. Her shoulders were bare, and her hair matted and stuck to her head in clumps. She was staring wide-eyed at her aunt, more scared than anyone Greg had ever seen. Other than that, though, she seemed to have stretched to proper Morphid height, her features sharp and beautiful in every respect.

He shook his head in awe. Just then, Ashby and Perry arrived, stopping at the threshold, question marks stamped on their faces. Greg held up a hand, prompting them to stay back.

"How do you feel?" Mirante asked in a gentle tone that sounded foreign coming from her. She was sitting on the bed, holding Finley's hand, her back to Greg. Portos stood on the other side, a hand absently rubbing his chin.

Finley cleared her throat and looked from Mirante to the old Sorcerer. Greg was reminded of the disoriented feeling, the clumsiness of his limbs, the sluggishness of his thoughts right after he morphed. It wasn't a pleasant experience, not even after a normal metamorphosis. There was no telling how Finley felt.

The girl shook her head and pressed a hand to her forehead. "I don't know," she croaked.

"Amazing!" Portos murmured. "I've never seen or heard of such a thing."

Finley looked up at him. "What do you mean?"

"Well—"

"He means," Mirante interrupted, raising her voice in irritation, "your metamorphosis was a bit out of the ordinary, a bit too fast. But everything seems fine. You feel alright, don't you?"

"I . . . I guess." She stared at her hands, wiggled her toes under the sheet. "I look so . . . big."

"That's perfectly normal, dear." Mirante smoothed her hair back.

Abruptly, her gaze flicked back to her aunt. "What about my mark? What is it?"

"You haven't gone through the last stage yet. But we'll know soon."

Finley's chest shook with a sob. She pressed her hands to her face.

"What? You're not crying, are you?" Mirante asked.

"I thought the day would never come," she said, her voice wavering. "I thought I would be forever Casteless."

With a jerk, she peeled her hands off her face. "What if this is it?" she demanded. First her eyes settled on her aunt but, almost immediately, they darted toward Greg who was peering from behind the wall.

"You!" she exclaimed.

"Shit!" Greg cursed under his breath. He pulled back, but it was too late. Finley would spill the beans and their plan would go down the shitter.

Perry lifted his hands in question. Greg shook his head and cursed again.

"What are you three doing there?" Mirante had come around the corner. "I thought I asked everyone to leave."

"Um, we were just wondering how Finley is doing," Ashby said, stepping into the room and waving at the girl.

"Hello." He did a double take, his black eyes opening as wide as quarters.

Greg might have warned him to close his mouth before he caught a fly, but there was no time for that. He stepped to Ashby's side.

"Yeah, we were—" Greg started.

"These three . . ." Finley interrupted.

Greg continued, talking over her. ". . . worried since her stasis was so short. Less than twenty-four hours. Phew, that's crazy."

" . . . were thinking of—" Finley stopped abruptly. "What?!" she turned to her aunt. "What is he talking about?" The question was shrill. Panicked.

Mirante practically barked at Greg. "Did you *have* to mention that?"

Portos shook his head and sighed. "Not the smartest thing to bring up at the moment, kid."

Greg gave him a "what the heck?" look. The Sorcerer himself had been about to do the same just a few minutes ago before Mirante interrupted him.

Finley clutched her sheet tighter than before. "Something *did* go wrong! Oh, Fates, I'm still a failure."

"We don't know that," Mirante said.

The girl started to hyperventilate.

Greg took a step back. "We should get out of here," he whispered sideways at Ashby, but he was still gawking.

Greg elbowed him, but it seemed to have no effect.

"Calm down, Finley," Portos said gently. "This half of the metamorphosis went well. There's no reason to believe the final stage won't."

The Sorcerer's calm tone and demeanor seemed to soothe Finley. She nodded and relaxed her death grip on the sheet. She closed her eyes and after a big inhale opened them. She was staring right at Ashby.

Oh, shit!

She was bent on screwing up their plan, just when they'd gotten what they needed to make it work.

Finley's eyes filled with resentment. Greg waited for Ashby to speak up, to come up with something else to stall the inevitable, but the princeling had been struck mute by the pretty girl.

"Mirante," Finley began, "you . . . you should . . ." She coughed and swayed a bit. "I should tell you . . ." But before she could say another word, her eyes rolled into the back of her head and, like a wet rag, she went limp and passed out.

The final stage had claimed her. Only Fate knew what she would morph into. With his luck, she'd become someone who would completely wreck his chances to get to Sam.

They needed to get out of here. Now.

ℰꙨ Chapter 40 ℭℛ
Ashby

Ashby dragged his feet as he walked down the hall, his thoughts stuck in an endless loop that played an image of Finley's face over and over again.

Mirante had pushed them out of Finley's room, ordering them to leave her alone and let her rest. "You surely remember how exhausting and disorienting metamorphosis is. The last thing she needs is all of you stressing her out with *your concern*."

Finley had changed so much.

Ashby didn't know why this upset him so. Maybe it was because he'd expected her to stay the same, to never morph. She had been perfect the way she was. Nothing had needed to change.

The nature of this thought made him pause, literally.

"What in bloody hell is wrong with you?" Perry asked, looking back over his shoulder as Ashby trailed behind.

"The pretty girl got his tongue," Greg said.

Perry looked as confused as Ashby felt. "What?"

"Don't be daft," Ashby spat. He pushed past them and headed for his own dilapidated bedroom.

Greg caught up to him. "We have to get out of here before Finley wakes up. The moment Mirante hears what we're planning, she'll lock us up."

"Greg's right," Perry said. "And if Finley is on the same accelerated schedule, we may not have long."

Perry and Greg pushed past the door into Ashby's room, but before he went in, he caught sight of Mateo—his father. It was becoming easier to think of him that way. He walked toward Ashby and stopped in front of him.

"You shouldn't worry about her," Mateo said.

Could he read his mind? Was that how his gift worked?

"I perceive no distress from her. I believe everything is okay, even if it doesn't seem so." He patted Ashby's shoulder and kept walking.

Ashby blinked at the floor, feeling disconcerted but reassured. He started to walk into his room, but Mateo called out.

"Son," he said, the word making Ashby's chest feel warm.

He looked at his father over his shoulder.

"Be careful." Mateo gave him a smile that was sad and strangely resigned.

After returning a quick nod, Ashby pushed past the door to his room and immediately began pacing. He hid his face from Perry and Greg to prevent them from reading his entangled emotions.

"Even if we leave, she'll still tell them," Perry said, continuing their previous conversation. "They might still try to stop us."

"*Might*," Greg said.

Ashby knew they should leave, if only to pacify Greg, but he was worried about Finley. What if, in spite of what Mateo had said, there *was* something wrong with her? What if all the stress they'd caused her had something to do with the anomalies she was experiencing?

And what about that look Mateo had given him? What did it mean?

"C'mon, Ashby. This is no time to hesitate," Greg pressed.

Tapering his desire to go back to Finley's room to check on her and deciding to trust Mateo, Ashby nodded. "Go get your things. We leave in ten minutes."

Greg didn't hesitate and left without a word.

"I don't like any of this," Perry said. "I have a bad feeling."

"It's bad all around," Ashby said. "There is no liking any of it, so just go pack and be ready to leave. We can even go back for Brooke, if you want."

That seemed to clear all of Perry's doubts, and he left without making things harder than they already were.

Ashby shook his head and took a deep breath. This had to be done. There was no other way to save Sam.

Within ten minutes, Greg and Perry returned, packs strapped to their backs. They both seemed readier than Ashby felt. At least they had something, better yet *someone*, to look forward to.

Finley's image flashed before his eyes, unbidden. It was ridiculous that his mind would play such a trick on him. He was as good as Casteless, while Finley, just a few rooms down the hall, was going through the last stage of her transformation, getting ready to receive her mandate from Fate, her path to a purpose and, perhaps, even her link to someone to share her life with.

Ashby secured his own backpack and stepped closer to make a circle with Greg and Ashby. The transfer potion was still in their system, and he was glad not to have to take anymore. He didn't think he would ever get used to the hideous brew.

Perry put his hand out. Greg laid his on top almost immediately. Ashby hesitated for a moment, then lifted his and was about to rest it on top of Greg's when the bedroom door burst open.

They froze and stared open-mouthed at the intruder.

Finley stood in the threshold, panting, a long, bare leg sticking out from under her sheet-dress.

"What the . . . ?!" Greg murmured. "She couldn't have . . ."

"Stop!" she croaked. "Don't you dare go anywhere!"

୫ Chapter 41 ୨
Veridan

Just as he'd expected, it took Veridan two hours to walk to Alas. He had climbed over rocks and fallen trees, had squeezed through thorny bushes, damaging his pants further, had developed a blister on his small, right toe. But he had endured, maintaining a steady pace that kept his heart beating at an uncomfortable rate.

Now he was here, standing at the edge of where the trees and bushes stopped, Morphid civilization enticing him and making his heart beat faster than the brisk walk had.

Forcing himself to pause and calm his idiotic giddiness, Veridan dusted his suit, then removed his shoe and used a bit of magic to heal the bothersome blister and clean his clothes. He wasn't going to limp into the city or look less than presentable.

He wished for a glimpse of the clothing worn by the city residents, but his suit would have to do. He was presentable in any case. He always made sure of that.

Veridan pulled on his sleeves, adjusting them, thankful for the cool air that had kept perspiration to a minimum. He ran a hand over his hair to slick it back, then took his first step onto one of Alas's cobbled streets.

Small houses lined the road, their walls smooth and clean, warm light shining from their windows. The general feeling he got was peaceful, organized, clean—though no people were in sight. Gas lamps illuminated every corner.

He resisted the urge to peek through a window and get a glimpse of someone other, someone better, than the Casteless man he'd seen by the cliff side.

Veridan pressed forward, moving toward the palace he'd seen, the jewel in the center of the city.

Gradually the houses began to change, getting bigger and more ornate. At a four-way intersection, he stopped and considered whether to turn or keep going straight. A faint sound—like that of a group of people—coming from his left helped him decide.

He kept a hand on his amulet as he went. Someone turned the corner ahead of him. Veridan caught a quick glimpse of the man as he passed under the gas lamp. He was undoubtedly a Morphid, tall and proud—a fine specimen, unlike the Casteless man. He had not noticed Veridan yet and was looking at the ground, seemingly lost in his own thoughts.

Veridan gave a nod of satisfaction and kept moving in the man's direction. He noted the trousers stuffed into tall boots, the loose shirt tucked in neatly, though rolled to the elbows. He checked for weapons, but there were none in sight.

When he was about twenty paces away, the man finally lifted his gaze. His dark eyes widened, and he abruptly jumped off the sidewalk and onto the street.

Veridan tightened his grip on the amulet, an incantation on the tip of his tongue.

"Your Eminence," the man said, his head bowed. "Apologies! I didn't see you."

Stunned, Veridan stood there, not knowing what to say or do. The man didn't look up or move. His hands were limp at his sides, his entire body screaming *I'm not a threat.*

Questions multiplied exponentially in Veridan's mind, but moving along seemed the most sensible thing to do. Given the level of respect the man was professing, it was safe to assume indifference was the appropriate response.

Reluctantly, Veridan kept moving, throwing backward glances. The man didn't move or change his demeanor until Veridan reached the corner, then he hopped back onto the sidewalk and disappeared out of sight at a hurried pace.

Following the sound of people to the next street, Veridan found himself on a busy street, illuminated more brightly than all the others. Judging by the varied signs over the buildings, this had to be the night or business district.

He paused, watching the scene before him. There were people sitting outside at small tables, sharing drinks and conversation—some on the sidewalks, others on jutting balconies and terraces.

The mood was light, relaxed. The conversation appeared civil, in spite of the presence of drinks and the late hour. The feeling of pride and satisfaction that had sprouted within him at his first sight of the city redoubled

No one noticed him as he stood there, away from the gaslamp, back pressed to the wall. He read the signs with ease, even though they were not written in English or any other language he'd ever seen.

It was fascinating and it meant that what he'd read in his grandfather's texts was true. There was magic in the land, not only in the people.

Companions' Oasis appeared to be an idyllic place for couples to dine.

The Actuary suggested a boring place that the likes of Council Member Dabworth would enjoy.

Brews & Amulets raised Veridan's curiosity into the red zone—though the place appeared closed at the moment.

The Hungry Moth seemed to be some sort of tavern and, after examining all the other places in the block, he decided he would head there.

With a deep inhale and a heavy weight in the pit of his stomach, Veridan stepped away from the wall and walked toward the tavern, his head held high.

He managed a few paces unnoticed, but soon a couple spotted him. They had been walking arm-in-arm, but promptly detached from each other and stepped aside to clear the sidewalk, giving him space and acquiring the same deferential pose as the other stranger.

Less surprised but equally puzzled, he walked on, wondering if his attire had anything to do with their attitude. They could clearly tell he was a foreigner, and that might be the way the Alas's citizens made visitors feel, if not at ease, at least safe from harm.

When he reached *Brews & Amulets*, he paused and turned toward the window display, both to satiate his curiosity and clear his mind from all the questions and suppositions that dulled his focus.

He attempted to examine whatever laid past the window, but his own reflection commanded his attention right away. He nearly gasped, but bit his lip instead.

His eyes were glowing a violent red.

℘ Chapter 42 ℘
Sam

Sam's heartbeat drummed inside her ears as she made her way down the dim-lit hall, each step as quiet as a cat's. When she got to the fork in the hall, she stopped and took a quick peek left.

With a strangled gasp, she pulled back. The guard had gone around the block, surely looking for the suit-of-armor tipping culprit. She cursed, then ran the way she'd come, the rush of adrenaline redoubling in her veins. Praying no one was around the corner, she turned and kept running. She passed the door to the cells and, for an instant, considered giving up and going back in—except that wasn't really an option.

Rounding the second corner, she skipped over fallen pieces of armor, careful not to kick anything. She hopped over the large chest piece. Noticing a familiar door down a separate corridor, she turned and headed that way. When they took her to Danata's office, she'd tried to memorize the twists and turns, and this seemed familiar. Her heart slowed by a fraction when the hall widened into a large area adorned with bookshelves and uncomfortable-looking couches that must have belonged to someone's aristocratic grandmother.

Padding across a thick rug, she headed for a set of tall, gilded doors. There, she paused to gather her courage and give her heart a moment to rest from the cardiac havoc it was enduring.

A loud *ding* made her jump almost a foot in the air. She felt like a fool when she realized it'd come from the behemoth clock that stood regally to her right.

It was midnight.

One millimeter at a time, Sam eased one of the gilded doors open to no more than a crack. She peered out with one eye and was glad to discover a clear path to the Regent's office. No one stood guard, but she didn't trust it could be this easy.

Sam pulled back and waited.

The clock ticked noticeably as she marked the seconds. After about six minutes of biting her nails, steps echoed behind the door. She held her breath, her ears tuned to the sound of leather soles slapping on the polished stone floor. When she was sure whoever was outside was retreating, she peered out again.

A guard was at the office's door, testing the handle. It didn't budge. After a nod to himself, the man continued on.

Sam marked the time before stepping out of her safe spot, then rushed to the office's entrance. Her feelers went ahead, diving into the lock mechanism and unlocking it.

After a compulsory look both ways, she slipped inside, closed the door behind her, and pressed her back to its carved surface. Sweat dripped down her back in one long, cold line.

The hall and its many desks were empty, their computer monitors displaying matching screensavers of the Rothblade coat of arms.

Reluctantly peeling her body away from the door, Sam walked down the middle aisle. Moonlight filtered through the large panel of windows on the right, illuminating her way.

Her shoes sank into the plush runner rug as she followed its length to Danata's office. The smoked glass door had its own security box. Sam opened it with her feelers, unsurprised that the Regent didn't trust her own workers.

The inside of Danata's office was darker, and Sam had to let her eyes adjust. Maybe it was her imagination, but the temperature seemed to drop a few degrees, probably to match the Regent's petrified heart. After the creepy feeling passed, she walked around the desk, her fingers sliding across the top as she went. Her eyes roved around, looking for anything of interest. Nothing lay on the desk except a phone, a crystal paperweight with a snow storm frozen in its depths, and a leather desk pad.

Sam knelt on the other side of the desk—she didn't dare sit on the executive chair for fear of turning into stone—and pulled on one of the side drawers. To her surprise, it opened, revealing such mundane things as pens, tape, and paper clips. She opened the other drawers, saving the one over the chair for last. As she'd hoped, this drawer held the first thing of real interest.

Feeling like some sort of thief, Sam pulled out a stack of papers. She thumbed through the pages, her fingers shaking. She scanned through columns of numbers that seemed to detail the castle's expenses. As interesting as the sums appeared to be, she forced herself to move through the stack.

A page with the header "Conscription Ball Schedule" caught her attention.

She stopped, setting the top sheets aside.

The paper detailed the date and time for some sort of event.

14th October.

Gate Opens —8 P.M.

Welcome ends — 9 P.M.

The schedule went on, marking the time for introductions, commingling, conscription ceremony, even wining and dining.

Sam frowned, racking her brain for today's date.

She had absolutely no idea. She'd completely lost track of time. At first, she'd made an attempt to mark the days, but it had been impossible without a window to the outside world. When Veridan and Danata took her, it had been September the 28th, she knew that much. By her estimate, around two weeks had passed, but there was no pinpointing the exact number of days. Eleven? Thirteen? Fifteen?

Sam moved to the next page. It contained more information about the ball. She leafed forward through a guest list, more figures about expenses for food, decorations, and extra security. When she'd perused the entire stack of papers, Sam put it back in the drawer, ensuring everything looked the way she'd found it.

Next, she turned her attention to the bureau behind the desk. The first section she inspected contained several rows of hanging folders stuffed with more financial reports and dossiers describing different programs, even one that explored the topic of "Decreasing Numbers in the Morphid Population." It was all very interesting, and Sam would have loved to read them all, but nothing was really useful. And neither was the section of the bureau stacked with several decanters of the amber liquid she'd seen Danata drink with such relish. Sam wondered what it was and guiltily wished for a bit of poison to drop into one of the bottles.

Mostly disappointed with her findings, Sam exited the office, though not without a backward glance to make sure she hadn't left anything out of place.

There had only been one thing of interest, but she needed to confirm its relevance.

Had they held the ball already? Was it tomorrow? Or was it taking place even as she skulked among the castle's shadows? There was an easy way to find out.

Sam walked to one of Danata's minions' desks and shook the mouse. The screensaver went away and was replaced by a login screen with a snow-peaked mountain for a background, and the current date and time in one corner.

Bingo!

12:23 A.M.
Wednesday, October 12

The relief she felt at knowing the exact date and time was unexpected. How could something she'd always taken for granted ground her so much? She hadn't realized how aimless she'd felt, but now, she seemed to fall back into place, back into time, and became very much aware of the days Danata had stolen from her.

So in two days, this *Conscription Ball*—whatever that was— would create a distraction for the many people who worked in the castle, especially Danata and Veridan whose names had been peppered all over the schedule. There was no telling how busy the guards would be with all that "extra security" they'd have to perform. The guests might try to steal the heirloom silverware and eighteenth century vases, so the two rude Americans locked up in the dungeon might be easily forgotten for a few hours.

The sound of muffled voices yanked Sam back into the moment. She dropped to all fours and hid behind the desk, holding her breath. Her lips moved silently in a litany of *please, please, please.*

She imagined two guards, talking outside, commiserating on how bored they were, how useless it was to patrol the corridors. She willed them to move along.

But no such luck.

The door opened and someone walked in.

Damn.

"Don't be long," a male voice said.

Closer, a female voice responded with a scoff. "Easy for you to say. You don't have *Vitorio Carso Pestile* breathing down your knickers."

Sam wrinkled her nose at the ridiculous name.

"Thank Fates for that," the man said.

The door closed. Steps padded on the carpet. Sam curled tightly into a ball, as if that would stop the woman from seeing her if she came to this desk.

Sam's ears filled with the *boom, boom* of her heart.

From the sound of it, the woman was in for a long night of work. Cursed words danced in an endless stream inside Sam's mind.

She was screwed.

℘ Chapter 43 ℚ
Greg

"Stop! Don't you dare go anywhere!"

Greg stared at Finley, unable to believe she was standing there after she'd slipped into the second phase of her metamorphosis only minutes ago.

He waited for a stream of Mirante's people to pour in behind her, but instead, the girl stepped into the room and closed the door. She was panting and wore a desperate expression that might make anyone think she'd been running for her life.

"Finley," Ashby said, "I'm sorry, but we have to leave." He gave a nod to Perry to proceed with the transfer spell.

Greg tightened his grip over the Sorcerer's hand. No way was he being left behind again.

"I won't tell on you!" Finley blurted out. "Take me with you." There was a plea in her voice.

Ashby yanked his hand back, breaking contact with Perry.

The Sorcerer muttered a bad word and rolled his eyes. "Don't mind me. I'll be here all day, waiting for you to make up your mind."

"What is it?" Ashby asked.

Finley shook her head, eyes roving around the room as if the answer was pinned on the walls. "I . . . I'm not sure."

Her shoulders dropped, the intensity she'd brought with her disintegrating like butterfly wings. Greg recalled the confusing nature of the *calls* he'd received when he first morphed. They had come and gone, making him feel crazy.

"Finley," Ashby approached tentatively, "what is your mark?"

He put a hand on her bare arm. Their eyes locked. She shook her head again. Ashby nodded at her, asking for permission to look. For a moment, it seemed she would refuse and run back the way she'd come. That type of blinding, deafening, paralyzing panic had been familiar to Greg in the beginning. It took time to get used to the intensity of the calls, and practice to understand their final purpose. Details came in pieces which could be maddening. Greg had driven all the way to Indiana in search of someone named Sam. He'd had no idea why and hadn't learned the exact reason till much later, when Sam confessed he'd saved her life the day he reached West Lafayette and called her with the excuse of needing math lessons.

After a long moment of hesitation, Finley gave Ashby a half nod and allowed him to walk behind her to check the mark at the base of her neck.

Greg watched Ashby's expression closely as he took in the sight of Finley's mark. A line formed between his eyebrows, a frown that grew tighter and tighter the more he looked. In turn, Finley watched Perry and Greg, panic growing like a dark stain in her green eyes.

"What is it?" she asked, almost breathless.

"You . . . you are a dual?" Ashby said in a guarded tone that made Greg think this was the least relevant aspect of the girl's mark.

Greg was almost afraid to hear the rest. He couldn't imagine what had made Ashby go so pale.

"One of your castes . . ." Ashby continued, "I don't recognize it. I've never seen this shape." He lifted a hand as if to trace whatever he was seeing, but in the end, he refrained.

An unknown mark was scary enough—especially in this time of Keepers, Weavers and Rippers—but the fact that Ashby seemed more reserved about the caste he *had* recognized made Greg shiver.

Had Finley morphed into something worse than Danata?

"Your other caste . . ." Ashby swallowed, "I know well."

"Oh, Fates!" Finley seemed at the verge of tears. "What is it?"

"You're a Regent."

෮ Chapter 44 ෬
Ashby

Ashby took a step back as Finley turned to face him.

"A Regent?" She shook her head. "But that's impossible!"

The room was getting smaller, the walls looming as if ready to crush him. Ashby's lungs seemed to lock, while air crowded uselessly inside his throat. There was no reason for this reaction. The Regency was already lost to him. The moment his mother ripped him from his Companion his fate had turned to dust. Why should this upset him so?

Fate had seen the gap his *ripping* from Sam had created and made sure to provide a Regent. This time one without a Companion—like Danata—because Finley's other mark was definitely not a gray wolf, which was Ashby's own mark.

Was this what Mateo had somehow sensed?

"I can't be a Regent. I can't," Finley said.

"Ashby, are you okay?" Perry asked.

"I'm fine," he answered too abruptly, proving that he wasn't fine at all. He'd thought he'd come to terms with the void his life had become, but this was too much. He'd thought he'd found a friend in Finley, but Fate's wicked sense of humor had decided to make her a rival instead.

"I don't want this," Finley said. "I'm nobody."

But already her tone was different, and not only because the metamorphosis had changed her voice. She also stood straighter, sounded more assertive, and held everyone's gaze.

Ashby let out a sharp laugh.

"What's so funny?" Greg asked.

"I guess this means Sam isn't meant to be Regent either," Ashby said, hating the mixture of sarcasm and satisfaction in his voice.

"I'm sorry if this seems insensitive," Greg said, "but she doesn't give a crap about being the Regent."

"This is messed up," Perry said. "There are five people with Regent marks and only one Regency. Last time something slightly similar happened, your mum *fake-killed* Roanna, and three people disappeared for years. What will happen now? Fate has lost its bloody mind!"

Perry was right. Fate was mad.

Keepers falling in love. Rippers tearing Companions apart. Too many Regents to determine a clear line of succession.

Morphidkind was falling apart.

"You two can fight it out, if you want," Greg said. "Like I said, Sam doesn't care about being Regent. Her aspirations are more humble than that."

"What now?" Perry asked.

Greg wasted no time answering. "Nothing of immediate relevance has changed. We should leave. Now."

"No," Ashby said. "We need to think about this. Portos might be able to figure out what's going on."

"No, no!" Greg said emphatically. "We can't stay here. We have to go. Sam needs us. She will screw up our plan." He pointed at Finley.

"Mirante might . . ." Ashby trailed off, not sure of what to say and how to say it.

"We *have* to go," Finley suddenly blurted out. "Please, now."

Ashby exchanged confused glances with Greg and Perry.

"Why?" Perry asked.

"I don't know why. I just know we have to."

"It's a call. Must be her other caste, whatever it is," Greg said. "Unless this happens to Regents, too." He gave Ashby a raised eyebrow.

The only call Ashby had ever experienced was the one that led him to Sam, and that wasn't really a call, but a built-in compass that had pointed to his Companion up until the moment his mother severed their vinculum.

Ashby shook his head to indicate Regents didn't experience calls.

"Let's go!" Finley urged, looking truly scared.

"I think we'd better do what she says." Greg turned to Perry. "Give her some potion."

Perry raised his eyebrows at Ashby, waiting for an order. Ashby hesitated. What if he made a mistake? Loud voices out in the hall snapped him from his indecision.

"We need to leave before they find me!" Finley hissed, so panicked that she was forgetting to hold her sheet close to the right places, making a flash of heat travel up Ashby's neck.

Perry got a small flask of potion from his pocket and extended it in Finley's direction. "Just in case," he said when Ashby frowned at him.

She drank the potion without hesitation, barely making a face. Next, she sidled next to Perry and looped her arm in his.

"Ashby, what's it gonna be?" Perry urged.

A knock at the door made him jump. "Is Finley in there?" a husky voice asked.

"Please, Ashby," Finley begged, her eyes wavering as if she were about to cry. "I can't tell you why, but every cell in my body is screaming we should get out of here."

Perry put a hand out. Ashby took a step in his direction, his own hand going up slowly, trembling under the weight of the two choices.

The door opened and two of Mirante's burly helpers peered in. "There she is."

Ashby looked over his shoulder. His gaze locked with one of them. He must have seen something in Ashby's eyes—guilt?— because his expression flipped from casual concern to distrust.

"What are you all doing?" he asked, stepping cautiously into the room.

"We're getting the hell out of here," Greg said, yanking Ashby's hand and pressing it to Perry.

"Do it, Perry!" Finley pleaded.

Ashby had no idea which decision was best. The consequences of either one went too deep to properly contemplate in the short seconds left to them. All he could do was follow the path they'd already laid out, even if Finley had inserted herself in the middle.

He nodded his assent.

Perry wasted no time. The bottom fell out, even as Mirante's men hurled themselves at them.

They disappeared into nothingness, that space between here and there.

℘ *Chapter 45* ℘
Veridan

Veridan's shock nailed him on the spot, the window display acting like a cheap mirror. Nothing beyond its surface seemed to exist, only his reflection.

Red eyes.

He had red eyes in this realm. This must have been why those people deferred to him, calling him eminence and giving him a wide berth.

Earth Magic.

It had to be his caste. It was the only explanation that made sense.

The shock dissipated slowly. As it seeped out of him like magic from a weak amulet, he allowed his eyes to see past his reflection. A narrow table topped with a red cloth lay beyond. Amulets, small pouches, mortars and pestles of wood and stone, and other trinkets littered its surface.

Brews & Amulets.

A shop that would make humans laugh and point as if it were a joke, but which was perfectly normal here.

Veridan turned away from the window, now aware that the color of his eyes gave his caste away. He headed for The Hungry Moth, holding his chin higher than before. These people knew he was someone of import. A righteous feeling grew inside of him.

He'd always known he was above most Morphids and, definitely, filthy humans. He felt more vindicated by the minute.

As he pushed open the heavy door to the tavern, he was greeted by the din of cutlery and conversation.

Eager for more information, he headed to the back of the room where a barkeep stood behind a tall counter, doling out tankards of some frothy drink Veridan could only assume was beer.

A few men sat at the front, atop tall stools. Most wore simple attires of trousers and loose shirts, but one of them sported a long cape with a hood. Veridan headed to the open seat next to the better-dressed patron.

A wave of silence followed him. Each table he passed grew quiet. The customers stopped their conversations and set their utensils down as they became aware of his presence.

No one said anything or stood from their chairs. They simply set their hands on their laps and stared down at the table.

When he reached the counter, he looked at no one but the barkeep. The man was thin, with a sparse, graying beard, and nubby hands that appeared to be in constant motion. He was in shirtsleeves and wore a stained apron.

He touched two fingers to the center of his forehead and inclined his head. "Welcome to The Hungry Moth, your Eminence. What may I serve you today?"

"I'll have what he's having." Veridan pointed to his right where the man in the hood sat nursing a tankard. He had no accurate idea of what barkeeps served in this realm, so it was a safe request as well as a way into conversation.

The barkeep twisted his mouth disappointed, but set to fulfilling the request.

As Veridan had expected, the hooded man turned to face him—except, to his dismay—it wasn't a man.

Instead, an extremely beautiful woman with eyes as red as his own glared back at him.

"My . . . my apologies," he said with an uncharacteristic stammer. "I didn't realize—"

The woman put a hand up and waved it with an air of nonchalance.

"I'm used to it," she said. "Though you might want to reconsider your order. This brew is terrible." She took another sip from her tankard, regardless. "Can't complain when it's free, though." She shrugged.

So that was why the barkeep had seemed displeased. The brew was free—perhaps because he was a Sorcerer.

"Not from around here, I take it." She looked Veridan up and down.

"No, not at all."

The barkeep delivered his drink and backed away without a word. Veridan considered not tasting the *brew*, but who was he kidding? Of course, he would taste it. He'd waited too long to get here to say *no* to whatever this realm had to offer.

"Indeed, terrible," Veridan said after taking a swig.

He shared a smile with the woman.

She put out a hand. "My name is Fina Rothblade."

Veridan nearly choked. He put the tankard down and thumped a fist against his chest.

"Now, it's not that bad." Fina winked.

Rothblade! This woman shared Danata's surname. What were the odds? Rothblades, Dabworths, Silvercreeks, and many others had left Nymphalia hundreds of years ago. Was she a distant relative of Danata? Had he come all this way to be made fun of by Fate? Typical.

"Charles Veridan," he said.

"I can't fathom where you come from, Charles," Fina said. "Your garbs are unlike anything I've seen before, and I've seen a lot."

Veridan thought to correct her, but he liked the way *Charles* sounded in her deep, contralto voice. He examined her clothes in turn, noting the fine quality of everything she wore. She was dressed like a man, with form-fitting trousers tucked into tall boots of supple leather. The inside of her cloak was lined in a silken material and edged with velvet. Her shirt was the only slightly feminine garment. It clung tightly to her chest, pushing up her exquisite bosom.

"I like them, don't mistake my meaning," she said, raising an eyebrow in a provocative way. "But they're certainly not from these parts."

He didn't know what made him do it, but he leaned closer and whispered in a playful tone, "If I told you where I come from, you wouldn't believe me."

She laughed. "I don't think there's anything you could say or *do* to surprise me."

Laughter to match Fina's bubbled in his throat. It had been a while since he'd felt light enough for a half-sincere chuckle, much less the full, husky sound rumbling in his chest now.

"Don't be so sure," he said.

"So what brings a *mysterious* Sorcerer to our humble city?"

Two things got his wheels turning. Firstly, she knew he was a Sorcerer, likely by the color of his eyes, as he'd suspected. Secondly, Alas, in spite of its beauty and size, was considered humble. He couldn't help but imagine what a non-humble city would look like in this realm.

"Running from the Unmaker?" she said with a dry, unamused laugh.

"The Unmaker?" The words slipped out.

Fina gave him a sideways glance from over her tankard. Veridan bit his tongue, upset at the involuntary way he'd revealed his ignorance.

"I guess you *can* surprise me," Fina said after swallowing. "I thought everyone had heard about *him*. It's all everyone talks about. I'm sick of it." Her original good mood seemed to have soured. "First the Ripper and now this. No one cared when Integrals were being torn apart right and left, but they care now."

Veridan's stomach gave a twist. Bile rose into his throat. What was this? What inescapable fortune had befallen his kind?

"Are you good there? You look sick," Fina said.

"I'm fine," Veridan assured her. "Can you tell me more about this . . . Unmaker?"

"Not until you tell me where you've been hiding. If there is a place where no one's heard of Altos Bluestone, that's where I want to go."

Veridan considered for a moment. Certainly no one had heard of this Altos Bluestone in London or anywhere else in his realm, for that matter. Certainly, Fina could go there to forget about this *Unmaker* and whatever it was that worried her. But could he gain something by taking her there?

Tired of all the years of waiting and eager to learn all he could about Nymphalia, he threw caution to the wind.

"I come from a different realm, and it's definitely never heard of the Unmaker," he said.

Fina turned to fully face him, a look of hunger in her eyes.

So he added, "A place that doesn't belong to Morphids, but it's ripe for the picking."

ℰ Chapter 46 ℛ
Sam

Sam had been crouching under the desk for a few minutes now. The office worker had sat two desks in front of her—thank God for small miracles—and was now typing away at her computer.

The seconds seemed to pound inside Sam's head, reminding her how long she'd been gone from her cell.

She had to find a way to make the woman leave—maybe a distraction like the one she'd created for the guard. Sending her feelers out, she perused the area.

The woman faced the door, her back to Sam. She sat straight as a rod, spreadsheets and documents arranged carefully on her screen. She had a cup of steaming coffee by her side and a small Thermos next to that.

Yep, I'm screwed, Sam concluded when nothing in the confines of the office sparked an idea. She knelt quietly, racking her brain.

If only the electricity went off . . .

Wait a minute.

The card readers by the doors had microchips in them, the same bits computers ran on, right?

Wasting no time, Sam directed one of her vinculums into the computer's CPU. From her basic Tech class in school, she knew computers had different parts for different functions. Long and short term data storage. A processor to compute things. Fans to cool everything off, and other things she couldn't remember.

Now, if she only knew which was the processor, she could short it to cause the most damage.

Inside the computer, Sam found a labyrinth. There were slots, small chips in neat rows, cables, plastic bits, metal bits . . . and she had no idea what any of them did—not like it mattered since *broken* was what she needed, though.

Picking at random, she touched one of the microchips and sent a surge of electricity into it. At first, nothing happened, but after a moment, the worker banged her mouse.

"Oh, now what?" The woman tried the keyboard next which seemed to still be working fine. She went back to the mouse and banged it a few more times. "Bloody brilliant!"

The woman stood, her chair rolling backwards. Sam felt triumphant until the woman stomped across the aisle and took the mouse from one of the other computers.

Oh no, you don't.

Sam went back to examining the other computer parts and, this time, picked one of the bigger chips. It read "Intel" on top, maybe the CPU? If not, she would zap part by part until nothing salvageable was left. And if any of the other computers in the room allowed the woman to do her work, Sam would fry those, too.

Focusing all her energy, Sam sent a strong surge into the chip. A loud pop and sizzle sounded around her, followed by a shrill scream.

Sam pressed a hand to her mouth, her vinculum recoiling and sending a painful current through the length of her body. She squeezed her legs together as her bladder threatened to burst.

"Oh no, oh no! What did I do?" The woman sounded frantic and her loud yelp still reverberated in Sam's ears. She'd been in the process of plugging in the stolen mouse into the back of the computer when Sam zapped it, so she thought the electric surge was her fault.

Static had every hair in Sam's body standing on end, even her eyelashes. Her teeth felt on edge, but she'd fried the computer without being noticed.

The woman hurried to return the mouse, not daring to plug it in. She gathered her cup and Thermos and left the room in a hurry, slamming the door behind her.

Sam waited until she was certain no one was outside the office, then slipped out. She traced her steps back the way she'd come, trying to feel hopeful about the one piece of information she'd acquired.

She was almost to the corridor with the suit of armor, when a strange feeling rolled through her. Pressing her back to the wall, she looked left and right, sure that a guard was about to discover her. She listened for footsteps, but heard none.

Tense all over, she waited for the feeling to dissipate, but it only got worse. Something was terribly wrong, but she had no idea what. Could it be Jacob? She came away from the wall, trembling, and took a step in the direction of the cell, then froze.

Not that way, some instinct seemed to say.

Up until that moment, she'd always felt that following her instincts was a good thing, but this time it was the opposite. Even the cell sounded ten thousand times more appealing than going into the corridor to her right, which was where the sudden urge wanted to take her.

Sam shook her head, even as her feet changed course and took her to a closed door with no signs or adornments on it. For several minutes, she stood quiet, listening for any sounds on the other side. There were none.

A dark force beckoned her inside.

Hand trembling, she raised it to the knob and turned it. Locked. The simple lock posed no obstacle to her vinculums, and soon she was inside, heart pounding.

It was a bedroom with a bed, mirror, and dresser. Nothing more. Immediately, her attention turned to another door in the back. This one was small and inconspicuous, but it was there her instincts took her. Shivers raked across her back as she pushed into the room.

An enormous black miasma filled the back of the tight space, floating in mid-air. It throbbed like a giant's heart, emitting a low thrum that made her think of thousands of moaning voices.

The shivers on Sam's back morphed into violent spasms that shook her. She grabbed onto the door frame, afraid to collapse to her knees. She shook her head, unable to understand why she felt so violently ill. Through the fog of her confusion, she noticed her vinculums had embedded themselves into the dark cloud and were thrashing behind its viscous wall.

Black shapes that, for all the world, looked like hands reached for her as if ready to pull her into the cloying darkness.

Gasping, Sam pulled away, taking several steps out of the closeted space. Her vinculums retreated with her, but not entirely. A sharp tug on them made her spinal column feel as if it would snap in two. She almost screamed, but managed to swallow the pain even as it choked her.

Sam beckoned, beckoned, beckoned.

Her vinculums pulled out slowly, slipping out of the miasma one millimeter at a time. When they came out entirely, they fell limply in front of her. Their usual brightness and life gone.

She dropped to her knees and crawled toward them.

No no no!

Her fingers slipped through the strands as she tried to pick them up.

"C'mon. C'mon." Fingernails scratching at the cold, stone floor, Sam begged, "Please."

Just seconds ago it had been so easy to command her them and now they were . . . dead.

Tears spilled hot on her cheeks. She would never be able to get back in the cell, but that wasn't really what drove the fear into the very center of her heart.

What chilled her to the core was the fact that, with her vinculums dead, weaving herself back to Greg was now impossible.

ᔐ Chapter 47 ᔑ
Perry

Perry magically produced a wad of quids, trying to be as inconspicuous as possible. They were legal dollars from a large pile Ashby had instructed him to keep secure. After Veridan found them at The Plaza, they had gotten smarter about credit cards and using anything that belonged to the Regency.

Ashby took the money and walked back to the hotel's main counter, while Perry stayed back with the others in the small lobby. He took Brooke's hand and pressed it to his lips. She beamed up at him and wrapped her arms tightly around his waist, and it felt so good.

After transferring from the MORF's dilapidated headquarters to Brooke's backyard, she had driven them to a hotel on the outskirts of West Lafayette, a place where they could stay until the Conscription Ball.

Mirante would be mad, surely wondering what her niece had morphed into, but it was best to keep it a secret until they rescued Sam. The woman seemed loyal to Roanna, but Perry didn't trust her enough do the right thing once she found out there was a Regent in her family.

And then there was the matter of Finley's other, unknown caste. *That* was more worrisome than anything else. Perry sighed, already tired of all the mad castes that kept sprouting everywhere.

At least he'd met Brooke through the ordeal. He wouldn't tell her—not yet, anyway—but he was in love with her. Head over heels, actually. Who would have thought? The Morphid world had really lost the plot when Singulars fell in love with creatures of a different species. He chuckled to himself. She would slap him if he called her a "creature" out loud.

"Clue me in," she said. "What's so funny?"

He shook his head.

Ashby came back with four card keys and handed them out. In minutes, they found themselves in Ashby's room.

Greg was on the phone, ordering take out. He'd lived in West Lafayette and assured them he knew a good place that delivered tasty Greek food. Everyone was pretty much tired of Chinese and pizza. Only Brooke complained.

"Everything has those nasty kalapata olives."

"Kalamata," Perry corrected.

She pinched him.

"Sam loves them," Greg commented, his eyes going all faraway and wistful. He hid his face and hung up the phone.

Finley kicked off the sneakers Brooke had let her borrow and wiggled her toes. The pinky one looked very red.

"They're too tight," Ashby noticed.

"Oh, it's fine." Finley sat on an upholstered chair in one corner. She pulled her now long legs up and hugged them. She looked like a lost child with her ill-fitting clothes and forlorn eyes.

Ashby got on one knee and took her hand. "Any more calls?"

She shook her head.

Brooke gave Perry a questioning glance. He shrugged and turned away. The moment felt too intimate for some odd reason.

"Um, we'll be in my room," Perry said. "Call us when the food comes in."

"Yeah, me too." Greg got ahead of them, leaving the room in a hurry.

"Guess I'm not the only one feeling like I'm playing gooseberry?" Perry murmured.

"Gooseberry?" Brooke scrunched her nose in that adorable way she had.

"I think you call it third wheel or something."

"Oh, right," she said, giving Ashby a backward glance.

As soon as he closed the door to his room, Perry pulled Brooke in for a kiss. A thrill ran through his body as it always did every time their lips touched. He walked her backward toward the bed, still kissing her. He fell on top of her, a wave of desire hitting him right at the core. He stifled a groan.

So far, they hadn't done more than some intense snogging, but he was dying for more. They'd been with other people before, but they'd both had their reservations about sleeping together. Now, after being away from her for what felt like forever, he was wondering why he'd ever felt like having sex with her was a bad idea.

He deepened his kiss. Brooke arched her body under him, pushing her hips against his own. It seemed her reservations had gone the same way. Out the window. Emboldened, he slipped a hand under her shirt. She dug her nails into his neck, and the pain was sublime.

Perry's heart hammered like never before, not even his first time. He could hardly remember the girl who'd given him that initial taste of the forbidden, but he was sure he would never forget Brooke—not that he had any intentions of trying.

His fingers crawled upward, inch by inch. He went slowly, her every need and pleasure his first priority. Before, he'd been a bastard who only cared about himself. How things had changed.

Her neck tasted the way she smelled: sweet. She made a sound in the back of her throat, and he almost went mad.

"Perry," she said in a quick exhale of breath. "I think . . . maybe . . . we should . . ."

He stopped immediately and pulled away, hovering over her.

She smiled sheepishly. "I'm sorry. I just . . ."

"Shhh," he pressed a finger to her full lips. He lay beside her and pushed a stray lock of hair off her forehead. "You're beautiful."

She gave him the same look as the first time he'd called her that.

"Stop fishing for compliments. You know you're beautiful. More so than any Morphid girl I've ever seen."

"Now, you're lying," she scoffed.

"I've never lied to you, Brooke." He'd lied plenty to other girls, but never her.

"Really?"

"Really."

"Okay, tell me this then . . . do you think this plan will work?"

Perry threw his head back and laughed sadly. "Now, you're not playing fair."

"That means you don't think it will." Her eyes watered. She loved Sam like a sister, and this ordeal had been hard on her.

"It's no easy task, but I think we can pull it off. Ashby and I know that castle like the back of our hands. We can find her and get her out with no one noticing."

"Oh gosh, I hope so."

They lay quiet for a minute, holding hands and content to do nothing more than that.

"How was it . . . growing up there? Were you happy?" she asked.

Thus far, Perry had avoided thinking about that. All he'd ever believed about his past had turned out to be a lie, and his emotions were too conflicted to consider. What Danata had done to his parents was horrible. And Jules, her life had been destroyed, everything stolen from her. It was cruel.

Yet, beyond the natural sympathy anyone might feel toward her situation, Perry had a hard time feeling anything more. He'd had a good life at Rothblade Castle. Maybe he hadn't had parents, but he'd had a brother.

Did that make him a bad person? What would Brooke think of him? He took a deep breath and spoke the truth.

"Yes, I was happy. Ashby and I . . . we had good times."

"Good. I'm glad," Brooke said to his surprise. She caressed his cheek. "Don't let what's happened taint that. None of it was your fault. You were just a boy and didn't know better. The old woman's bitterness is justified, but it doesn't mean you should make it your own."

Perry swallowed the knot that formed in his throat and blinked rapidly at the ceiling.

"Aw," she kissed his forehead. "Why so emotional?"

"Because . . ."

The hell with it.

"Because I love you, Brooke."

๛ *Chapter 48* ๙
Veridan

At the mention of a "different realm," Fina pulled Veridan to a table in the far corner of the tavern.

He explained everything, watching the Sorceress' expression for the smallest change. There was none. She remained the same throughout, listening without blinking. When he finished, Fina remained impassive, her gaze never breaking from Veridan's, as if she expected him to cave in and admit it was all a lie.

Finally, she said, "Who put you up to this?"

He frowned. Not what he'd expected her to say. "No one. I speak the truth," he said simply. He wasn't the kind to grovel, and he wasn't about to start now.

She looked him up and down, the same way she'd done when he first entered the tavern. "The story is ludicrous, beginning with the fact that our kind doesn't cower to lesser beings. But your *costume* . . . well . . . it's simply ridiculous."

Veridan fumed. He was wearing his best Loro Piana suit. If anyone was ridiculous it was her with that vampiresque cape and stable-boy outfit. All she was lacking was a smelly horse. He pushed his chair back, ready to leave before he lost his temper. He'd been wrong to listen to his instincts. This woman hadn't been the right person to confide in.

"Was it Banall?" she demanded.

Veridan placed a hand on the table and began to stand. Fina changed her voice to a deeper tone, imitating someone—Banall, he imagined.

"I can just hear him . . . *those Rothblades, they're a bunch of fools, always rambling about the Repression Exodus, thinking they're cleverer than the rest of us.* What did he offer you? Where are you supposed to take me so he can beat me senseless?"

Veridan froze—half sitting, half standing.

"Repression Exodus?" he asked, his insides turning to water. So maybe Rothblade wasn't such a common last name, after all. He sat back down.

Fina leaned forward, teeth bare, looking like a feline with her claws out. It wasn't hard to imagine her leaping over the table and scratching his eyes out.

"Vasco Rothblade," Veridan said, "relative of yours?" He was the Morphid who led the exodus out this realm to the human one.

"Everyone knows that," she growled. "You had the right idea a second ago. Get out of here before I tear your head off."

Veridan wondered how much she knew about her ancestor. "Doubters are just dreamers with broken hearts," he said.

"What?"

"Nothing." He paused. "Listen, this conversation is counterproductive. We could sit here hours trying to convince each other, and we'd both lose—perhaps even our heads." He touched his neck and gave Fina his most charming smile.

"Exactly my thoughts."

"I can take you there. Right now." Veridan stood and adjusted the sleeves of his jacket. "Your ancestors truly found a way to leave Nymphalia. I'm not sure, but it sounds to me like things are . . . less than optimal around here again. Or perhaps I should say *still bad.*"

She looked up at him from under her pinched eyebrows.

Veridan pulled out one of the orthotopes from his pocket and placed it on the table. "I trust you know how to use one of these." He showed her his own stone. "It leads to the foot of the portal I created to come here. I will wait for you there. Ten minutes. No more."

He walked out of the tavern. He wanted Fina to come, to meet him at the top of that mountain, amongst those trees. The desire to see her face again was strong—enough that it'd probably be better if she stayed behind.

It was ridiculous! He'd just met her, and already he missed the red gleam in her eyes. He wondered what color they would be away from Nymphalia's Earth Magic. Dark? Light? Would it matter?

As soon as he found himself on an empty street, Veridan used his orthotope and transferred himself to the clearing in the forest. The glow of the portal and the sharp scent of pine filled his senses.

He waited.

Ten minutes passed excruciatingly slow. She wasn't coming. Veridan cursed and stepped toward the portal. Frustration filled him. Unable to leave, he turned away from the magical doorway and paced, granting Fina a few more minutes. Other than coming to this place, he hadn't wanted something so badly in a long time.

A pop sounded behind him. Veridan's heart stuttered. He turned slowly to find the Sorceress standing there, the portal shining at her back. He exhaled in relief, feeling more ridiculous still.

Fina was crouching, a chain dangling from her hand. She was clutching her amulet, ready for anything. She was expecting an attack and yet she came.

Veridan stood straight, hands at his sides, showing his open palms. "There's no one but me," he assured her.

Her eyes darted around the clearing, and when she caught sight of the portal her agitated breathing came to an abrupt halt. She turned slowly, backing away from it at the same time.

Putting himself in her shoes, Veridan considered what to do. After a quiet moment, he approached the portal and stuck a hand into its very center.

"I will go first." He wanted to say more. *"Please, trust me. Believe me."* But he refrained, sensing that it would work against him.

He stepped into the light and, this time, knew she would follow. She'd taken that first leap of faith. She was ready to dream again.

And she did. Her hand poked through just seconds after he set foot inside the nebula. He thought the place would scare her, but when she came across, her eyes contained only wonder.

Quickly, Veridan took her beyond the darkness. Once out, she pulled away from the nebula, blinking at it, a million questions etching her features.

Veridan took her hand and led her out of the small alcove and into his chamber, his heart hammering with a schoolboy's excitement.

He didn't notice the slumped shape lying on the floor until he nearly tripped on it.

"What is this?!"

The girl, Samantha, lay pale and immobile in the middle of his chamber.

✍ *Chapter 49* ☙
Greg

Two days proved to be an eternity, way longer than the previous two weeks. But, finally, the day for the ball was here. In just a couple of hours, they would transfer back to England and attempt to get into Rothblade Castle.

Three of them were in Ashby's hotel room, making sure they had everything they needed. With Finley as part of their group, their plan had changed to include her, which added one more unpredictable variable that Greg didn't like one bit. As if all the other risks weren't enough, now they had a freshly morphed girl with an unknown caste. The fact that she insisted on going with them due to her untrained calls was the cherry on top.

He would keep an eye on her, though. If these calls were leading her to Sam to cause any type of harm, he would take care of Finley, no matter how fond Ashby seemed to have grown of her.

As if she'd read his thoughts, Finley peered at him from her spot on the bed. She looked sheepish and uncomfortable without Ashby in the room.

An elaborate gown lay next to her, the dress she would wear to the ball. She was waiting for Brooke to come out of the small bathroom where she'd gone twenty minutes ago, promising to hurry.

Greg tugged on his bow tie. He felt ridiculous in a tuxedo. He'd never worn one before, and it was as uncomfortable as he'd imagined.

There was a knock at the door. After confirming through the peephole that it was Ashby and Perry, he let them in.

"I've settled the bill and paid up to tomorrow, in case we need to come back," Ashby said, strolling into the room.

Perry hesitated at the door, giving Greg a strange look.

"Are you coming in or not?" Greg asked.

He snapped out of it. "Ah, sure." He walked in, avoiding Greg's eyes.

Greg glanced back and forth between Ashby and Sorcerer. They were both wearing tuxedos too, though they seemed more at ease in them. The two had gone downstairs to settle the bill, Ashby dragging Perry with him for a private word. Clearly, Perry hadn't liked what he'd heard.

"Is something the matter?" Greg asked.

Perry shook his head. "Nothing."

Greg didn't believe him. "No, really." He wrapped a hand around Perry's bicep, halting his progress. "What happened?"

"Nothing, just Ashby being a wanker, as usual. He . . . um . . . he suggested that maybe I should let Jules do the transformation spells, but I can do them. She made me practice a couple of times, and I know what I have to do."

Ashby and Perry exchanged a look. Greg tried to understand the vibe between them. There was too much history between the two to fully comprehend their dynamics, though. In the end, he shrugged and let Perry go.

"Next." Brooke waltzed out of the bathroom, wearing a midnight blue gown that went down to her ankles. Her hair was pinned back with perfect curls cascading onto her shoulders.

Perry wolf-whistled, admiring her by taking an exaggerated walk around her while Greg bit down a pang of envy. He wished Sam was here, showing him how beautiful she looked in a new dress.

Finley picked up her dress and rushed into the bathroom next. Greg hoped she wouldn't take as long as Brooke. They only had one set of make-up and hair implements, else they would have gotten ready in separate rooms. Why hadn't anyone thought of buying a separate set?

After checking his watch, Ashby said, "We have plenty of time. The contracted limousine will wait for us as long as necessary."

"I don't know about you guys, but I'm getting nervous," Brooke said.

Perry stood in front of her and rubbed her bare arms up and down. "You can still stay, you know."

"I know, but I won't be a coward. Sam needs me, and I may be able to help in some way. You never know."

"You never know," Perry echoed. "Okay, turn around. Time to make you a Morphid."

Brooke faced away, exposing her bare back to the Sorcerer. Perry held his amulet in one hand and traced a circle at the base of her neck as he spoke a string of unintelligible words under his breath.

Slowly, like a dark stain of water seeping through paper, a dark mark appeared on her skin. At first it was but the rough outline of a circle, something a child might have traced. Then, the center began to fill with minute details that soon acquired the shape of a gray wolf and a staff, the dual caste of a Companion and a Council member.

When the spell was done, Brooke rushed to the mirror behind the door to admire Perry's handy work.

"Neat!" She touched it. "It feels bumpy, like yours."

"It has to look as real as possible to pass scrutiny," Ashby said.

"That was easier than doing ours," Perry said, sounding puzzled. "I thought it would be the other way around."

"Guess it's easier to do it from scratch, than to modify it," Ashby said.

Perry had worked on everyone's marks earlier, changing his and Ashby's to gray wolves since they would play the part of Companions to Finley and Brooke. Greg, for his part, sported a Seeker caste while he would pretend to be Brooke's brother, there to accompany her in such an important occasion. Finley's, of course, was another gray wolf and staff like Brooke's—now she didn't have to go as a Regent and risk being murdered on the spot.

"Shall we get started with your face," Perry asked Ashby.

"Um, why don't you do Greg first?"

"Wimp!"

Greg had also been the first one to get his mark modified. And now, he had no trouble being the first to get his face *tweaked*. He would die for Sam. This was nothing—even if Perry screwed up and turned him into Quasimodo.

He stepped forward without a word.

"It may hurt a little," Perry said as he set to the task, all jest gone from his expression.

The amulet was in his hand which Greg understood was only necessary for spells that required the most power and concentration. Immediately, Greg's face began to tingle. It was a strange sensation that made him tense all over. He closed his eyes tightly and willed himself not to panic when his mouth seemed to inflate like a balloon.

Perry went on whispering his spell, his free hand brushing Greg's ears, nose, and forehead at different points in the process. The tingling morphed into a dull sort of pain along his jaw and brow.

"Holy cow!" Brooke exclaimed. "That's just weird." Ashby *shooshed* her, reminding her that Perry needed to concentrate.

When the Sorcerer declared the job done, Greg cursed and bent over, pressing both hands to his face.

"It freakin' hurts."

Every bone in his face felt as if it was being stretched by some medieval torture device, while his fleshy bits felt as if he'd gotten sunburned in hell.

"It will pass in a few minutes. It won't be 100% painless, but bearable. I enlarged some of your bones and magic is stopping them from going back to normal. Just a few structural changes are enough to make anyone look very different. Your own mum wouldn't recognize you."

Rubbing his face, Greg walked to the mirror and looked at himself.

"Shit!" Even he didn't recognize himself. His gut did a twist. Everything was bigger. His nose was thick at the nostrils. His chin jutted out. His ears drooped like an old man's, and his forehead made him think of damn Frankenstein. He felt like a freak, though he supposed there were people with similar features. At least, he was still attractive enough to pass for a Morphid.

Perry stood behind him, a sly smile on his face. He looked proud of his work, and he ought to be. The differences were uncanny and had Greg feeling as if he was losing his mind. He hadn't imagined it would disturb him so much to wear someone else's face, but it was bizarre.

"How long did you say this will last?" He'd paid little attention to the details before. It hadn't seemed to matter. Now, he was impatient to go back to normal.

"Until I release the magic holding everything in place."

"Well, make sure not to get yourself killed. Though, I guess I could ask your grandma to fix me, if you do."

"Don't call her that," Perry said in a serious tone.

Greg put both hands up in apology. "Can some Tylenol help with this pain?" He pressed on his now protruding chin.

"Hardly." He turned to Ashby. "Next!"

He got to work on Ashby immediately. Now, on the other end of things, Greg watched with fascination as Ashby's features shrunk, the exact opposite of what had happened to Greg.

Ashby bit his lower lip through the entire process and gave a loud gasp when Perry announced it was done.

"Oh, God! It looks excruciating." Brooke was pale. "Not looking forward to it at all."

"You'll be fine," Greg said. "It hurts less already."

"How do I look?" Ashby asked, lifting his hands in a demonstrative fashion. He turned his face this way and that.

"Um, like that little kid in *The Sixth Sense*," Brooke put it.

Greg nodded. "Yeah, you're right. It's the smaller eyes, I think."

Ashby was on the way to the mirror when Finley stepped out of the bathroom. He stopped mid-step and stared, speechless.

"Finley! You look beautiful," Brooke gushed. "That dress is perfect on you."

"Very nice." Perry nodded in agreement.

Finley blushed, then her eyes searched Ashby who was still standing speechless. Her mouth fell open when she noticed his new face, but she processed her surprise like someone very used to magic and its effects. She smiled at Ashby as if waiting for a comment from him, but he managed absolutely nothing.

Breaking the uncomfortable silence, Greg said, "Excellent dress choice."

Barely acknowledging *his* altered features, Finley thanked him with a smile that didn't help hide her disappointment at what she must have interpreted as indifference from Ashby. She couldn't have been further from the truth.

Oddly, Greg felt happy for Ashby. Maybe he didn't have to be a broken Companion anymore, which should do wonders for the guilt Greg felt sometimes.

"Alright, Brooke, you're next," Perry said, rubbing his hands.

"Finley, you're lucky you don't have to do this. From what I can tell, it hurts like hell." She faced Perry. "Don't you dare make me ugly!"

"I couldn't if I tried."

"Aw, aren't you two charming?" Greg teased.

"You're one to talk. Have you seen yourself when you're with Sam?"

Another pang hit him and must have shown on his face because Brooke quickly apologized, calling herself an insensitive idiot.

"Don't sweat it," Greg told her. "We'll get her back today."

"Damn right we will!" she said, just as she got a new face.

❦ Chapter 50 ❧
Ashby

Ashby couldn't take his eyes off her. Finley looked resplendent in her emerald gown, a small pin keeping her bangs from her forehead and a delicate amount of makeup accentuating her green eyes. His heart beat out of control, and he couldn't comprehend how it was possible to feel this way for someone who wasn't his Companion.

And now he wondered . . . had he ever felt this way with Sam?

He shook his head, realizing it had been different with her. All impulse and blind determination. No nerves, no fear of being rejected, even when he saw the way she clung to Greg.

No, this was different. This was all doubt, sweaty palms, and butterflies in his stomach. He had no idea what to do, how to act. What would Finley think, if he . . . if he caressed her cheek, brushed her naked shoulder with eager fingers, kissed her?

He shook his head again.

"You alright, mate?" Perry asked. "Having a seizure or something?"

"Uh, no. I'm fine. Are we ready then?" he asked, checking his friend's impressive magical work.

Brooke looked nothing like Brooke. Her eyes were pale gray, her nose slightly hooked, and her face shaped like a heart with a narrow chin and high cheekbones.

"Gray eyes, really?" Brooke stood in front of the mirror. "I don't like them. They make me look cold, and I'm fiery."

"You certainly are," Perry said in an insinuating tone.

Ashby rubbed the back of his neck. Perry in love . . . what a mad Morphid world this had become. His gaze traveled to Finley, involuntarily. Something fluttered in the pit of his stomach.

"It's time," he announced after quickly checking the time.

It was 1:00 P.M. and the ball began at 8:00 P.M. Western European Summer Time. After they transferred, they would have one hour to get their limousine then drive home.

Home.

The word felt stale. Was Rothblade Castle still home? It didn't feel as if it were.

Would it ever be again?

His heart squeezed when some strange premonition told him it wouldn't. He turned away from the thought and told himself it didn't matter.

They gathered around Perry. Ashby's hand ended up on top of Finley's as they readied to depart. He looked pale, almost pasty, next to her rich tanned skin. They exchanged a quick glance, then looked away.

Home. The word echoed inside him, full of meaning once more. He glanced sideways at Finley, daring to imagine the impossible.

"At your command, Ashby," Perry said, eyes darting toward Greg.

Ashby couldn't help but glance in his direction, too.

Greg frowned, looking back and forth between them. His eyes filled with distrust all of a sudden. He suspected something. His hand twitched on the pile.

"Do it!" Ashby exclaimed as Greg began to pull his hand away.

Perry issued the spell and they all transferred. The last image to flash before Ashby's eyes was Perry's regretful face. He hadn't wanted to do it this way, but Greg was Ashby's only bargaining chip.

℘ Chapter 51 ℭ
Greg

Instincts screamed inside Greg's head.

Something was wrong.

The way Perry had looked at him, then back at Ashby. Were they about to betray him somehow? No, it couldn't be. And yet . . .

He began to pull his hand away.

He hesitated. Ashby gave the order. The world snapped and his body turned to sand, dissolving, falling, whirling endlessly without direction. He waited for the familiar sensation to pass. He'd transferred enough times to know what came next.

But he went on waiting, waiting, waiting for his body to coalesce and become whole once more.

It didn't.

His senses didn't return. Instead, he remained blind and deaf, left only with the endless plummeting sensation and the feeling that he was immaterial, made of nothing but dust.

Where was he? How long had he been here? Was he even breathing?

Panic filled the space between the crevices, the craters between his scattered particles.

He was dying, dissolving. How could he live without a heart to pump life into his brain?

How long had they been planning to betray him, to kill him this way?

The image of Mirante and Ashby talking in hushed tones in the dimly lit conference room of the dilapidated hotel popped into Greg's mind.

Had it been since the beginning?

Ashby had gone from refusing to help him to suddenly being willing to go against MORF's leader, and like a desperate idiot, Greg had fallen for the act.

If he'd had a mouth, he would have screamed. As he was, he managed little more than to feel more scattered and insubstantial. He tried to calm down, tried to gather himself, but it was impossible. His thoughts were a whirlwind.

What if they leave me here to die?

Worse . . . what if I can't die and I'm left here forever?

Then—deprived of his sense of time as he was—the worst thought of all occurred to him.

What if he'd already been here an eternity?

ℰ Chapter 52 ℛ
Sam

Sam lay on the cot back in her cell, head slumped, arms limp at her sides. She stared at the ceiling, her eyes vacant. There was a void in the middle of her chest, an emptiness that no amount of reasoning could help her ignore. She'd tried to tell herself it didn't matter, that everything would be all right, that MORF, her parents, her friends would rescue her, that Greg would still love her, no matter what, that she would be whole without her connection to him.

But it all felt like a lie.

If she'd had more tears, she would have shed them now. But she'd cried for two days. Or was it less? More? She'd cried since opening her eyes to Veridan as he had sneered down at her in *that* room.

"Close that door," the Sorcerer had told a woman Sam had never seen.

The black miasma that had lured her in was shut away.

"How did you get in here?" Veridan demanded.

Sam stared past him, urging her vinculums to wake up. They didn't. That's when the tears began.

"Why aren't you in your cell?" Veridan pressed, taking her by the shoulders and shaking her to a sitting position.

Her answer was more tears.

"Who is she?" the woman asked.

"No one."

"And *no one* makes you this upset?" the woman asked.

"She's the Weaver."

The woman's eyes went wide. It seemed Veridan had told her about Sam.

"I want her," she said.

"And you will have her," Veridan said, then turned back to Sam. "Did Danata put you up to this?"

The question puzzled Sam. Why would Danata do that? But she couldn't make herself care. There was a bigger, all-encompassing thought in her mind: Greg. She had forever lost the connection to her Integral. She'd lost Ashby and that had been painful, but this was excruciating, crippling. When Danata tore her from Ashby, Greg had been there to anchor her, to pull her from the oblivion that almost took her away forever. Now, she had no one.

"Answer me, girl. What is wrong with you?!"

The Sorcerer had no way of telling her vinculums were dead. Only Danata would be able to see what had happened to them, but she'd only cared to look when there'd been something to rip. Now, there was nothing.

"Fine. You don't want to talk? Have it your way."

Veridan pressed a hand to her throat and uttered a short spell. A heavy weight wrapped around her neck, trapping even her meek sobs. He'd rendered her mute, but what did it matter?

The High Sorcerer had then pulled a cord in a corner of his room and, in minutes, guards came to take Sam back to her cell. They dumped her on the cot and left her alone until the next morning when Danata and Simeon came to interrogate her. But Sam wouldn't have told them anything, even if she'd been able to talk. Veridan's muting spell was still in place, which probably meant he didn't want Danata to know about the horror shop he kept in his room.

"I am too busy at the moment to waste my time with you," Danata growled at her. "But you *will* tell me how you got out of the cell."

The Regent had been furious and, under different circumstances, it would have given Sam satisfaction to see her face so crimson. But as she was, Sam hadn't even felt indifference. She'd felt absolutely nothing.

"This stupid ball is more trouble than it's worth," Danata had complained as she walked out of the cell, making sure to point out that Simeon would be outside her door around the clock.

Like it mattered anymore. Sam was worse than useless, now.

Every bit of her felt dead, even her hope.

❧ *Chapter 53* ☙
Perry

"Where is Greg?!" Brooke exclaimed as soon as they materialized in a dark alley in Manchester, a nearby city to Rothblade Castle.

Perry took a step out of their circle and looked around. He exhaled in relief when he verified no one had seen them appear out of thin air.

"I left him behind," Perry lied.

It felt like a dagger twisting in his gut to tell her this, and he hated Ashby for forcing him to do it. She would be so mad when she found out he was lying.

Damn oath! He would have refused Ashby if he could have.

"What?! Why?" she demanded.

"It isn't safe for him," Ashby said. "You know Veridan holds a grudge against him. Sam would kill us if something happened to Greg."

"But you said there'd be a sword for him inside the castle to defend himself," Finley said.

"I lied. He wouldn't have gone along with a plan that left him behind. The truth is . . . he's too impulsive, and I was afraid he would ruin everything."

"Yeah, but . . ." Brooke looked conflicted. "He's gonna kill you two, you know."

"He won't," Ashby said. "He'll be too happy to see Sam to remember he was mad."

"I wouldn't be so sure about that," Brooke said. "We should go back and get him."

"There's no time. C'mon." Ashby walked out of the alley and turned in the direction of the limousine rental place.

Perry followed, shaking his head.

"Tell him something. Convince him." Brooke pulled on his sleeve. "We need Greg. He can fight."

He pressed forward, mumbling that he was just following orders.

As planned, the limousine was waiting for them in front of the rental building, the tuxedo-clad driver waiting on the sidewalk. Ashby exchanged a few words with him, and the man opened the door.

"Why won't you do something?!" Brooke stepped in front of Perry, blocking the way.

Teeth clenched, he answered, "You know I can't go against Ashby. I'm sorry."

He walked around her and, rudely entered the limo before her.

Inside, they sat in silence and faced each other. Brooke brooded and uttered curses under her breath. Finley looked back between Ashby and Perry, a sort of understanding in her green eyes. She seemed to know what was going on and still chose not to say anything.

Silence accompanied them to the very front gate of Rothblade Castle and was promptly replaced by oaths when Ashby announced they'd arrived. Brooke went pale and wrung her hands over her lap. Ashby pushed to the edge of the seat, then moved back, making a great effort to look relaxed.

The limousine stopped. Ashby lowered the window and put on a smile. Before he had a chance to say a word, an ill-humored guard ordered them to get out. Ashby seemed at the verge of protesting, but closed his mouth when Perry cleared his throat. Instead, Ashby repainted the smile on his face and got out. Everyone else followed suit.

They were ordered to stand in a long queue of guests while their vehicles were diverted away from the castle.

"What a bother," one of the guests in the queue complained.

Perry froze for as second as he recognized Margaret Obryen, one of the council members. Then he relaxed, remembering his altered appearance.

"Is this typical?" Ashby asked, faking a deeper tone of voice.

"No, it's not typical. It's ridiculous." Margaret Obryen shook her head and took the opportunity to go into one of those rants that seemed to be her specialty. "How can she put council members through this embarrassment? I dare say not even the common folk deserve this."

Margaret Obryen gave everyone an earful when she made it to the front of the queue. Still, she had to submit to a metal-detecting wand and had to present her mark before she was allowed past the gate.

"Your name?" the guard demanded of Ashby when they reached the front of the queue.

"Ezra Oliver," Ashby said.

"Not on the list."

"I'm accompanying my Companion. She morphed into a council member just a few days ago." Ashby put on a proud smile and presented Finley.

The guard narrowed his eyes, looking displeased. "Step aside. You'll have to wait until we process everyone else."

"But—"

"It's that or go back the way you came," the guard said rudely.

Ashby clenched his fists, but stepped aside. Perry and Brooke received the same instructions and were also forced to wait until the queue cleared.

"Well, can we go in now?" Ashby asked.

"Someone else must decide that. He'll be here in a moment."

"You mean you made us wait all this time so that—"

Finley entwined her fingers with Ashby's, effectively stealing his ability to speak. "Forgive him. He's just a little nervous for my sake. We'll wait."

The guard grunted, sparing a dirty look in Ashby's direction.

"This sort of treatment in unacceptable," Ashby managed as he stared at their interlaced hands.

"If you cause a scene, it will attract attention." Finley broke contact and proceeded to smooth her already smooth dress.

"I'm sorry. You're right."

Every window in the castle glowed with warm light. The path to the main door was illuminated with small candles inside of paper lanterns. Pages came and went, escorting guests in as they approached the grand entrance.

Perry and the others waited another ten minutes before someone bothered to come for them. It turned out to be his mother's insufferable secretary Vitorio Carso Pestile.

"My apologies for your wait," he said, barely taking note of their faces. "It is, as you may be able to imagine, a very busy night. And now, not one, but two unregistered council members. I'm flabbergasted. Please, follow me. Someone will inspect your marks."

They exchanged nervous glances as the man led them toward what had once been the carriage house, not toward the castle. Two guards followed behind.

"Of late," Vitorio rambled ahead of them, "the political situation has been a tad delicate. Perhaps you have followed the Morphid underground news and are aware of things." He looked back over his shoulders. "No?"

No one said anything.

"A pity," Vitorio continued, "that we have to take these strict precautions, but I'm sure you understand."

"We certainly do," Finley said. She seemed to be the only one with her head 100% in the game.

They entered the carriage house. The guards also stepped inside, closed the door behind them and took posts flanking the door.

Two other people, a man and a woman, were already in the room. They stood in front of one of the massive bookshelves Ashby and Perry used to climb when they were little.

Perry's insides solidified into stone when the man turned around and faced them. He wore a pleasant smile that would have fooled a group of strangers. Perry knew better.

"Good evening," Veridan said. He offered an arm to the woman who accompanied him and ambled closer. "I am the High Sorcerer, and this here is Fina Shardwald."

He didn't bother to explain who she was. His date? Veridan had never had a date. Not that Perry knew. And he would have never imagined such beautiful and self-assured woman to go for someone like Veridan.

They stopped a few paces away. Veridan's eyes glided over them. The smile fell away from her lips, and his eyes narrowed. He examined everyone, taking extra interest in Ashby.

Abruptly, his attention turned to Perry. The High Sorcerer slipped a hand into his pocket. Perry itched to take a hold of his amulet, but that would give him away.

"Two council members and their Companions?" Veridan asked.

"Yes," Finley stepped forward. "My name is Finley Malone. My apologies, I had no time to announce my arrival. It might have saved you the inconvenience."

Veridan didn't pay her any mind. Instead, he jerked a hand back. Perry's shirt burst opened, his amulet snapping from its chain and flying straight into Veridan's hand.

With a spell of his own, Perry tried to get his amulet back, but he couldn't garner enough energy to go against the High Sorcerer's surprise attack.

"Did you really think this would work?" Veridan asked.

Fina stood crouched by his side, eyes roving around wildly, alert to any attack.

"It's alright, dear. They are harmless."

Ashby had been right. It was impossible to get into Rothblade Castle without being detected.

Now, they were just where Ashby wanted them to be.

⚬ Chapter 54 ⚬
Ashby

"I invoke my right to see the Regent," Ashby said, his tone firm and confident. Not even the High Sorcerer could undo the magic the request carried. At Rothblade Castle and by some ancient magical force, the invocation was binding, even if many were not aware of it. But, Ashby had been taught this as soon as he had enough sense to understand.

Veridan laughed. "And you think that will help you? She's ready to see your head roll, *boy*."

"Then let's waste no time."

"As you wish."

They left the carriage house through the back door and entered the castle likewise. After winding through a few corridors, Veridan left them in Danata's office under the care of the guards. The ball had barely begun, but the Regent would have no trouble excusing herself.

They waited in silence, though Perry's eyes expressed his discontent too clearly. He was obviously still fuming over what he'd been forced to do. Ashby had hated invoking the power of his oath against him, but it had been the only choice.

Ashby had known from the moment he'd made his decision that Perry would refuse to help and that, for the first time since his friend had sworn fealty, the oath would have to be invoked.

Still, it hadn't been easy. Perry was loyal by nature, and it seemed he'd grown fond of Greg and Sam.

If only he'd been able to leave Finley and Brooke behind. But refusing to bring them along would have raised even more suspicions. As it was, Greg had nearly figured it out. Ashby trusted the girls would be fine, however. Danata had no reason to bother with either of them, as long as she didn't find out Finley was a Regent.

"We're screwed," Brooke said. "All that preparation and planning for nothing."

It was never meant to work, Ashby thought, but said nothing.

The door to the office opened and Danata burst in. She stopped, one hand on the door knob, her eyes eagerly darting from face to face.

Her features soured. "What kind of joke is this? Where is Ashby?"

"Right there," Veridan walked in and pointed at Ashby. Fina was nowhere in sight.

Danata frowned at Ashby. He felt his stomach roil with the same ill-content that had been brewing there since she cut their filial bond. He'd thought that seeing her might ease the hatred he'd developed toward her, but that was not the case. Instead, the emotion solidified and took root.

"I tried to explain, but . . ." Veridan said when the Regent continued to gape at them in confusion. "They have used a transformation spell."

The High Sorcerer took out his amulet and whispered under his breath.

Gasps of pain echoed through the room as Ashby, Perry and Brooke grabbed their faces and bent over in pain. Ashby's bones creaked like old doors as they went back to normal. It took a long minute to recover his wits and straighten to finally face the hateful woman who had once been his mother.

"It *is* you," Danata said, a strange fascination filling her violet eyes. She cocked her head to one side and looked him over as if he were an attraction at the zoo.

"It is me, *Mother*."

She flinched at the word. Clearly, it disgusted her as much as it did him.

Danata finally let go of the door and walked further into the office. "And what sort of misconception brings you here?"

"I came to bargain," Ashby said, keeping a close eye on Veridan. The Sorcerer was intent on him too, watching the proceedings with care.

Ashby bided his time. He'd counted on Veridan's presence and watchful eye, after all.

"Bargain? I don't bargain with traitors."

Ashby did his best to look contrite.

"You betrayed me!" Danata shouted.

"I made a mistake. I was mad after you tore me from my Companion. I didn't understand that I would be better off without her. I see it now, though."

"What?! You bastard!" Brooke exclaimed, leaning in his direction, but Perry held her before she got her claws into Ashby.

Danata threw her head back and laughed. "You expect me to believe this little act?"

Surreptitiously, he slipped a hand into his pocket, hoping Brooke's outburst had provided some distraction.

"Samantha won't weave our broken vinculum," Ashby continued. "She cares nothing for me. You showed me that. Now, her mother wants the Regency, and there'll be no place for me in that scheme."

"Nah ah ah." Veridan shook his finger. "Take your hand out your pocket."

Damn! He clenched his teeth.

Slowly, Ashby pulled out his hand, fingers wrapped around a glass sphere.

In one swift motion, Veridan cast a spell that tore the sphere from Ashby's hand and caused it to levitate close to the ceiling. The Sorcerer moved back, increasing the distance between them.

"What is that?!" Danata demanded.

"Nothing to panic about," Ashby said in a reassuring tone. "It's just my bargaining chip. A transfer void."

Veridan lifted a brow, eyes fixed on the floating orb. It glowed purple and white, a current twirling inside like a tiny galaxy.

"Well?" Danata probed her High Sorcerer.

Slowly, the sphere descended and landed on Veridan's hand. He examined it closely, turning it in every direction, then probing it with a bit of magic.

Satisfied with his inspection, he asked, "Who's inside?"

"What is he talking about?" Brooke asked Perry in an urgent whisper.

Perry looked away, shame bright on his cheeks.

"Greg," Finley answered for Perry.

Veridan's features lit up like those of a kid in front of a Christmas tree. "Is that so?"

Ashby nodded. "A token to prove where my loyalties lie."

"How could you?!" Brooke exclaimed. "We trusted you."

Danata stepped from behind her Sorcerer and faced Ashby. "Prove it."

"Veridan, would you oblige?" Ashby asked. "You took Perry's amulet."

The High Sorcerer's distrustful gaze lowered to the sphere. He considered it for a moment, then put it on the floor and kicked it. The sphere rolled across the floor and came to a stop close to the opposite wall.

Veridan began on a spell while everyone stared at the sphere, transfixed. Ashby slipped a hand into his pocket once more.

A burst of energy sprang from Veridan's fingers and crashed against the sphere. The purple haze inside it darkened for a moment. Brooke pressed a hand to her chest and took a step toward the sphere. Perry held her back.

Smoke billowed from the top of the orb as it dissolved. The smoke took a vaguely human shape and gradually solidified into a bewildered Greg, features unaltered. He blinked, swaying on his feet. It took him a long moment to regain his wits and focus on the gaping audience.

❦ *Chapter 55* ❧
Veridan

Veridan had nearly given up on exacting revenge against Greg Papilio, and now the boy had been delivered on a silver platter.

Who would have thought Ashby had it in him to do something like this? Though Veridan had no reason to be surprised. He was Danata's son, after all, raised in comfort and spoiled since the day he was born. Of course the idea of not becoming the next Regent, of being no one, had scared him enough to stab the lame Keeper in the back—not that Ashby lacked reasons to want Greg out of the way. He'd taken the insipid girl away, too.

Greg's mouth moved up and down in a silent babble. Judging by his stupefied expression, Ashby had done a magnificent job of pulling the wool over the Keeper's eyes.

"Quite unexpected," Danata said with a raised eyebrow and an amused tone. "I appreciate the sentiment, but this boy is useless to me. I would have much preferred Samantha's mother over her pathetic *boyfriend*."

"That shouldn't be hard to arrange," Ashby said.

"He'll be quite useful to *me*." Veridan gave Greg a satisfied smile.

"What the hell did you do, Ashby?" Greg demanded.

"He betrayed us," one of the girls said. "Perry, too." She stepped away from the Perry, black tears streaking her face.

"I had no choice, Brooke. I'm sorry," Perry whined like a coward.

Greg's fists clenched. He crouched, his chin dipping while his gaze smoldered in Ashby's direction. He was losing his composure. Veridan licked his lips, already savoring what was to come.

Greg charged forward like a bull blinded by rage.

With an almost imperceptible flick of his hand, Veridan released an attack toward Greg's chest. As the magic traveled through the air, Veridan's memory flashed back to that awful day when Greg had nearly strangled him, even as he'd employed his entire magical arsenal against the Keeper. For a panicked instant, he feared the same might happen now, but then the magic reached Greg and his spine arched as he convulsed and then dropped to the floor.

"Stop!" The loud girl, Brooke, shouted.

Veridan turned slightly, ready to blast her into silence, but Perry got a hold of her and kept her from interfering.

"Let me go, you traitorous bastard."

Turning his attention back to Greg, Veridan enjoyed the sight of the boy's twitching body. He had a hand on his chest, fingers curled into a claw over the hole in his burnt shirt. His eyes rolled white into the back of his head, and a groan rumbled in his throat.

"You will not embarrass me again." Veridan reached a hand in Greg's direction, smiling. "I told you there—"

"Catch this!" Ashby snapped.

A shrill scream followed.

Veridan whirled, throwing a protective shield around himself. But it wasn't his neck he should have been worried about. It was the Regents'. Literally.

Ashby stood behind his mother, pressing a sharp dagger to her neck. For a frozen instant, Veridan thought it an empty threat, a useless stunt he could easily diffuse with a disarming spell. That was until a trickle of blood slid down the Regent's neck, staining the silken material of her evening gown.

Danata's eyes were beacons of confusion and terror. A gurgling sound escaped her lips as she tried to say something. Her legs went limp. Ashby eased her to the floor, never letting go of the dagger, as if to guarantee the wound would remain and do its job.

Veridan's heart pounded with the shock of it. Ashby had killed his mother. He would have never thought the princeling had it in him, but he'd been so mistaken. In his shock, Veridan didn't notice Perry was holding an amulet until the young Sorcerer issued a quick incantation and disappeared from view.

Veridan whirled around, looking for him, expecting an attack from the back. None came.

Brooke and the other girl stared at Ashby in horror. They hadn't known his plan.

Ashby knelt by Danata's side, peering into her face as she choked on her own blood. He held one of her hands, and stayed there until the Regent exhaled her last breath.

The traitorous son closed his mother's eyes with a thumb and forefinger, then slowly stood. His dark gaze swiveled to Veridan's who was still surrounded by the shimmering sphere of his protective spell.

"It's over," Ashby said.

"Over? Over?!" Veridan laughed. "It hasn't even begun."

"You are no longer the High Sorcerer."

Such fool to think this was what Veridan cared about.

"Stand down, and we'll be lenient."

Veridan scoffed. "Such pretentiousness."

Abruptly, Perry materialized behind Veridan with the familiar pop of a transferring spell.

Veridan moved aside, strengthening his shield against an impending attack from the young Sorcerer, but Perry was tending to Greg instead, healing the wound on his chest, his own protective barrier surrounding them both.

No matter. Veridan would enjoy riddling all of them with holes when it was all said and done. He glanced at Ashby. He and the girls were also under Perry's shield, a strong protection that would take time to pierce.

"For once you've been good for something." Veridan told Ashby, casting a disdainful glance at Danata's lifeless body. "Good riddance. She served her purpose, and she served it well."

Ashby frowned, confused. He could not begin to imagine Veridan's true aim, his lifetime dream that was, at last, only moments from coming to fruition. He and Fina had planned it all in the last couple of days, for what better time than now, when the entire Council was within the castle walls.

But this princeling boy could only see what was right in front of his nose.

"The Regent is dead, long live the Regent," Veridan mocked. "Is that what you think? Such narrow views."

He began to back out of the room. He'd wasted enough time here. There would be plenty of chances to hunt all of his enemies later.

"I don't want the Regency," Ashby said, inching toward the door as if to block his exit. "It's the last thing on my mind."

"How honorable!"

"Roanna is the rightful Regent. Or perhaps there's even another."

For some reason, Ashby cast a glance in the direction of the unknown girl. But Veridan couldn't care less about any of it. Soon, there would be a new Morphid order, and it wouldn't involve any of these people.

By now, Ashby was fully blocking the door, as if a good-for-nothing would be able to stop a Sorcerer. How ludicrous!

"You have to pay for what you've done," Ashby said. "For your many years of complicity to Danata."

Veridan laughed. "If you only knew! Now, get out of my way and quit wasting my time."

Ashby looked over Veridan's shoulder, hesitating. After a moment, he shrugged and stepped aside, ushering him with an exaggerated hand sweep.

He walked forward, but a tingling in the back of his neck made him stop. Slowly, he turned and found Greg on his feet. A sword was in his hands, held at a cross-body angle and reflecting the overhead light. There was a murderous look in his eyes and undeniable purpose shaping his brow.

Fear, like poison fumes, rose in Veridan's chest. Rage quickly mixed with it. How could he still be scared of this boy? He had no powers. The sword meant nothing. It took years to learn how to properly wield any sword, much less a magical one.

Untrained or not, the boy launched at Veridan in his typical reckless fashion. The sword led the charge, accompanied by a battle cry that savagely ripped from Greg's throat.

ℰℴ *Chapter 56* ℛ
Greg

They had betrayed him and now he was dying.

His chest was an inferno that would boil his heart to nothing, but maybe not before Veridan hit him again. The Sorcerer was standing over Greg, a smile twisting his mouth.

"You will not embarrass me again. I told you there—"

"Catch this!" Ashby's voice rang in his ears.

Veridan turned away. Something was happening, but Greg's head was swimming, and all he knew was that he was sinking. His eyelids fluttered closed. Something popped next to him. His eyes snapped open again.

Perry was kneeling by his side, lips moving in a fast blur.

Greg tried to push him away, but his hand swatted at empty air. He was seeing double from the pain.

"Calm down," Perry whispered in his ear. "I'm healing you."

Yes, you do that so I can kill you.

The pain started to ease. Perry pushed something solid and cold under his arm, then rattled a string of sentences that sent Greg's head spinning even faster.

"Here's the sword. I fetched it for you. This was all part of Ashby's plan. It's going well so don't ruin it. Just do as I say."

Ashby's plan?

"When you are able to get up, squeeze my hand, and I'll lead the charge."

When he felt normal once more, it took all Greg had not to strangle Perry but, for once, he managed to keep his impulses in check long enough to understand the situation.

He squeezed Perry's hand. The Sorcerer helped him stand.

Veridan was headed toward the door, Ashby blocking his path.

"You have to pay for what you've done," Ashby said. "For your many years of complicity to Danata."

Veridan laughed. "If you only knew! Now, get out of my way and quit wasting my time."

Ashby looked over the Sorcerer's shoulder, his gaze locking with Greg's for an instant, then he shrugged and stepped aside, sweeping his hand in invitation. Veridan took two steps forward, then as if sensing the danger, stopped and slowly looked over his shoulder.

Greg wasn't supposed to lead the charge, but he couldn't help himself, especially when a look of utter panic registered on Veridan's face. With the sword clasped tightly in his hands, he didn't have to cower from the Sorcerer. Maybe he should have— the sword didn't make him immune—but there was no way in hell he would shrink from this evil.

He ran toward Veridan, the sword raised. Perry followed close behind him, shooting bolts of energy from his hands. They crashed against Veridan's shield and dissolved into nothing.

The older Sorcerer released a bolt of his own. Greg angled the sword to deflect the blow but, to his surprise and relief, it dissolved, too. Perry had also surrounded them with a protective shield.

Panic still in his eyes, Veridan rushed backward out of the office and into a bigger area lined with desks. As he went, he released a few more useless attacks.

Emboldened by Perry's protection, Greg ran faster, sword held high in the air. Knowing the sword would cut through their barrier as well as Veridan's, Greg crouched low, feigned to one side, then twirled in the opposite direction. The blade cut the air, slicing through Perry's shield first, then Veridan's.

Greg braced himself for the impact of metal against bone, pointedly aware of the fact that he was about to kill someone, but willing to carry that load if it meant saving everyone else and ridding the world of a vile creature.

He forced his eyes to stay open, even as they fought to close and spare him the gruesome sight. Instead, what they forced him to witness was Veridan's disappearing act just as the sword came within mere inches of cutting him in half.

Carried by momentum, the weapon swung wide, missing Perry by an inch.

"Bloody hell," Perry exclaimed, leaning backward and taking a hand to his neck. "Damn, the bastard is fast with spells!"

"Where did he go?!" Greg growled.

"He could be anywhere by now."

Greg was oddly relieved. He wanted Veridan dead, but maybe he wasn't so eager to become a murderer. Besides, there was only one person he cared to find.

"Where is Sam?" he demanded.

"My guess would be the cells," Ashby said from the door to the office where Greg had materialized from his time in limbo.

"Take me to her, now!" Greg demanded.

"Perry, you take him. I'll stay here." He stepped to one side and pointed toward a limp body on the floor.

Greg couldn't see the woman's face, just her black hair spilling around her head and a crimson stain at her neckline. Brooke and Finley stood past the body, pale and speechless.

"Who—?" Greg began.

"My mother."

"Is she . . . ?"

"No. She's not dead. It's just a sedative. The blood is fake."

"Oh, thank God!" Brooke exclaimed.

"We thought it would make anyone on her side stand down," Ashby continued, "but Veridan seems to be up to something of his own."

"We?" Perry asked, clearly as clueless as Greg.

"Mirante and I. We didn't want to rely on your acting abilities. It had to appear real." Ashby turned back toward the office. "I'd better get MORF in here to help. We have to find Veridan before he causes trouble."

"C'mon, take me to Sam," Greg said.

"Okay." Perry led the way, and Greg followed, heart hammering as they rushed through endless corridors.

I'm coming, Sam. I'm coming.

ℰℴ *Chapter 57* ℭℛ
Sam

Sam slept fitfully, tossing from side to side. Nightmares assaulted her from the moment she closed her eyes.

A huge, dark monster roiled above her. Darkness-covered hands stretched in her direction, reaching, reaching, eager to pull her in.

She startled awake. The feeling that something was terribly wrong soaked her skin. Bringing her manacled hands to her face, she sat up and stared at the floor.

What if she never got out of this place? What if her destiny was to weave people over and over so Danata could tear them apart again?

Despair gripped her heart.

As horrible as that thought was, though, it was that dark thing she'd seen in Veridan's room that disturbed her the most. She had no idea what it could be, but her spine turned to ice every time she thought of it.

Evil was the only word that came to mind whenever she tried to describe it.

A sound outside the door made her muscles tense. Muffled voices, too loud not to be shouts. Still, she couldn't make out what they were saying.

Something crashed against the door outside. Sam jumped to her feet, heart thumping. She'd figured they'd leave her alone tonight since the ball was taking place, but . . .

She thought of her vinculums. They had shredded that cup and could do the same to someone's face, but then she remembered they were dead.

She pressed her back to the back wall, eyes wide and on the door. For a moment, everything went silent, and her heart skipped a beat for Jacob. Were they here to get him? Panicked, she took a step forward, but she was thrown back against the wall by the force of an explosion.

Limp as a rag, Sam slid down the wall and hit the floor. Her ears rang and red sparks danced in front of her eyes. She blinked to dissipate them, then wished she hadn't. Veridan was standing amid the billowing smoke with Simeon lying battered or perhaps dead behind him.

Something tugged inside of Sam. It felt like one of her vinculums, but it was probably just her fear. Her widened eyes could not leave Veridan's.

The Sorcerer threw a glance over his shoulder, then rushed into the cell. Sam cowered against the wall as if to melt into it, but there was no escaping, not even by scratching at the Sorcerer's hands as he grabbed for her.

"I don't have time for this," Veridan spat, throwing a spell directly into her face.

Sam went rigid, unable to move a muscle. After another quick glance over his shoulder, Veridan yanked Sam away from the wall, laid her flat on her back, and pulled a small vial from his jacket's pocket.

The word "no" rose in Sam's throat, but it just stuck there.

Veridan poured the glittering, green liquid into her mouth and pressed a hand over her lips and nose. He didn't remove his hand until she swallowed, and the potion had time to set into her empty stomach like a load of bricks.

The Sorcerer took hold of his amulet and issued the transfer conjuration. Sam tried to fight, to will herself into staying. The cell was preferable to wherever Veridan wanted to take her.

Sam's stomach lurched as the spell took hold. Steps echoed outside her cell, and just as she began to dissolve someone appeared at the door.

"Sam!"

Greg!

He rushed toward her, a hand extended in her direction, but it was too late. The cell fell away as Sam tumbled into nothingness.

❧ *Chapter 58* ☙
Ashby

After getting in contact with MORF and summoning a few trusted guards, Ashby left his unconscious mother in their care and set out in search of Sam, with Brooke and Finley right behind him.

"Which way are the dungeons?" Brooke asked, looking right and left off the hall outside Danata's office.

"They are not really *dungeons*, but this way," Ashby said.

They'd barely taken a few steps when Perry and Greg turned the corner, running at a full pelt.

"Where is she?!" Brooke asked.

"Veridan took her just as we got there. He used a transfer spell," Perry said.

Greg was breathing heavily, sword in hand, and looking ready to behead Veridan or whoever stood in his way.

Ashby thought for a moment and, for some reason, remembered what he and Perry had once seen in Veridan's chambers. The Sorcerer was up to no good, and something told Ashby that the dark, sinister blob Veridan kept in his room had something to do with it.

"Follow me. I have a feeling he didn't go far," he said, turning and running toward the north end of the castle.

Steps echoed through the halls as they ran, blindly turning corners and knocking furniture down in their haste. When they made it to Veridan's chamber, Ashby tried the door, but it was locked.

"Perry, can you open this?" Ashby asked.

"But of course." Perry waved a hand over the lock, then twisted the knob. Nothing. He winced. "It might take me a few minutes. The bastard has sealed it with magic."

Perry tried one more time with the same result. "Um, I'll keep working on it."

Ashby banged on the door.

"I doubt he's going to just let us in," Brooke put in. "Can't one of you just give it a good kick?"

Greg stepped forward and, without preamble, released an explosive kick close to the lock. He bounced back and hopped on one foot, wincing in pain.

"Well, that was a bad idea," Brooke quipped. "Sorry, Greg."

"Maybe if we all push at once," Finley offered.

Ashby ran a hand through his hair, trying to figure out what to do. Perry was still casting spells as he clung to his amulet, but it didn't seem as if he would be able to bridge Veridan's magic.

An explosion inside the room rattled the door and made the walls tremble. They all exchanged wary glances.

"I almost got it," Perry said, sweat dripping down his forehead. If a lock was giving him this much trouble, what could he do against Veridan?

Greg threw a few more kicks at the door. The wood dented where his heel struck. The hinges groaned.

"Wow," Brooke said under her breath. "Perry, you might want to give it a rest. I think Greg's got it."

Perry gave her a mean look and tried harder.

"Sorcerers," Brooke said with a roll of her eyes.

A few seconds passed, then Perry exclaimed, "Got it!"

The lock clicked opened. They rushed inside, Greg leading the charge just to run into another barred door.

Perry pushed to the front. "It should be easier this time," he said as he got to work.

Greg readied his sword and stood firmly, his shoulders rising and falling at an accelerated rate.

"Oh, God, Sam," Brooke said, biting her nails in worry. Finley put a hand on her arm to console her.

Just as Greg seemed ready to explode into another fit of useless kicks, the narrow door to Veridan's alcove cracked open.

Wasting not a second, Greg rushed in, the sword ready for the kill.

๑ Chapter 59 ca
Veridan

Veridan didn't have to travel far. Going to his chamber within the castle was possibly the shortest transfer he'd ever performed, but maybe the most crucial.

"Good, you got her," Fina said with delight. "Let me check her mark."

"No time for that. Things have changed," Veridan said. "Her Keeper has just arrived."

"I thought you said they had been ripped."

"Yes, but he's relentless. He wields a Sorcerer-forged sword, now. But we don't have time for explanations." Veridan pushed past the door into his small alcove. The nebula floated, throbbing and roiling as if the souls trapped inside knew what was coming.

"It's fortunate I was able to convince everyone, then," Fina said.

Veridan hadn't stopped to contemplate any other possibility. Fina had promised to act fast, and he had trusted her to deliver. He hadn't been wrong.

Fina followed him into the alcove, the girl floating behind under one of her spells. He had to smile at that. It was as if the Sorceress could read his mind. She would make an excellent partner against humans.

"They await on the other side, atop the mountain," Fina said.

"How many?"

"Seven Sorcerers and five Warriors," she responded.

Veridan was momentarily awestruck. She had gathered twelve Morphids of powerful castes in such a short time.

It was regrettable how, in this realm, Morphidkind had been unable to prosper, but their numbers had been so low since the beginning that it had been an uphill battle. Now, however, with fresh blood from Nymphalia, it would be much different.

An insistent pounding came at the door. Magic reinforced the wood and lock but, depending on who was on the other side, it might be only a matter of time before they broke through.

Fina looked over her shoulder from the alcove's threshold.

"Expecting someone?" she asked, taking a hold of her amulet.

Behind her, the girl's eyes swiveled in their sockets, as if to scream for help.

Veridan cursed. He needed time to go into the nebula and open the portal for his guests. They would also need space to disembark, especially since a battle was knocking at their door. This room was entirely too small.

As he searched for an answer, his gaze stopped on the wall to his left. He pursed his lips and raised an eyebrow, considering. He wouldn't need this chamber any longer. He wouldn't need the stupid castle, for that matter. His sights were on far more than just an isolated corner of the world where he could hide and subsist.

He tightened his grip on his amulet as the pounding at the door became violent. A quick spell issued from his lips and the wall exploded outward, ancient stones spitting into the night sky like cannonballs. When the dust cleared, a hole as wide as a limousine stretched before them. Crisp air blew into the small alcove. With a flick of his hand, he shut the door and applied a magical seal that should hold his pursuers for a few minutes.

"Help me," he said to Fina, as he cast a gentle spell toward the nebula.

Fina joined him as soon as she realized his intention. She cast a similar spell, and the nebula began to move through the hole. It went past the stone wall and floated outside in midair. Fina and Veridan followed it, stopped at the edge of the demolished wall, and kept pushing. The nebula traveled over the topiary, as they directed it to a small clearing in the far end. There, they deposited it with care, then leapt down to the garden minutes before the door to the alcove burst open.

They stepped softly onto the grass below, their landing cushioned by magic. Samantha floated behind them like a dog on a leash. Laying a hand on Fina and the girl, Veridan transported them to the nebula with a quick spell. They appeared behind a tall hedge that hid them from view. The seclusion of the spot would buy Veridan the time he needed to open the portal and set his scheme in motion. As an extra measure, he released a few spells around the area that would disguise their presence to the casual eye.

Satisfied, he took Fina's hand in his and smiled down at her. She smiled back, her eyes glinting with an intensity that made him want her. Oh, what a delicious future awaited him. Fate was a poor architect compared to what he was able to accomplish.

Hand in hand, they stepped into the nebula, ready to change the world.

ꙮ Chapter 60 ꙮ
Greg

"Damn it," Greg cursed, rushing to a huge hole in the stone wall.

They were gone, leaving behind no clue of where they'd gone. Again. The garden below was empty, no sign of Veridan or Sam, just tall shrubs in obscenely manicured shapes.

Ashby joined Greg and peered out.

Behind them, Perry said, "That *thing* is gone."

Greg and Ashby turned to Perry who was gesturing toward the far corner.

"What *thing*?" Brooke asked, but Perry shook his head and didn't offer an explanation.

"Perry, can you figure out where they've gone?" Ashby asked.

The Sorcerer walked closer and surveyed the garden, a hand on his amulet. After a strained moment, he shook his head. "No, there's a concealment spell of some sort, but they couldn't have gone far, not with that . . . thing." He exchanged a look with Ashby. "They're down there somewhere." He narrowed his eyes into the dark night.

"The thing, the thing!" Brooke exclaimed, exasperated. "What the hell are you talking about?"

"We don't really know what it is," Perry said. "All we know is that it's a nasty bit of dark magic that can't be good."

Greg didn't care about some stupid, indescribable thing. Only Sam mattered. He turned, faced the hole, then leaped down. Behind him, Brooke's panicked voice called out his name. Greg landed in a crouch twelve feet below. He looked back over his shoulder to find the four of them peering down with surprised expressions.

"I guess you don't care about *the thing*," Perry called out with a sigh. "Everyone," he put a hand out. "Let's go, unless you feel like jumping."

Three hands landed on top of Perry's. The spell came quickly and, in a dizzying jolt, transferred them down to the garden next to a massive swan-shaped bush.

Ashby stepped away from the bush. "Let's find, Sam."

"Took you long enough," Greg said, slipping off his uncomfortable jacket and bow tie and flinging them to the ground. "They're near." He shook his head. "I don't know how, but I can sense Sam."

At first, when he'd been running with Perry toward the jail cell and he'd felt a tug in the depths of his soul, he thought he'd imagined it, but when they burst into the cell and found Sam in Veridan's grip, the pull had been so strong he almost fell to his knees.

He could have slammed his head against the wall as Sam disappeared right before his eyes. They'd been too late, and the awareness he'd felt in his soul, the familiar Keeper instincts trying to come to the surface, had disappeared with Sam.

But now it was back, which meant he was on the right track, and Sam was not far. He closed his eyes and tried to focus. The others quieted, understanding what he was trying to do.

His heart gave a twinge as he thought of Sam at the mercy of the evil Sorcerer, but he shut the fear away and focused on that remnant of who he'd been before Danata tore him from his Integral.

Sam was his guiding force, his beacon in the storm. He'd been lost without her, but now that he was so close, her light—no matter how dim—would lead him back to her.

His heart lurched to one side. Greg's eyes sprang open.

"This way," he said and headed left, around a hedge as thick and tall as a wall. His eyes might be useless in all the damn shrubbery, but his heart was true, better than any compass ever created.

ℰ Chapter 61 ℭ
Sam

Veridan and that woman had disappeared into the viscous, black cloud, and Sam still couldn't believe her eyes. Were they gone forever? It seemed too good to be true and didn't explain why Veridan had bothered to take her from the cell.

She lay flat on the soft grass, unable to move a muscle. She had physically exhausted herself trying to break free, and it was no use. Instead, she focused her mind on staying calm and calling out to Greg with all her might.

He was close. He had to be. She felt her instincts trying to alert her. There seemed to still exist a phantom connection between them in spite of all the turmoil. Or was it just hopeful thinking?

One of her vinculums began glowing again, getting brighter by the second, letting her know he was on his way. So, Sam nurtured this strand as best as she could, all the while hoping she'd be able to weave them back together.

Frozen as she was, time became immeasurable. Seconds, minutes, or maybe even hours blended together. The only meter was the rhythmic throbbing of the black blob, shifting shape and casting an ominous shadow over her. She watched it warily, afraid it would swallow her as it beckoned for her, pulling at her heart like the cries of a thousand children.

A sudden sound broke through the quiet garden. Sam's heart picked up its uneven pace. Her eyes swiveled from side to side as she strained to find the source of the noise.

"Sam!" Greg stepped from behind a tall rose bush. He spared one cautious glance at the blob, then rushed to her side.

Relief, like a tidal wave, washed over her. His name jumped to the tip of her tongue, but froze there, unable to break free. He ran a hand down the side of her face, tears sparkling in his blue eyes. His gaze traveled down the length of her body, ensuring she was alright.

"Thank God I found you!" He took her hand, and his warmth seeped into her, making her feel more alive than she had in weeks.

Ashby, Perry, Brooke and a strange girl appeared behind him. Sam would have laughed hysterically if she hadn't been a statue. They were all here. Joy and relief bounced inside her, looking for a way out.

"What is wrong with her?" Greg asked. "She can't move."

"Immobilizing spell," Perry said, taking a knee next to Sam. "Hey, there," he said with a wink. "Looking a bit peaky, are we? I'll have you back on your feet in no time."

Sam so wanted to hug the young Sorcerer as he gripped his amulet and started issuing an incantation. First, her manacles came off and a few seconds later, her limbs began to tingle. It started at her fingers and toes, then her wrists and ankles. She'd just regained sensation around her shoulders when, suddenly, a hole yawned open in the middle of the blob, and Veridan and many others stepped into the garden.

Everyone turned, stepping protectively in front of her. Sam found herself half frozen and half able to move. Without taking his eyes off the blob spawns, Greg helped Sam stand, then held up a sword.

She braced herself against his back, trying to keep her balance on barely responsive legs. Peering over his shoulder, she settled her gaze on Veridan. The Sorcerer stood proud against the riling backdrop of the evil, dark miasma. The fear he'd always shown in Greg's presence, since his first attack at the gas station, seemed to be replaced by an air of haughty confidence. Looking at his companions, it wasn't hard to imagine why.

A dozen other Morphids stood with him, all displaying the same superiority. The woman who had been with Veridan before was there too. She stared at them with a natural hostility, as if she were used to being at war and this was just another battle. They wore strange clothes, suited for some sort of cosplay event or a medieval fantasy novel. Seven of them wore long capes clasped at their necks by amulets, much like the ones Veridan and Perry carried. The other five wore garments which fit them like gloves. Tight pants molded to their legs and disappeared into supple, high boots. Leather armor on top of fitted shirts protected their chests. Shiny swords hung from wide belts, turning her insides to water with fear.

The situation didn't look good. The strangers had just been birthed by a noxious cloud, for Pete's sake. And not only that, their expressions were murderous. How lucky for them to find a group of potential victims.

Veridan's gaze paused a moment on Greg, then quickly moved to Ashby.

"I never thought you had murder in you, Ashby," the Sorcerer said. "I'm impressed."

Sam lowered her head, hiding completely behind Greg. She put her hands over her ears, trying to drown out the rhythmic throbbing of the blob. It still called to her, though more desperately than before and threatening to drive her insane.

Do something Do something Do something!

Her Morphid instincts screamed, though unlike before, they didn't seem able to tell her exactly what to do. There was one thing she knew she could do, however, something she'd wanted to do since Danata ripped Sam's last vinculum.

"W-what is the meaning of this?" Ashby asked, his voice wavering at first, but quickly growing firm.

At some level, Sam registered her friends' predicament, but it felt like little more than a bad movie playing in the background. Her task at hand was more important than anything else. Squinting overhead, Sam located her vinculums. One remained as charred and dead as before, but the one that had linked her to Greg was bright and alive.

Calling the vinculum to her hands, Sam got to work, weaving the strands with practiced dexterity. She'd done it so many times by now that it'd become second nature. By controlling the luminous energy generated by weaving broken links, she made herself whole again.

As the last strand snapped into place, Sam's heart jumped. A jolt of energy traveled down her body, shocking life back into her limbs. Something metal clattered to the ground as Greg let out a gasp and fell to his knees. She followed suit, the jolt too much for her legs.

"Sam!" Brooke tried to kneel by her side but was warned away by Veridan.

"Don't move!"

Sam stared into Greg's contorted face. His eyes were clenched shut, and his mouth pressed into a hard line. For a moment, she thought something had gone wrong, but then he let out a sigh of relief, his warm breath blowing on her. His features relaxed, and his eyes sprang open.

"Sam," he said in a quiet whisper.

His eyes glimmered with unshed tears. He lifted a hand to brush her cheek and smiled.

"Thank you," he mouthed.

Left to her own devices, Sam would have gone on lying on the cold ground, staring into Greg's cerulean gaze, but Veridan wouldn't have it that way.

"Take them, too," the Sorcerer commanded. "The boy is a Keeper. Take special care."

"A Keeper," a female voice said with some surprise. "Haven't seen one of those in some time."

Greg tensed, gave Sam a slow nod, then jumped to his feet, turning to face their enemies in one quick motion.

๛ Chapter 62 ๏

Greg

Greg's chest hummed with power, making him feel as if he could take over the world. He was whole again, part of Sam as it was meant to be. The joy of it all had been so great that it'd dropped him to the ground. Then Sam's beautiful face had been right in front of him, her honey-colored eyes full of enormous relief and happiness, reflecting his exact emotions.

But the moment of peace had been short, and now he stood in a crouch, faced with five oddly dressed Morphids. Veridan was one of them, a satisfied smirk twisting his lips.

Energy coursed through Greg's veins, the magical power his Keeper abilities granted him whenever Sam was in danger.

"Are Keepers truly immune to magic? I've never fought one," a snobbish-looking woman asked to no one in particular. She stood next to Veridan, frowning with bored curiosity.

"Why don't you ask your chicken-shit friend?" Greg said.

"Chicken-shit?" the woman echoed.

"Swords will work better on him," Veridan said in response.

But before he even finished his sentence, the woman shot a ball of purple fire straight at Greg's face. The energy hit true, making Greg's entire head prickle, tinting everything violet. He blinked away the colors as the magic gathered in his chest. There, it roiled, looking for a way out. With a jerk of his arm, he obliged, releasing the energy into one of the unsuspecting Morphids in front of him.

The man went rigid and, with a muffled cry, dropped to the ground.

One down, thirteen to go.

"Oh, my," the Sorceress said.

"Elgin!" One of the men wearing leather armor knelt by the fallen man, checked his vitals, then shot a murderous look at Greg. "You will pay for my brother's life." He stood in one fluid motion, drawing a sword and swigging it to kill.

Greg jumped out of the way, pushing Sam back. She staggered and fell behind a bush. The Warrior—Greg guessed the guy's caste as his energy felt exactly like Katsu's—sliced his sword upward, trying to decapitate him.

Dodging, Greg rolled to the ground and picked up his discarded sword.

The Warrior came at Greg, backed by others dressed exactly the same. More Warriors? They surrounded him. He cast a quick glance in Sam's direction. He couldn't see her, but his instincts told him exactly where she was and, for the moment, she was safe behind the bush.

With a unified war cry, all four Warriors charged Greg. A shield of his own creation went up around him. Swords clashed against it, sizzling on contact. One sword got through—a magically forged one, for sure—and he parried the blow just before it skewered him through the gut.

Relentlessly, the Warriors hacked at his shield. At first, few blows got past his defenses, and he was able to easily avoid them. But as the minutes ticked by, Greg grew tired. His shield weakened, and his sword arm began to burn from constantly blocking blows and occasionally attacking.

Here and there, he caught glimpses of what was happening outside his deadly circle and, from the looks of it, things weren't much better for Ashby and the others. As he fought, he kept track of Sam behind the bushes and grew increasingly worried as, instead of running to safety, she seemed to be moving closer to Veridan.

Greg eluded another blow and managed to graze his attacker's arm in retaliation. The woman cursed and immediately followed with a slash. The attack was fast and vicious, and only Greg's enhanced Keeper skills allowed him to block it.

This gave another attacker the chance to move behind him. Greg started to turn, but a sword cut at his back with lightning speed. Fire sliced down his spine. He growled as he felt something warm run down his back.

He fell to his knees and his attackers stepped up, closing the circle around him.

☙ Chapter 63 ❧
Perry

When four Warriors surrounded Greg and started attacking him, Perry barely had time to feel sorry for him before a challenge came his way. Judging by the amulets that held their cloaks in place, Perry had to assume the remaining Morphids were Sorcerers.

He had never seen them before, so they had to be dissidents. It was the only thing that made sense. All Morphids were required to register with the council, but Perry was sure this lot had not. They had to be rogue. Sorcerers were a rare caste, and there couldn't be this many outside of Danata's circle of control.

Veridan smiled at Perry as he leisurely approached. "And now, I'm finally free to teach you the lesson you deserve."

And with that Veridan unleashed a magical attack that only Perry's younger, faster reflexes allowed him to block. A jet of fire crashed against Perry's arm as he placed it in front of his face and issued a quick conjuration. Heat blistered his wrist until his defense took full form and was able to completely block the flames.

He bared his teeth, leaning forward, ignoring the pain and smell of singed hair.

Ashby, Brooke, and Finley tried to scurry out of the way, but Veridan ordered his henchmen to stop them.

Perry ducked and rolled out of the way, throwing a paralyzing spell that missed Veridan by a hair's breadth. The jet of fire turned to ice and nipped at Perry's ankles as he kept rolling and tried to think of spells to throw at his opponent.

Then Veridan bent a spell that circled Perry, hit him in the back and pinned him to the ground, immobilizing his entire body. He struggled to reach his amulet, but he might as well have been crucified to the lawn. A pair of polished shoes entered his vision. Even though he couldn't look up, he didn't need to. He knew perfectly well who wore them.

"Finally pinned down like the roach that you are," Veridan said.

"Let him go, Veridan," Ashby commanded, his voice heavy with authority.

Perry would have frowned if he'd been able to move a muscle. Had Ashby gotten a hold of an assault rifle or something? Because if he hadn't, he had no business sounding so confident.

"Quiet!" Veridan ordered.

Someone chuckled, entertained by the situation.

Bastards! As soon as I get free, I'll fry your brains.

But how would he get free? The amount of magical power he was able to wield without touching his amulet was not enough to break loose. Where was Portos? Why was MORF taking so long to make an appearance? He hated to admit it, but at this point, MORF seemed like their only hope.

Without a warning, Perry's hands jerked behind his back where they seemed to turn to rock. He flew upward and floated to join a line of other immobile figures. Ashby, Brooke, and

Finley dangled a few feet from the ground, their hands at their backs, too.

Perry's eye darted around assessing their situation. They were surrounded by eight or nine Sorcerers while Greg still fought against the armed blokes. But where was Sam? Had she gone to fetch help?

Veridan looked them up and down, then turned his attention in Greg's direction just as the warriors around Greg parted, revealing his prone shape on the ground.

"No, Greg!" Sam popped from behind a bush, ran toward her Integral, and foolishly threw herself at him.

Seriously?! Perry would have rolled his eyes, if he could have.

Grand. They were done for, now. Really done for.

℘ *Chapter 64* ℂ
Sam

There was blood everywhere.

Sam's hands hovered over Greg's back, wanting to touch him but afraid to hurt him. There was a gash on his back that went from his right shoulder to his waist. Blood soaked his white shirt in a huge crimson stain that made her heart shrink in fear.

"Greg!" she whispered, leaning closer to look at his face.

His eyes sprang open. He tried to move, but winced in pain.

"You'll be alright. Don't move," she said.

He had healed before, that day a homeless Morphid had forced poison down his throat at the soup kitchen. His Keeper powers would heal him from this wound, too, wouldn't they?

"Well, isn't that touching?" Veridan said in a more toxic tone than usual.

Keeping a hand on Greg's shoulder, Sam looked up at the Sorcerer.

He grinned, all the fear he had ever shown in Greg's presence gone. He had needed a gang of armed Morphids to take him down.

"Coward." She spat the word.

A woman stepped next to the Sorcerer, her eyes surveying the captives. "This was easy."

"I told you," Veridan said as he twisted a hand in Sam's direction and seized her with his magic.

An invisible hand wrapped around Sam's throat, and she rose into the air, kicking her feet to no avail.

Greg stirred, groaning as he tried to get up, but one of his armed opponents pinned him down by placing a boot on his back.

"Let me go!" Sam demanded in a weak, strangled voice.

"Hello, little Weaver," the woman next to Veridan said.

There was a certain hunger in her eyes, the same kind that had been in Danata's gaze every time she'd forced Sam to use her weaving skills with Anima.

A shudder ran down Sam's body. And, in that moment, she knew she'd rather die than remain captive to Veridan and these people, whoever they were.

"Fina, would you mind *holding* her for me?" Veridan asked, a sickly caring look in his eyes.

He liked this woman. Sam felt like throwing up at the thought of that spawn of hell caring for anyone in that way.

The woman, Fina, took over by extending a hand in Sam's direction and holding her up in the air. The Sorceress cocked her head to one side and examined her as if she were a rare bug.

The blob throbbed behind Fina, pulsing, making it almost impossible for Sam to concentrate. The voices hadn't stopped calling for her. Moreover, their shrill cries inside her head had redoubled. Her temples pounded in unison with the black miasma.

As Veridan walked away, Sam tried to follow him with her gaze, but her eyes kept losing focus, lids closing heavily as the blob insistently beckoned.

"It seems your Regency didn't last very long, my dear Ashby," Veridan said, looking up at Ashby's floating shape.

Ashby's Regency? What did he mean? Was Danata dead?

"You mean *he's* the Regent?" Fina asked. "I thought you said it was a woman, the Ripper."

"And so it was," Veridan said, "but Ashby, her beloved son, decided her reign had lasted long enough. He saved me the trouble of dispatching her myself. She did help me gather some considerable energy, and I am not ungrateful." He gestured toward the blob and directed his next comment at Perry. "Isn't it marvelous? I bet Portos never accomplished anything half as powerful. You should have picked me as your mentor, and not that imbecile. Quite the mistake you made."

"What now?" the man with his boot on Greg's back demanded. He seemed tired with Veridan's monologue and ready to slice more people open.

"Kill them all," Veridan said with a nonchalant flourish. "They'll be no use us. Except the Weaver, of course. I know you want her, so you may do with her as you please,"

"No!" Greg protested weakly from the ground. As he tried to push up again, his captor kicked him in the side of the head.

Sam knew she should scream, call out for help, do something, but her head was a thick haze and everything around her had turned black. First it was her fingertips. They turned so dark and slick they looked as if she'd dipped them into a barrel of crude oil. She shook her hands trying to get the disgusting stuff off, but instead, it climbed up until it reached her elbows, and she became convinced a black hole was devouring her.

Desperate cries for help reached her ears. She craned her neck in all directions, trying to identify the source. Whoever they were, their pain must be agonizing. She felt it herself, the anguish, the desperation, the need for release. Clasping her hands over her ears, she shook her head. She wanted to—

Leave me alone! I can't think!

The clamoring stopped.

Sam took a deep breath and opened her eyes.

The blackness on her hands had turned to light, the most beautiful, white iridescence she had ever seen. It was the same beauty she'd grown used to seeing in vinculums, but a million times brighter, a million times more.

As Sam's instincts had a moment to settle, the realization came to her like a crashing wave. She gasped, shock paralyzing her heart for a moment. She lifted her eyes away from her luminescent hands and allowed herself to look back at the blob once more.

What a minute ago had been roiling blackness was now a sphere as bright as the sun. It pulsed just the same, but there was nothing dark or evil about it anymore. Its surface shimmered with dancing rainbows of color, still calling to her but in a much different way. A single voice rose from the many that had plagued her mind for the past few hours. It was unlike any voice she'd ever heard, and it spoke, not in words, but in warmth, emotions, and gentle changes in color.

It spoke of its suffering and imprisonment.

And it pleaded for release.

A release Sam could provide because, as the silent voice reached out with its warmth, she finally understood what the blob was and why it was able to communicate with her.

The energy that had pulsed so darkly and now opened up to let her in was made up of vinculums. It wasn't hard to guess how it had coalesced into one place or how it had come to be under Veridan's control. He'd been with Danata for years while she systematically tore Morphids apart. Somehow, he must have figured out a way to harness the vinculums' energy just as the Ripper performed her wicked deed.

Tears fell down Sam's cheeks, unbidden, as the agony from the trapped souls washed over her. No one but a Weaver could comprehend the magnitude of the pain Danata and Veridan had inflicted.

And no one but a Weaver could provide the release they needed.

Letting her instincts flood her and take full command, Sam reached out to the blob, her fingers moving in a synchronized beckoning motion. The effect was immediate, a rush of energy that came to her like an avalanche. It poured over her with blinding quality, immersing her senses in what felt like a dimension made of starlight.

Something red flashed against the luminous white, an energy that tried to stop her but was unable to penetrate through her cocoon of energy. She ignored it.

Tendrils wrapped around her, each one demanding her full attention. They tugged at her, projecting their suffering and their desperate need for freedom. For a moment, the energy around her was so overwhelming that Sam was sure she would lose herself and there would be no escape. And it was ironic that she had Danata to thank for the strength and refined awareness of her Weaver powers because, without the Regent's relentless cruelty, Sam would have never gained the necessary skills to withstand the volley that came at her from every direction.

Taking command of her powers, she pushed away the insistent souls pressing against her. Her hands worked fast to gather each separate source of energy.

Like a composer she felt the pitch, the unique feel of each torn vinculum, and cast out in search of their perfect match. Many were there, waiting, ready to join to its twin and become whole again.

Others had no match anymore, but as Sam unweaved their strands with care and compassion, they were released into the ether and seemed to exhale in relief.

She worked in a frenzy for what felt like an eternity, but might have been seconds. Her fingers moved at speeds she had never seen before. And not only that, she discovered that her own charred vinculum, dead throughout this ordeal, now glowed and was helping her weave and unweave as needed.

Like fireflies, the unweaved souls fluttered away, no more pain, no more anguish. Only oblivion. While those that were lucky enough to still have a match drifted upward, together once more, tearing free from the prison Veridan had made for them.

Sam didn't know how long she had been working or how frantically her fingers were weaving, all she knew was that the unrelenting cries which had plagued her finally stopped, leaving an eerie silence behind.

Everything around her went still, but only for an instant. The dark energy that had kept the souls bound began rotating in a wide circle, quickly forming a whirlwind that blew Sam's hair in every direction.

Not quite sure of where she was, Sam looked around wildly and realized she was floating mid-air, her clothes flapping, her hair whipping her face. Below her, bushes jerked from side to side, leaves rustled and figures scrambled, fighting against the massive winds.

In her trance, Sam had forgotten about everyone else. Even Greg.

Her gaze flicked to the spot where she'd last seen him. She caught a glimpse of him, his black hair stirring in the wind, his fingers clawing the dirt as he fought against the dragging force of the storm raging around them. Sam had only enough time to wonder how to reach him when whatever force had kept her in place dissipated and she went tumbling head over feet into the spinning storm.

ɛᴑ Chapter 65 ᴄᴙ
Ashby

The man with the sword walked toward Ashby and the others, a look of utter contempt and indifference in his eyes. It seemed that slaying people bored him, though he had no trouble doing it. He'd slashed Greg and pressed a dirty boot to his injured back as if he were nothing but a dog. Now, he was ready to follow Veridan's command to kill them all.

Where had these people come from? How had they colluded with Veridan to do this, whatever this was?

The man lifted his sword, ready to strike Brooke. Perry's eyes widened and practically screamed "stop," but he was as helpless as Ashby to actually do anything.

A roar of anger and impotence filled Ashby's chest. Wasn't there anyone who could help them?

As if in answer, the Sorceress who had a hold of Sam let out a shriek. "What is she doing?"

Everyone's attention snapped to Sam's floating shape.

Tendrils of light were wrapping all around her. They were floating away from the black orb from which Veridan and the others had come. They stretched toward Sam like hands reaching for salvation out of the dark waters of an evil ocean.

Veridan's face disfigured into a mask of panic.

"No!"

He ran toward Fina, his Sorceress accomplice, a hand on his amulet and a spell on his lips. Red electric rays shot from his fingers and flew directly at Sam. They crashed against the blinding white light that protected her, but quickly dissipated, having no visible effect.

"Help me!" Veridan ordered, his high pitch tone revealing his fear.

Ashby held his breath, fearing for her. Greg drew to his hands and knees on the ground, making a monumental effort to stand and defend her, but collapsed again.

Fina and the other Sorcerers took hold of their amulets and, in unison, released their own attacks on Sam. Their magic tangled with whatever energy had taken hold of her but, again, it seemed useless.

Unrelenting, Veridan and the others tried once more. The brightness around Sam seemed to dim as light fluttered away from her like Chinese lanterns on their way to the heavens.

Without warning, Ashby fell to the ground with a *thud*, the paralyzing spell barely causing more than an uncomfortable tingle around his body. Perry, Brooke, and Finley fell next. Perry scrambled to Brooke's side and wrapped her in his arms.

"You're okay," he assured her. She hid her face in his chest, visibly trembling.

Apparently the Sorcerers were too preoccupied with attacking Sam to keep their prisoners in check.

"What is wrong with her?" Ashby yelled to Perry over the clashing magic.

"I'm not sure," he said, squinting into the light, his hair beginning to stir with the incredible wind. "I think . . . I think it's vinculum energy, coming from that blob."

Vinculum energy?

But how could have Veridan amassed the energy inside a black, roiling glob? The answer came to him all at once, it was so obvious. That's what the Sorcerer had meant when he said that Danata had been useful.

Ashby's hair lashed against his eyelids. He pushed it away, fearing the sudden surge of wind. The current whirled all around, trapping them in a huge, tumbling sphere. He took hold of Finley's hand and pulled her closer.

"What's happening?" she asked.

Ashby shook his head at a loss for what to say or do.

The Warriors leaned forward into the wind, their feet planted firmly on the ground. The Sorcerers' capes flapped in the wind, as they continued to issue incantations against Sam. Wind roared in Ashby's ears. He put an arm in front of his face to block the flying debris and peered up at Sam.

She seemed to be the epicenter of whatever had turned their world into a category four hurricane. Most of the light around her had dissipated, leaving her suspended in midair. Her long hair whipped about. Her eyes were closed, and she glowed like a small sun. Then, as if someone had cut her moorings, a gust of wind caught her, and she tumbled in the direction of what remained of the blob.

Without thinking, Ashby let go of Finley's hand and launched in Sam's direction. He managed to take two steps on solid ground before his feet were swept from under him, and he also flew toward the darkness. It revolved like a large drain, sucking in anything in its way.

Dirt, leaves, branches, and other bodies were caught in its siphoning force.

Ashby angled his body in Sam's direction, trying to reach her. He screamed her name, but could barely even hear himself. A branch struck his brow, breaking the skin and sending blood into his eyes.

Sam noticed him and also angled her body toward him, arms outstretched.

They came within inches of each other, their hands almost touching, but someone flew between them, knocking Ashby's arm to one side. A cape came loose from the person's back and plastered itself against Ashby's face. He struggled to pull it off as it blinded him, doubling his panic.

Just as he managed to throw the cape to the side, Sam slammed into him and wrapped her arms around his waist.

A moment ago, he'd felt as if he could help her, but now that he had her, he didn't know what to do. The wind was so powerful it had uprooted bushes, which were now caught in the whirl, threatening to take off their heads.

They went round and round, each lap shorter than the last, headed straight for the coalescing blackness at the end of the vortex.

Ashby looked around, desperately trying to find a way back down, but it was almost impossible to discern anything in the chaos. They took another tumble which brought them closer to the ground.

The legs of one of Veridan's Warriors kicked in the air as he held on to a bush. Ashby tucked his head in to avoid a boot to the face just as the bush became uprooted and flew off with the Warrior. He tumbled along the ground until a black tendril wrapped around his leg and pulled him to the bottom of the funnel where he disappeared like a roach in a sewer drain.

Fates!

If one of those things touched them, they were dead. Just as he'd finished processing that thought, Sam jerked to one side, helping them avoid one of the inky tentacles.

More of Veridan's people were pulled into the narrow tip of the vortex where Ashby imagined the giant blade of a food processor, mincing everyone to pieces.

They spun around another lap, moving ever closer to their doom. He looked into Sam's eyes, and a silent message passed between them. It was acceptance in her eyes, the same that had suddenly flooded him with a strange sort of calm. They would die in the roiling darkness, and there was no escape.

Hope died within him.

At least, they'd undone Veridan's plan as well as Danata's. MORF would come, and everything would be okay with the council. Roanna would retake the Regency, and hopefully everything would be better for Morphids.

Suddenly, they jerked to a stop. Sam still had one arm wrapped around his waist while their legs kicked wildly behind them. He was so disoriented from spinning that it took him a moment to realize what had held them in place while the rest of the world tumbled.

Greg.

&o Chapter 66 os
Greg

A strange wind picked up around the garden while, through clouded eyes, Greg stared at Sam floating in midair, wrapped in light. Even as Veridan and his Sorcerers unleashed magic in her direction, his Keeper instincts told him she was safe, protected by the luminous power that surrounded her.

But as a hurricane like those he'd come to fear as a kid in New Orleans began to whip the top of the bushes, his Keeper senses spiked. Danger was upon his Integral.

Acting purely on instinct, Greg reached for his sword and gripped its handle, taking advantage of the Warriors' distraction. Fighting against the pain that split his back, Greg got to one knee with the aid of the sword. The wind assaulted his eyes, obscured his vision, and pushed against his sizable frame with disturbing force. Still, something told him this was just the beginning. Things were about to get much worse.

Obeying the dire warning that twisted his gut, Greg got to his feet, lifted the sword and stabbed toward the ground with all his might. Pain shot across his back, and he nearly fell to his knees but managed to sink half the sword's length into the earth.

A gust of wind hit him, nearly flinging him into the air. He grabbed for the sword as an anchor, almost missing it. Several of the Warriors were whisked up like leaves, but he held on tight, even as his back felt as if it would split in two.

The wind continued to pick up. His feet came off the ground, clothes fluttering in the savage gale. He was trying to readjust his grip when his instincts flared up and more adrenaline exploded into his veins. He glanced up just as Sam and Ashby rushed past. He flung out his arm, attempting to catch her, but he missed her by a few inches.

"Sam!" he screamed.

Her eyes darted to his as if she'd heard his cry, which was impossible in the roaring vacuum. She and Ashby spun upward and away from him, their eyes filled with desperation.

Greg switched his grip on the sword to angle his body better. When Sam came back around, he would not miss her. His gaze followed her trajectory around the vortex. Her eyes were also locked on his as she neared. Resolutely, she reached a hand out and wrapped her arm around Ashby's waist.

"I got you," Greg mouthed.

When they came hurtling by, Greg clasped his hand around her wrist and braced himself for the violent tug he knew was coming. Like the force of some immense gravity, the vortex and the combined weights of Sam and Ashby yanked on him. His ribs, shoulders, and elbows popped as his body stretched in an effort to hold the sword on one end and his friends on the other.

If he'd thought he might be torn in half before, he was certain of it now. Every fiber of his body ignited with pain. He clenched his teeth, growling as his sternum stretched to a breaking point. At any moment, his ribcage would crack open, and his insides would spill out to be carried away by the churning storm.

Suspended, they flapped like human flags, then the sword shifted and they lurched toward the black hole. Sam's grip began to slip. He tried to tighten his hold, but he was already giving it all he had.

His eyes locked with his Integral's, and he silently begged her to hold on. She shook her head, her face scrunched up with the massive effort of holding her weight and Ashby's.

Greg's gaze searched Ashby's. He had slipped from Sam's hold and was holding on to her leg, quickly slipping further and further down. His blond hair flapped from one side to the other, out of control. His brow was furrowed with effort, but also something else.

Greg didn't know how, but he knew immediately what that something was.

"No, Ashby!" Greg yelled into the storm, but his cry was lost and never reached him.

For an instant, Ashby's dark gaze met Greg's. There were so many emotions in his eyes that Greg felt his heart break in two. Regret, terror, resignation.

And at last, a sad smile and a silent farewell.

"Noooo!" Greg yelled as Ashby let go of Sam's leg, rushed toward the spinning darkness that had already swallowed Veridan and his evil Morphids, and disappeared into the void like a drop of water into a drain.

The force that was trying to rip Greg in two diminished. Sam stopped slipping from his grip, and the sword seemed firmer on the ground. And yet, he knew with certainty his strength would not last much longer. He'd lost a lot of blood, and his adrenaline had nearly burned out.

If this was the end, at least he was with Sam. He couldn't really ask for more.

Their eyes locked. Sam's resigned expression mirrored the way he felt.

"I love you," she mouthed.

He mouthed it back, just as his hold on the sword grew more tenuous.

One finger at a time, he lost his grip and then they were airborne, headed straight into doom.

ᔕᄀ Chapter 67 ᏕᏕ
Sam

Greg came at her as his grip on the sword gave.

He pulled her into his chest, and she threw her other arm around his neck and squeezed as hard as she could.

They were headed into death, and she would cling to him all the way there.

Spinning into the wind like pieces of lint, they flew toward the bottom of the funnel, following Ashby's path. He had let go. He was gone and, now, they would go with him. They had started this together, and they would finish it together. There was consolation in that, at least.

The inky blackness that had held all those Morphid souls prisoners roiled, ready to devour them. Sam closed her eyes and buried her face into Greg's neck.

Everything went silent.

The wind stopped.

Gravity took over.

They plummeted to the ground, tangled in each other's arms. Greg let out a muffled *humph* as Sam fell on top of him. Other things fell around them. She heard them drop, but didn't dare open her eyes to see.

They weren't dead but, if that was the case, where had they gone?

Still, Sam didn't dare look.

Rushing steps. Someone calling their names.

She knew that voice.

Sam's eyes sprang open. She looked around and realized they were still in the garden. They hadn't gone anywhere. The place was destroyed—torn bushes, branches, and leaves everywhere—but it was still Rothblade Castle.

Greg blinked at her, wincing from pain. She got off him and pressed a hand to the side of his face. He was drenched in a cold sweat.

"Sam! Greg!" Someone ran up to them and stopped.

Sam peered up. It was Perry with Portos at his side.

"Greg's hurt," she said. "Please, help him."

The two Sorcerers dropped to their knees.

"I'll take care of him," Portos said, taking hold of his amulet.

Perry nodded, then raked stiff finger through his hair, a desolate expression on his face. His gaze darted around the garden and kept going back to the spot where the blackness had been.

Tears pooled in his eyes. "He's gone. Ashby's gone," he said in a sob.

Ashby had, in the end, given Sam and Greg the chance to live. He had selflessly let go, knowing Greg was losing strength. He had bought them only a few seconds, but it had been enough.

The last time she'd talked to him, she'd told him terrible things and, now, she would never have a chance to take them back. He had come to her in New York, and she'd refused to weave their vinculums back together. She had caused him so much pain. How could she ever forgive herself?

Sam held Greg's hand as Portos mouthed incantations over his prone shape. The thought of Ashby was more than she could bear, so she focused on Greg instead, while a silent prayer for forgiveness played in the back of her mind over and over again.

She could only hope that in his heart of hearts, Ashby had come to forgive her—even if she would always hate herself for her twisted nature.

✌ Chapter 68 ✌
Greg

After Portos healed him, Greg clung to Sam with the firm idea that he would never let her go. She held onto him the same way, sobbing and shaking her head against his chest. At intervals, the urge to make sure she was real seized him, and he would hold her face between his hands, drinking in her every feature. He kissed her forehead, her eyelids, her mouth, and pulled her in again.

MORF had come to help and not a second too late. Now, they were running around the garden, shouting orders and trying to keep the ball guests from getting in the way. Chaos went on around them, but his Keeper instincts were quiet. He'd seen Katsu kicking a branch and looking disappointed that he'd missed the fight. He'd have to thank him for his lessons and patience.

Sam was safe.

And they were together. That's all that mattered.

"Sam," a tentative voice called behind Greg.

Reluctantly, they let each other go and turned. It was Brooke, her hair a tangle a top her head.

"Brooke!"

The girls embraced each other, crying.

"I thought you'd get pulled into that thing for sure," Brooke said. "If Portos hadn't shown up when he did…"

So Portos had stopped the siphoning storm. He'd save them. How could he ever thank him?

"Um…" Brooke scratched her neck, looking hesitant. "There's someone who wants to meet you."

Sam frowned and exchanged a glance with Greg.

He nodded, letting her know it was safe, then took her hand. "Your mother, probably."

Sam's eyes went wide, and she looked worried all of a sudden.

"You don't have to if you're not ready," Brooke said. "She said she would wait. She understands."

"No, it's fine," Sam said.

Greg could feel her nerves, her concern, but he also felt her strength and curiosity. He didn't know what had happened to Sam in the time they'd been apart, but he could sense she'd changed. There was something fierce in her that hadn't been there before.

They walked past a big tangle of fallen branches. On the other side, a group of people waited, including Roanna, Bernard, and Portos. Worry etched their faces as they seemed lost in intense discussion.

When Greg and Sam approached, the conversation stopped, and they turned to face them.

Roanna pressed both hands to her mouth as if in prayer. Relief, joy, and a wealth of other emotions showed on her features.

"Celestine," Roanna said in a choked sob. She approached cautiously and stopped a few paces away from her daughter.

Greg let go of Sam's hand. She gave him a weak smile, then focused all her attention on Roanna.

All the emotions that washed over Sam at that moment hit Greg right at his core. His knees went weak with the weight of her feelings, and he experienced them as if they were his own. And later, when he tried to find words to describe the moment when his Integral reunited with her mother and father, he was unable to.

Sam simply had felt too much.

Epilogue
Sam

Sam's mother—it still felt strange to call Roanna that—stood in front of the council. The large hall brimmed with people, hundreds of eyes directed toward the dais and the rightful, reinstated Regent.

Sitting at the front row with Greg on one side and her father on the other, Sam couldn't help but admire her mom. The way she had handled the last two weeks with such poise and magnanimity was extraordinary, and definitely more than Sam would have been able to manage.

Roanna's understanding and patience with all of those loyal to Danata, her restraint upon learning about the Morphid state of affairs, the forbearance she displayed during Danata's trial, and the public letter of absolution she'd addressed to her sister were all more than Sam could imagine herself accomplishing. Roanna had even expressed some regret at the life imprisonment the council had swiftly bestowed upon the Ripper. Though she thoroughly understood the depth of Danata's crimes against so many Morphid souls, Roanna couldn't help but blame the nature of her caste and whether early intervention—had they known her caste—might have set Danata on a different path.

Sam smiled up at her beautiful mother as she inclined her head to thank the High Sorcerer, Portos, for the golden crown he'd placed atop a red velvet cushion.

Next to Sam, her father beamed, an expression of absolute love on his face. He took turns looking at his wife and then at Sam, as if he expected them to dematerialize at any moment.

"No one can ever tear you two apart again," Sam told him often enough. "I wouldn't let them."

"To think you were the one who weaved us together. Our own daughter!" Bernard would respond, always seeming unsure of whether or not that was a good thing.

At the end of the ceremony, the crowd filed into two massive dining halls set out for a feast. Roanna and Bernard sat at the head of the biggest table to ever exist in the history of tables and began the lavish meal after a few quick words of thanks to the staff and guests.

Roanna had wanted a simple ceremony, but the council had prevailed, arguing that a proper celebration would leave no doubts as to who was in charge.

Sam sat to Roanna's right, her mind popping with thoughts and questions about her future. Greg took her hand under the table and gave it a reassuring squeeze, sensing, as he always did, her inner unrest.

With Ashby gone, the job of Regent hung over her head. The idea of being the leader of the Morphid world had never appealed to her, and that sentiment had not changed. Ashby had been groomed for the life, and he'd had the instinct to serve his people while all Sam wanted to do was pick up a spatula and cook. Roanna said to give it time, that as Sam settled into her caste and new life, things would change. Sam didn't think so, but she knew better than to totally dismiss the possibility. Her mark *did* have a crown in it, albeit small. There was no telling what altruistic urge may guide her in the next week, perhaps something which would make her swear off soufflés for the rest of her life.

It was still incredible to think that she'd found her parents. It would be hard to explain to James and Rose, but it wasn't something she could keep putting off forever.

Sam leaned forward to find her friends down the table.

She spotted Jacob first, seated on a cushion because he didn't want to look so little among all the tall Morphids. He was smiling, eating a buttered roll and enjoying it thoroughly. He wore a huge smile that made Sam think he would be fine, in spite of it all. Sam's parents had decided to adopt him, and he had been inordinately happy about it. He'd even taken to calling her "sis" every chance he got.

Next to Jacob sat Mateo, frowning at his plate. He looked so sad all the time, but seemed to have found some solace in Perry, who never tired of telling him stories about his son. He had helped Sam in New York while she checked on the homeless to make sure they'd been healed after destroying Veridan's awful creation. Busying himself with the welfare of those needy Morphids had helped cheer him up a little, though not much.

Perry and Brooke sat next to each other, taking bites off each other's plates. Sam was glad to see a smile on Perry's face, since there hadn't been many of those lately. It had been impossible to sustain a good mood after what had happened, but Perry seemed to find it harder than anyone to move on. Losing his best friend and the only family he'd ever had was proving more than he could handle, even Brooke and his long-lost grandmother didn't seem enough at times.

Only Portos's theories of what might have happened seemed to give Perry a spark when he was down, and he would often snap out of his quiet daydreaming to say, "I do think Ashby's alive. Veridan may have been an arse, but he was a wicked Sorcerer— even Portos admits it and is more certain every day that Veridan created a passage to a different dimension. What if Ashby finds his way back?"

It was a nice wish but, even if the portal idea was true, how would Ashby get back? Sam doubted Veridan would offer any help in returning or would have the means to make it happen. Giant blobs of vinculum energy weren't something you found at the mall. It had taken years for Veridan to build what Sam had unraveled—at least that was the general consensus.

The idea that Ashby was alive should have offered some comfort but, in truth, it didn't. It only opened Sam's mind to more incessant questions. Had he gone to a nice place? An awful place? Was he suffering? Hungry?

In all his gloom and sadness, Perry seemed to be more positive about that possibility, though. He was sure Finley—a girl the boys had met during their time with MORF—was with Ashby. Apparently, one of her castes was Regent, and he seemed to think Fate had a plan for them. He also said she was a dual with a second, unknown caste that was sure to help them wherever they'd gone.

"You should have seen her," Perry told anyone who would listen. "She just threw herself at the portal after it swallowed

Ashby. I was trying to help her, get her away from the pull of the storm, but she just charged right after him. No fear. No hesitation."

At least that thought was comforting. If Ashby was alive, there might be someone with him who cared enough to risk her life for his sake. He deserved that along with all the things Sam could never give him.

Wherever Ashby was, in spite of it all, he held a place in Sam's heart.

***

Sam and Greg stood in the north garden. Perry had said it'd been Ashby's favorite place in Rothblade Castle, so it felt like the right place to do it.

The vinculum that had joined Sam to Ashby was still there, weakly fluttering over her head. She didn't know why, but its presence was a constant source of unrest for her.

And it wasn't just a psychological unrest brought on by guilt.

It was also physical—like an ache or a deeply-embedded splinter that would allow her no respite.

Greg squeezed her hand, then set it free, knowing she would need it.

"Are you sure about this?" he asked, yet again.

All along, he'd been able to sense her turmoil. The first few days after Ashby was taken, the uncomfortable tug had been gentle, not hard to send to the back of her mind. Sam had thought it would go away, so she hadn't mentioned it to Greg. Still, he'd known something wasn't right.

But as the weeks went by, the discomfort grew until it had reached a crescendo that, at times, felt as if it would drive her insane. Worse yet—as in tune as Greg was to her emotions—it had started to affect him, too.

"I'm sure," she said.

Ashby was gone, now. And even when he'd been here, Sam had refused to restore their link. What, then, would be the point of holding on to this vestige of what had once been?

Sam took a few steps away from Greg and stopped in the center of the garden. Colorful flower beds and neatly trimmed rose bushes surrounded her. Their sweet perfume mingled with the scent of freshly-watered potting soil. Her father kept the garden, and it was lovely.

The morning was crisp and no clouds marred the deep blue sky. There were many gray days here in England, and this beautiful morning felt like a good moment to let Ashby go.

With a deep breath, Sam lifted her hands and called the torn vinculum to her. It was slow to obey, but it came to her nonetheless.

In comparison with the vinculum that linked her to Greg, this one felt insubstantial to her Weaver instincts. Holding it between her fingers sent a shudder into her soul.

She sensed it would take but a simple few touches to unweave this frail reminder of what could have been. So she held it for a long moment, knowing that once she undid it, there would be no turning back.

I'm sorry, Ashby, she said inside her mind as if in a prayer. *You didn't deserve any of this. You had a great, uncorrupted heart. I see that now. I wish Fate had found the right Integral for you.*

A tear broke free and slid down her cheek.

Goodbye.

Sam strummed her fingers once, the way a guitarist might play a beautiful chord.

The tug on her soul stopped.

She exhaled.

And somewhere, across a thin membrane of time and space, a sigh of relief broke through the lips of a blond boy with onyx-black eyes and a heart of gold.

Fate had run its course.

THE END

ACKNOWLEDGEMENTS

Oh, man! This book took forever to finish.

Greg, Sam, and Ashby have been with me for many years, and I guess it was hard to let them go. I started writing Keeper in 2007. So you can say, Weaver is overdue.

There were other projects in between, all important, but maybe not as precious as this one.

Many of you have been waiting and asking for the conclusion of this series. I'm glad to finally be able to offer Weaver to you. I hope you will love it as much as I do.

My eternal thanks go to Bret Williams. He gives, gives, gives without expecting anything in return. I hope all the smiles we have together help balance the scales. You are the best.

Thank you, Isabella. You are my bright little star. I'm so lucky to have you. I know how much you love this series. Maybe I'll do that novella you've been begging for ;)

Thank you, Greg and Sam and Ashby. It was so great living your adventures. I will miss you.

FOR NEW RELEASES, GIVEAWAYS
AND MORE, VISIT

WWW.INGRIDSEYMOUR.COM

www.ingramcontent.com/pod-product-compliance
Lightning Source LLC
Chambersburg PA
CBHW051322250626
47155CB00007B/2414